FOR A HEART COME HOME

ANCIENT SONGS
BOOK 5

LAURA STRICKLAND

ARE YOU SIGNED UP FOR DRAGONBLADE'S BLOG?

You'll get the latest news and information on exclusive giveaways, exclusive excerpts, coming releases, sales, free books, cover reveals and more.

Check out our complete list of authors, too!

No spam, no junk. That's a promise!

Sign Up Here

www.dragonbladepublishing.com

Dearest Reader;

Thank you for your support of a small press. At Dragonblade Publishing, we strive to bring you the highest quality Historical Romance from some of the best authors in the business. Without your support, there is no 'us', so we sincerely hope you adore these stories and find some new favorite authors along the way.

Happy Reading!

CEO, Dragonblade Publishing

ADDITIONAL DRAGONBLADE BOOKS BY AUTHOR LAURA STRICKLAND

Ancient Songs Series
For a Warrior's Heart (Book 1)
For an Exile's Heart (Book 2)
For a Wild Woman's Heart (Book 3)
For a Viking's Heart (Book 4)
For a Heart Come Home (Book 5)

The Three Sisters MacBeith Series
Keeper of the Gate (Book 1)
Keeper of the Hearth (Book 2)
Keeper of the Light (Book 3)

*Do our ancestors travel with us
In the binding of our souls?
In trails well traveled and tales remembered.
In ancient songs that we hear not with our ears
But with our hearts.
Is there a surer way for spirit to travel
Than by the magic of love
That brings us home?*

~ Finlay the Bard

*I*N THE HALL *of a western chief deep in the Scottish Highlands, a bard sings and plays upon his harp, telling ancient tales of his host's ancestors. Four tales he has told this night, holding his listeners in thrall.*

But now the hour grows late. The ale has flowed, the feast is finished, and Finlay the bard judges that his listeners will soon require their beds.

A long evening of entertainment it has been, during which those gathered have heard of a long-ago, valiant warrior. A third son sent to perform an impossible task. A princess of ancient times with a bold heart. A Viking maiden strong in spirit. Courage and endurance and love so impossible, it can do nothing but exist.

He coaxes from the strings of his harp one last, bright, glittering cascade of notes and sets the instrument aside. The magic that holds the room wavers but does not break. His listeners still watch him with wide eyes.

It matters little what his audience thinks, or even the noble chief. Finlay has told each and every tale this night for the benefit of but one listener—the tall young woman with the ashen-blonde hair who even now blinks and tries to shrug her way from what she has heard.

Can she so free herself? He can only hope not, for the story is not done. The rest of the tale cannot be sung but must be lived out here and now, in present time.

Those of whom he has spoken tonight are not gone. They live on, if in other guises. He is still here, as he has always been, and pledged to one woman alone. If she does not see him and know him for who he is, then no song he ever sings will serve to complete the magic. The wheel of the years will continue to spin, but he fears his heart will never come home.

CHAPTER ONE

Western Scotland, early fourteenth century AD

"GRAND, MASTER FINLAY! That was just grand," Chief Anders MacMurtray cried warmly, getting to his feet in respectful enthusiasm. "A magnificent evening's entertainment ye ha' given us, worthy o' the bards o' old. Truly, 'twas a fortunate day yer travels brought ye to our door."

Katrin MacMurtray, standing at the rear of the hall where she had listened long to the bard's tales, shook the magic of them from her head and eyed her father, the chief. A big man was he, tall, with graying ash-brown hair that had once been the color of her own and gray-blue eyes. Wide of shoulders but spare of weight, he now looked a bit unsteady on his feet, perhaps from the quantities of ale he had consumed but more likely, so Katrin suspected, from the long journey upon which the bard had taken them all.

Back, far back into the world of Da's ancestors and her own.

How was it this Finlay, a wandering minstrel who had turned up at their door seemingly by chance, knew so much about their forebears? Katrin supposed it must be part and parcel of his vocation, and his living, to know and carry these things. He earned his way by making those whom he entertained feel important, larger than life, the stuff of legends.

He had done a magnificent job of it.

Even she, beyond all else a practical woman who usually spared little time for nonsense or fancy, had got caught up in it all. The grandeur, the heroism. The love. That alone had brought tears to her eyes a few times. Could there ever exist love such as the bard described?

Captivated by the question, she eyed him. Finlay, the bard. They did not know his last name, if he possessed one. Such men tended to roam the country far and wide, staying with anyone who would have them for as long as profitable, till the tales and songs ran out, at which time they merely moved on.

They'd hired such visitors before, usually older men, some who traveled on horseback and with their own attendants.

Finlay had arrived alone, his harp—a beautiful instrument in its own right—in a pack on his back along with all his other possessions. And he was not aged. Rather, he could not be above a score and six years or so. Tall and slender with a graceful mien. Long, auburn-red hair that he kept braided with silver ornaments woven through the strands. A face neither handsome nor otherwise, but clever and mobile, that added a certain charm of expression to the stories he told. A wonderful, mellow singing voice that could be soft as a spring breeze, or angry as a swarm of hornets.

Green eyes. He had the deepest green eyes Katrin had ever seen. Graceful hands on the harp strings, some of the fingers tattooed. And, as she had to admit, a rare talent.

There had been moments this evening when Katrin had been so carried away by the magic he wove that she felt she experienced it, rather than merely listened. When the glorious notes from his harp had lifted and carried her like a wee boat on the sea. When she'd almost been able to feel the warmth of a love so strong, not even time could sunder it, and had nearly felt the promise of kisses dropped into the palms of her hands.

Such fancy!

It had been good for Da, though, having the diversion. And quite possibly good for the rest of the clan's folk also. There had been too much grief of late, with the country torn apart and war flickering all around them like flames that refused to snuff out.

The death of her brother, Geordie, had so wounded Da's heart, and her own. She should be grateful, aye, to Finlay for showing up and sharing his gift, if only for the distraction of it. Yet there was something about the man…

Perhaps the way those green eyes of his insisted on seeking her out wherever she was in a room, on touching her again and again before drawing in the rest of his audience. What was his interest in her? She was but the daughter of the house, remarkable only for being far past the age to wed, who saw to the management of her father's keep and meant naught to a traveling bard.

Perhaps, she thought now as the audience stirred and, emerging from Finlay's spell, remembered where they were, he merely realized he relied upon her good favor as much as Da's, for retaining their hospitality.

It must be important to a man who made his living on the move, especially on such a foul, wet night as this one. For the sea lay restless beyond the rocky shore, and rain crashed down so hard she'd been able to hear it even above the music. Indeed, at times it had seemed to become part of the story Finlay told, elemental and beyond the expression of words.

Aye, Finlay would be glad of a warm bed this night.

She watched as Da stepped up to the bard, who was situated near the head of the hall. Katrin had herself wandered the chamber while he sang, seeing to the comfort of their guests, as was her responsibility. In truth, after the first of Finlay's tales she had found it difficult to keep still, except at those moments when his playing wove around her so intimately, she forgot herself. Almost—*almost*—became someone else.

Now she moved forward, exchanging words with the departing clan's folk in passing. None of them would forget what they'd heard here tonight.

Aye, and when she drew close enough, she could hear that Da continued to praise the bard. Finlay, who stood nearly at a height with the chief, took the accolades humbly, with no signs of conceit.

He merely smiled, and even as Katrin joined the two men, he said in his musical voice, "I am pleased, Chief MacMurtray, if I brought ye some pleasure. 'Tis all the reward I require."

"Still and all," Da said, the remnants of the magic Finlay had summoned still visible in his eyes, "I do no' ken when I ha' enjoyed aught so well. Ye took me right out o' mysel', ye did."

Finlay's smile put twin dimples in his cheeks, visible despite the reddish beard that grew there. Not a full beard such as Da or, indeed, Katrin's late brother had worn, but more a suggestion that it had been over long since he'd employed his razor.

Geordie. She could not let herself think of him. Even though…

Her brother's death, which occurred in a terrible accident while he was training to fight for a free and independent Scotland, had changed all their lives irreparably. She had lost her closest friend. Da had lost the pride of his heart. And the clan now stood without an heir to take up the reins should—God forbid—anything happen to its chief.

She looked the bard in the eyes. Och, indeed, and extraordinary eyes they were now that she got so close a look at them. Green as the fir trees that grew on the rise above the keep.

"A fine evening's entertainment, Master Finlay," she congratulated him. "But ye will be tired now and eager for yer bed. Let me show ye where ye will sleep."

"Mistress—Katrin, is it?"

"Aye. Come along wi' me." She leaned up and kissed her father's cheek. "Good night, Da. I hope ye will sleep well."

"Wi' all those pictures o' my ancestors in my head? Och, if I do sleep, I do no' doubt I will go to dreaming o' voyages and battles."

Katrin smiled at him, one of the rare smiles she reserved for those she loved. She hoped his dreams were pleasant. Since word of Geordie's death had come, since the terrible day his poor body had returned home, he'd had little true rest.

As had she.

"You had best wrap up your harp," she told Finlay. "I am

sorry to say we must go outside to reach yer quarters. Ye can hear the rain."

Da stepped away to his departing guests. Katrin stood and watched as Finlay wrapped the instrument in an oiled cloth, employing great care.

"'Tis a bonny instrument," she observed. Carved it was with scrolled lines and leaves, fashioned from a deep, burnished brown wood.

He glanced up from his task, granting her another of those flashing smiles. "She is my greatest treasure."

"She?"

"I call her Brada. All the most favored harps are granted names, ye ken."

Such fancy! But Katrin had to admit, the instrument deserved a name. To look at him, she would not think so humble a traveler could boast such an instrument. The rest of his belongings—the frayed pack, the shabby boots, the clothing not fine but worn with a certain flash—did not match it.

"Ye never fashioned such a harp yourself?"

"Och, nay. 'Twas made for me in Ireland."

"Ye ha' been to Ireland?" She had not, though she'd always harbored a secret desire to see the place. Especially now, in light of the tales he had told.

"Och, aye. Mistress Katrin, I ha' been most everywhere in the Celtic world, learning and collecting songs. Erin, Wales, the Isle of Man. Even to Brittany."

"Aye, so?" That impressed her, though she would not let on. Katrin was a woman who rarely admitted to being impressed by anything. "Well then, if ye ha' finished bundling the grand harp, follow me."

"Aye, thank ye."

They went out into the driving rain, Katrin pulling the hood of her cloak, which she'd retained against the cool damp in the hall, up over her hair. She went swiftly, and Finlay kept up with long strides.

Katrin had a sudden vision of him loping over heather-clad hills on those long legs of his, heading God knew where.

She stopped in front of a low hut and pushed her way in. Lit a candle with dripping hands.

"This is one o' the huts where we billet our visitors' attendants," she explained as he stepped in behind her. She gazed about. The place suddenly looked too plain for a man of his talents. A bit doubtfully she said, "I hope ye will be comfortable enough here. 'Tis yours for as long as ye wish to stay."

"I shall be more than happy here." But focused once again on Katrin, he barely spared a glance for the small room.

"If there is aught ye require, ye will come to me."

"I surely will."

"Then I hope ye enjoy a good rest."

"I do no' doubt it, mistress. Thank ye."

Carefully, he set down the harp. Began to remove his cloak.

Past time for Katrin to leave. And yet—inexplicably she hung back, watching as with neat movements he shook out the wet garment and hung it from a peg set in the wall.

"Tell me, Master Finlay—"

"Aye?" He turned to face her. Rain glittered like jewels in the red of his hair.

"How is it ye know so much of my family's history? Or—was the better part o' all that made up? Grand tales to flatter my father, perhaps."

"Nay, and nay." He straightened. "'Twas all the truth I told."

Katrin felt a thrill. Those stories! Those grand, brave, and wonderful people!

"But how? How could ye know all that?"

His deep-green eyes met hers and the smile touched them like light through a forest.

"'Tis my job to know, mistress. A bard is no' just a singer. He is a carrier o' history. A keeper o' old truths and ancient songs."

To be sure, he had a magical tongue, did this man. And clever with it. What he claimed might, or might not, be true. He wanted their patronage.

But ah, a part of her, practical or not, wanted to believe. Believe in such a love as that of which he'd told, one that stretched across the ages.

"Ye do no' remember me, do ye?" Finlay asked suddenly.

That had Katrin swinging back to face him. "Should I?"

A wry smile curled his lips. "Perhaps no'."

"Ye ha' never visited here at Murtray before, have ye?"

"I have, long ago. Once when I was but a lad and apprenticed to the bard Caradoc of Snowdon, who taught me how to play. He did bring me here. I ne'er forgot the place."

"Aye? I regret to say, I do no' recall. I must ha' been very young."

"We both were." Was there some message in his eyes? But ah, her mind was still half caught in the dreams he'd woven.

"I will let ye sleep." She turned for the door.

"Thank ye, mistress," he said again.

Katrin went back out into the rain, still feeling curiously unsettled. He had given her only half an explanation as to how he knew so many details about her family's history, things even she had never heard before. That her ancestors had come from Ireland—well, aye, she had heard hints of that long ago. That among them had been a great warrior and a prodigal son. That she carried the blood of a Pictish princess, and aye, well, some Norse blood also.

That showed in the color of her hair. In her height. In her propensity, or so Geordie had claimed, to pick up a sword.

Aye, sometimes her fingers fairly itched for one.

How could Finlay know that?

She was tired, her mind stuffed with stories, and she must give it up for this night, at least, as impossible to know.

She needed her bed.

She might even sleep, if she could chase those dreams away.

CHAPTER TWO

F INLAY TURNED SLOWLY and surveyed the room in which he found himself. A poor enough chamber built of stone, barely furnished with a narrow bed and not much more. But someone had laid a fire and he had only to put flint to it in order to be warm.

He had subsisted in worse places, much worse, both back when he had traveled with Caradoc and later, on his own.

But he had hoped for lodgings in the chief's house, where he would be nearer the heart of things. He reminded himself he was but an itinerant musician who had turned up—felicitously, as Chief Anders claimed—for a few scant days or so. Rooms in the keep alongside the family were reserved for honored guests.

Which he was not.

He must be patient. On the whole, he was a patient man, one who took his time and thought through his decisions before he implemented them. Using that patience, he had wandered his known world picking up pieces and laying them together in his mind. Following a trail so ancient that at times he feared he would never reach its end.

Here, at the age of eight and twenty and no longer such a young man, he had found that end. As if the ever-turning wheel of life had paused, and at last he was where he meant to be.

He had only to await the rest of it. But och, when the heart was involved, patience was a difficult virtue to achieve.

He caught up the flint that hung from a cord beside the fire and hunkered down to strike the flame. The kindling had been well placed, and the flames rose swiftly, spreading almost magical warmth. Something to fight against the damp chill that threatened to invade him.

He rose and unwrapped the harp, wiping the last bit of moisture from her with a cloth he kept for the purpose, guarding her comfort ahead of his own. A prize she was, her price earned through a thousand performances, made to his order by the masters in Erin.

Brada.

Bradana.

An image of a woman's face swam through the mists in his mind. Wide, bonny blue eyes. Features a tad too strong to represent beauty but so beautiful, aye, to him.

He had followed her. *Followed.*

Longingly, he stroked the strings of the harp, knowing his fingers traced the trail of hers, evoking ancient songs.

Briskly now, for he despised self-pity, he turned from the harp and shed his wet clothing, donning instead dry garments from his pack before he lay down upon the cot.

He wondered by whom the tiny hut—one of a number, as he'd seen when Mistress Katrin led him here—had been occupied in the past. Other chief's servants or warriors, Mistress Katrin had said, which seemed a curious thing. Also perhaps messengers forced to take lodging overnight. Knights bearing military orders, who stopped on their way.

The stronghold, being old and reasonably prosperous, would accommodate such. He was provided a bed, as he would no doubt be offered silver come morning. Would he be expected then to leave? Go on his way up the road?

The kingdom of Scotland, caught in the midst of ongoing war, lay in chaos. Surely he might claim refuge here for a time.

He closed his eyes. Would he be allowed sleep this night? Some nights, he slept like a dead man. Others, the dreams and longings racked him and brought him awake time after time, alive with memories, some wondrous and some so terrible he could scarce endure them.

This night, the old gods blessed him and he slept without dreaming.

He woke to find the rain had flown, chased by a blustery wind from off the sea. He left his quarters neat, as was his habit, and went out to look at the day. He required, with a deep need, to view the place.

A glorious holding was MacMurtray's, situated at the very edge of the Scottish mainland and facing the Western Isles. The sea, dark blue today and edged with white combers, stretched wide, and contained a number of small, offshore islands lying like sleeping green dragons. A strip of shingle traced the shore like a stone necklace, and away to the south the path climbed to a headland. The settlement had spread northward to encompass what had once been a Norse encampment, some three hundred years before.

So much had changed.

So much had not.

"Master harper?" someone hailed him, and he spun where he stood. Chief Anders himself it was, with a couple other men at his side. Advisors, perhaps, beside whom Finlay had noticed him sitting last evening.

"Come and tak' yer breakfast," Anders invited him.

At the chief's gesture, Finlay joined the men. "Thank ye, Chief MacMurtray. I am indebted for yer hospitality."

"Nonsense. Ye more than earned it wi' the wondrous stories ye told. By my soul! I ha' never heard the like."

Anders MacMurtray was a big, bluff, hearty man scarcely a shade taller than Finlay himself, but two of him in bulk, with strong bones and shrewd blue eyes. His recent worries concerning the country's current state of upheaval, no less than the loss of his son, had scored deep lines in a face that had once been handsome, and carried the remnants still. A widower he was, and said to be much sought after by the widows of the district.

"I am very glad ye enjoyed my tales, Chief MacMurtray."

"Enjoyed? More than that, master harper—your tales lifted me fro' mysel'. I felt as if I'd been on a long journey."

"As are we all, chief."

Anders smiled. "Ye will break your fast wi' me." He turned to the men who accompanied him, one of whom Finlay now recognized as his seneschal. "Ye will see to the lodging for the new arrivals? They should be here by this afternoon."

"Aye, Chief MacMurtray."

The men hurried off.

Politely, Finlay asked, "New arrivals?"

"Aye. We ha' a troop o' Gallowglass warriors comin' in."

"Gallowglass?" Legendary mercenaries they were, warriors supposedly without equal. What need might MacMurtray have for such?

MacMurtray hesitated. "They are fine warriors out for hire. Mostly fro' Ireland, but they tak' their ranks fro' Scottish men too, who find themsel's at loose ends."

"Aye, Chief MacMurtray, I'm familiar wi' them. But I do wonder at yer need for them."

"Come, sit down."

Anders led Finlay into the hall, still being cleared after last night's feasting, which had run late. The room bustled. Maids hurried everywhere. A man raked out the fire, preparing to lay a fresh one.

Anders led Finlay to the head table where he'd sat last night. It had already been cleared.

"Sit, sit," Anders told him. He called to one of the serving women. "Bring us plenty to eat, lass."

So simple a command, *bring us plenty to eat*. Yet there had been times both when in Caradoc's company and after when *plenty* had been beyond Finlay's reach. When his stomach had been fair stuck to his backbone with emptiness.

He had always been assured of a welcome in Wales. But Scotland was where he needed to be. And at some of the land's dingier keeps he'd been turned away with no more than a snarl, despite his hunger.

Now Anders looked at him across the table with those shrewd blue eyes. "Ye will ha' heard about the death o' my son, Geordie."

"Aye, indeed, Chief MacMurtray. Ye ha' my sympathy."

"Geordie was as fine a son as a man could have. My wife— God rest her—gave me but the two bairns, a son and a daughter. But my Geordie was a lad of whom anyone would be proud."

"How long past did ye lose him?"

"Ye mean to tell me ye donna ken? Ye seem to know more than I, o' my family's history." Anders softened the words with a smile. "Ye've heard o' Earl John Randolph, of Moray?"

"Aye, so. A staunch supporter o' the king, is he no'?"

"I sent my son there into his service wi' a number o' our other warriors. The others came home, though he did no'. An accident on the practice field, it was said, and the others only returned carryin' him. Aye, and well loved he was. The wailin' o' the women when he came home thus would fair hurt yer ears."

"I see." So, Katrin had lost her brother in an incident on the training field. The mere thought of it sent a shiver down Finlay's spine. Truly and truly, the wheel of time did sometimes turn back upon itself.

"I lost my heir, and his only cousin dead also as a wee lad. There may be other members o' the family far flung. If there are, I do not know o' them. My daughter"—Anders paused again and scanned the room as if he expected to see Katrin there—"has nay agreed to tak' a husband. A stubborn, headstrong lass she is, and has refused every man who has come her way till, as ye may ha' noticed, she is well past the age o' marrying."

Was she? Katrin could not be above a score and six.

"So I ha' nay grandson from her, to whom I might leave the holding. Geordie had nay issue either, being too busy wi' training and fulfilling my obligations to tak' a wife."

Finlay said nothing. He was good at listening quietly.

"But," Anders went on heavily, "that is no' my concern now—though it will be, eh? I canna live forever. We are at war, and me wi' an obligation toward John Randolph to supply men. Since I ha' more wealth than men o' blood, I thought o' the Gallowglass."

Finlay nodded. A risky business, taking on mercenaries who could not always be trusted to keep from deserting. Though for all he had heard of the Gallowglass—orderly companies of some renown—they had their own code of honor.

Anders could have chosen worse.

The maid brought their breakfast. Anders set to it like a man without a care in the world, even though trouble still lay in his eyes.

"The troop o' Gallowglass I have hired will be mustering here, helping to train some o' my younger lads, and waiting for Earl Randolph's order to march south. That is why we are tryin' to find lodgings."

Finlay nodded.

"I hope, master harper, ye will oblige us by staying on and help to entertain them wi' yer grand stories, before we ha' to move out. They are mostly from Ireland, but as I know full well, ye will ha' stories fro' there, to their liking."

"I ha' stories fro' Ireland, aye." Besides the first he'd told here. "It is a generous offer o' your hospitality, Chief MacMurtray."

"Nonsense. I ha' never before heard a shanachie o' yer skill. It lightens my heart to listen to ye. Now eat yer breakfast. There is a busy day ahead."

CHAPTER THREE

WHEN KATRIN ENTERED the great hall and saw her father sitting with the harper, she frowned. A hundred things to do this morn and Da sat chattering away to the minstrel as if they had not a care in the world.

In truth, they had cares aplenty. She had herself been up before dawn, only vaguely glad the fierce rain had ceased while numbering the details in her mind. Since Ma's death four years ago, she—with the help of Da's seneschal, Angus—had seen to the running of this place, the small and gritty details that raised life here from subsistent to comfortable. Or so she hoped.

It was a role to which she considered herself singularly ill suited. She detested domestic chores, and, in fact, when Ma was alive, she had run from them at all cost. She had likewise avoided any offers of marriage.

Not that she failed to admire men—from a reasonable distance. She quite liked looking at them, some more than others. A battle-fit fighting man could stir her blood. But she'd yet to meet the man who was not more trouble than he was worth.

The idea of being tied to one in marriage? Bah!

Now she found her father sitting with the harper who was anything but a warrior, although…

As she approached the pair seated at the head table, she put her head to one side. There was something about Master Finlay. She could not lay her finger on what.

In truth, she supposed it was fortuitous she'd caught him here with Da after all.

"Excuse me." She paused beside them.

Finlay rose smoothly to his feet. She tended to forget how tall he was till she stood beside him, and she was no delicate flower. He did not look so when seated with his harp. For he was slim as a whipcord and graceful in his movements.

"Mistress Katrin."

"Good morning. I trust ye slept well, Master Finlay?"

"Tolerably well, aye."

He continued to look at her so, with such close attention. An odd fellow withal.

"Da, we are come up short on housing for the soldiers ye ha' hired. And that affects ye, Master Finlay, as I am sorry to say. I shall ha' to change yer lodging. That is, if ye plan to stay on wi' us."

He had entertained them all and done it well, but surely he must grasp that this was a house in flux. He might as well clear out of her way.

Da spoke from his bench, not having bothered to rise. "I ha' just finished asking Master Finlay to stay. He can help to entertain the Gallowglass."

Katrin tried not to let her annoyance show. "Shall we have need to entertain them? They are but hired soldiers."

"Highly honored ones. Captain O'Hanlon and his troop are famed across several lands. We were lucky to get them."

And foolish to pay them, Katrin thought. They did not come cheap. And now she would have to feed them—and feed the harper, if he was required to entertain them—until they marched out to fight this proxy war.

The preparation for which had cost her brother's life.

The pain of that kept on hitting her over and over again, sometimes when she least expected it. In a curious way, it seemed a very old hurt, as well as a fresh one—a thing Katrin felt more than understood.

This war would beggar them before it was done, in both

people and silver. Already too many lost. Not that she did not believe in the cause, she who possessed a loyal Scots heart. But…

She looked again at the bard. He stood yet on his feet, waiting patiently for her to speak. Ah, well, she expected a man who dwelt on the sufferance of others must acquire patience.

Yet when he looked at her, something besides patience lay in those green eyes.

"The long and the short of it is, master harper, if ye are to stay I shall have to move ye from yer lodgings. I can fit two soldiers at least into the hut where ye are staying. I understand most will billet out in the bailey, but"—she looked at her father—"O'Hanlon, ye said the leader is called, has requested lodging for his officers."

"'Tis no' a problem," Finlay said promptly.

Would he now choose to leave? Realize hers was a household under fierce demand and take himself off out of the way despite Da's insistence?

"I can fit in any small space ye can spare."

"Nonsense," said Da, speaking before Katrin could. "Daughter, ye will put him in Geordie's room."

"What?" Katrin drew a breath, and a scalding heat flooded through her. Ma used to say that was one of her faults—she reacted too swiftly and often without due thought, when her emotions became involved.

In this instance, her emotions were valid.

No one had entered her brother's chamber since his body had been brought home. Well, only herself in order to finger his belongings once or twice, to catch his scent. To throw herself on his bed and weep.

Geordie had been one of the few who knew her, truly knew her and accepted all she was.

Gone.

For the harper to step into his place—och, nay!

Finlay watched her face closely, and Da said with a carelessness that did not fool her, "We need the space, aye? And 'tis no' as if yer brother will be back again."

"But—" Katrin sucked in another breath between clenched teeth.

Finlay said, "I can sleep outside if need be. Or in the stable. 'Tis no' as if I have not done so many a time."

"No' beneath my roof!" Da thundered. "Such an honored and gifted guest as Master Finlay shall be offered the best accommodation we can provide."

"Aye, Da." Katrin did not look at Finlay now but at a spot in the air over his left shoulder. "Ye will ha' to gi' me a bit o' time. That chamber has no' been touched since—"

"There is nay hurry, mistress. We ha' the day long."

He had the day long to sit here beside the fire and talk with Da until, presumably, he was required to weave more beautiful music. A luxury they could not at this time afford.

But such decisions were scarcely up to her. She needed merely to make what her father decided upon happen. A singularly frustrating position in which to be.

"Sit back down and finish yer breakfast," she told the bard. "I will let ye know when to gather yer things and shift to—to the chamber here in the house."

He did not move until she walked away from him. She might well consider such a man, limited in his autonomy, to be weak. But aye, there was something about Master Finlay that, despite his gentle voice and biddable demeanor, declared him anything but weak.

He had spun tales of strong warriors and fearless women—all supposedly her own ancestors—as if he knew and understood them. As if he too possessed an utterly loyal and unflinching heart. A loving one. So how could she declare him weak?

There must be steel at the core of that graceful frame, and strength behind those green eyes.

And why was she still thinking of the harper when she had so much else to do?

She worked her way through several tasks before heading to

her brother's chamber, which lay only steps from Da's and her own. Outside the door she came to a dead stop, unable to lift the latch.

She had not entered here more than five times since their men had arrived home from their assignment with Earl John Randolph, bringing Geordie's body. She had dashed in here then to find clothing in which he could go to his grave—the finest he owned. She'd helped to wash and dress him too, though she could do nothing but weep all the while.

So powerful was the memory that standing here, with one hand on the latch and the other splayed against the oak panel, she almost expected to find him inside. There stretched out upon his bed, perhaps, or sitting at the window with his nose in a book, for he had a fine mind as well as prowess at arms. If she opened this door he would turn, smile the way he always did when he saw her, make some quip, and unleash that big laugh of his that always made her feel safe and loved.

How could that be gone? All his energy, all his warmth?

She used to talk to Geordie the way she did to no one else, just go on at him so much that she was surprised, looking back, he had not grown tired of her prattling. He'd always listened patiently. She'd complained to him about how she could not see why *she* couldn't be trained at arms. Was she not strong? Quick? Able to withstand any hurts she might acquire? Just because she was a woman, should she be denied the right to defend herself?

He'd given her training. Even stood up to Da, when their father learned about it.

It came to Katrin now that had she been his brother rather than his sister, and at his side in training as she wished, she might have prevented the terrible accident that resulted in his death. She might have kept him with her still.

She opened the door.

The room lay empty except for Geordie's belongings. Bright daylight came in through the single window, and the air from the door set dust motes dancing. The bed lay in shadow, almost as if someone did lie there. Items were scattered. Some of those garments she had flung about on that terrible day. But nay, Geordie had never been a tidy man.

It looked, despite the dust, as if he'd only just walked out.

With a sigh and an enormous effort of will, Katrin went in.

CHAPTER FOUR

NOT TILL LATE afternoon did Mistress Katrin come to Finlay once more, finding him standing in the open air watching some of Murtray's men drilling.

"I am sorry it has taken me so long to prepare your quarters," she told him politely enough, yet still with that edge of impatience that seemed to characterize her. "There was much to do."

"That is well," he replied easily, using it as an excuse to let his gaze rest on her. She appeared frazzled, her hair—which surely she had not touched since morning—in disarray, her clothing smudged with dust. Her cheeks appeared similarly smudged. Had she shed tears amid her duties? Despite all that, she was the bonniest thing he had ever seen.

Ashen hair she had, not blonde nor brown, thick and heavy, agleam in the afternoon light. A strong frame that somehow managed to appear utterly feminine. A stubborn chin and a proud nose. Eyes that defied the world to pity her.

Ah, he would not pity her. Love? Love was another thing. Had he not been born to love this woman?

"I am in nay hurry," he added. "Let me collect my things from the hut. 'Twill take no time at all."

She followed him hence, the two of them skirting the activity in the yard. When they ducked into the hut she gazed around. Likely she believed this was what he deserved, a clean, comfortable, yet plain accommodation. Not a favored chamber in the master's house.

He reached for his pack and she forestalled him. "I will tak' that. Ye carry yer harp."

"Mistress, I am used to toting my belongings all about Scotland and beyond."

"No matter. I can help."

He let her do so and, carrying Brada, followed her back through the busy yard into the house. It grew quieter as they ascended the stairs and headed along a stone corridor.

She paused outside a door, and he saw her shoulders set before she led him in.

"I ha' changed the linen and we ha' given the place a good sweep. Put my brother's things in storage. Ye will let me know if there is aught else ye need."

"I canna imagine there will be." Finlay let his gaze explore the room. He could understand why she did not want him here—a stranger taking up a place at the very heart of her home. "I shall be quite comfortable. Thank ye."

"Aye." The word sounded bleak.

"And I regret if I ha' caused ye extra trouble."

She looked at him then, the wide eyes—pale gray with a dark rim of blue around the irises—finding his. Holding.

"'Tis no fault o' yours," she allowed.

"Still and all—"

"I must go begin the preparations for supper." She turned away. He longed to reach for her hand, make her stay but a moment longer. Somehow, he refrained.

Yet she turned back almost as if she felt his desire. "Will ye play for us tonight?"

"Aye, mistress, to be sure, if your father requests it." And would that please her? Did his music find its way to her heart?

No way to tell, for she merely nodded and went out, leaving barely a whisper behind.

She did not want him here in her brother's room. Taking her brother's place.

He could not help that.

He placed Brada against the wall beside the bed and explored the place. It had been thoroughly if hastily cleared. The carved wooden wardrobe over against the opposite wall stood open and empty.

What had she done with her brother's things? Stored them, she'd said. And what did she imagine he, a wanderer, might have to fill that space?

He could not fill this space.

But after some thought, he untied his pack and went to the window to look out. The room faced the rear and a great stretch of garden. A woman worked there in what must be a space for kitchen herbs. Farther out, a kale yard and a wild tangle of flowers and fruit trees invited the eye.

He could still hear the sea. Even on a mild day such as this he could, as if it were the life's blood of this place.

It might lull him to sleep.

He turned back to survey the chamber and almost thought he caught a glimpse of a figure there. Big and bluff and hearty, with sandy hair like his sister's and great energy.

Ah, and would he have to share this space with a ghost?

"I mean yer sister nay harm," he said aloud into the air of the room. "Pray, do no' begrudge me."

Did the air of the chamber stir? A response, mayhap.

Och, enough of such fancy. He had come here, the end of a long, long journey, to turn dreams into reality.

If he could.

Even if it were more than fancy, sharing a chamber with a spirit was not about to deter him.

KATRIN ORDERED AN extra board laid that night for the Gallow-glass, but they did not arrive. All through the meal she half expected them to come crashing in, but by the time Finlay took up his harp, a certain peace had settled around the hall.

She'd meant to walk out once the entertainment began. Take some time away on her own. Mayhap hike up the slope to Geordie's grave where he slept beside Ma.

When first he'd been laid there, she'd gone every day. Stood fighting tears—for a warrior, even be she female, rarely wept— and indulging in memories. Now it had been a while.

But Master Finlay's music caught hold of her, persuaded and seduced her. He did not tell a tale this night, merely gave them glorious music that seemed to wend its way deep into her mind.

Leaning back from her bench against the wall, she closed her eyes and saw—

A small, close room made of wattle and stone. Surely she knew this place. It was dark in the tiny chamber, or nearly so. Beyond its walls, music played.

Music played, the same sort of music she listened to here in her father's hall. Light, tripping, graceful notes. A song she knew.

A man held her in his arms. Nay, not a man—the man, the one in all the world who possessed her heart. He held her and made love to her with such sweetness, such devotion, it fair convulsed her heart.

Such love. Such belonging. Love and parting.

They were to part.

Her eyes flew open. She found the hall just the same. The fire burning lazily. Da sitting as if spellbound by the bard's music. The others at their ease, drinking ale. And Finlay, Finlay with his head bent gracefully over the strings of his harp.

Everything just the same, yet nothing was the same. It felt almost as if, somewhere, a wheel had turned.

Why should she imagine such a scene as that one, even in a brief flash? It had never happened; she'd never made love with a man, any man, in a tiny room while harp music swirled around them.

It must be pure fancy, though she was not a fanciful woman.

But ah—had not Finlay told a tale of such? The two lovers, Deathan and Darlei, set to part and making desperate love together in a tiny chamber adjacent to his father's hall.

It must be that, which Finlay's music brought to mind. For an instant she'd imagined she was Darlei, that wild-hearted Caledonian princess held fast in the arms of the man she adored.

She stirred, took up a pitcher, and moved about the room refilling cups, even though there were two serving women already at that task. She could not keep still.

Finlay, as caught up in his music as she, did not glance at her. But she paused near him, the better to hear him play. The exquisite quiver of each string. The beauty of his hands moving across them.

He ended one tune with a shimmering flicker of notes and began another in an odd key, sad and beguiling, that once more sent her senses skittering away. An old tune it must be. Unfamiliar. *Familiar.*

Surely she'd heard it before, mayhap long ago in childhood, come from another harper's hands. Da used to invite in any that were passing. And she had a good ear.

She would have to ask Finlay where he got his tunes. From all over, he would likely say. Had he not told her he had gathered them in Wales and Brittany and Ireland?

She needed to ask him again, with more insistence, where he'd got the tales he had told. How he knew so much of them. She must sit and speak with him—

The tune ended and the spell broke. All at once, Katrin was able to move. People stirred. The evening was done.

She would, however, carry that last tune into her dreams.

She went out and walked, once the hall had cleared, through the soft dark of the evening. She could hear voices from behind her, the last of the clan's folk straggling home. A big treat it was for them to be called to the chief's hall so often, for a chance to listen to a harper of Master Finlay's ilk.

He had gone off already to his chamber. *Geordie's chamber.*

She listened as the voices died away, and the hiss and draw of the waves filled the night. There was no moon, but a stone path led the way up the slope to the graveyard.

Was anybody here? Hard to tell among the yew trees, the rowans, and the heather. She paused at Geordie's grave and began to speak.

"Are ye here? Are ye back in yer room? I swear sometimes I can feel ye, as if I might turn around and ye will be standing there. Is there somewhat ye want of me? Something ye need for me to do? If so, just say so. I will do anything."

Silence but for the sea behind her. Long ago, if the harper could be believed, this place had belonged to her ancestress's grandsire. Bradana's.

Katrin's roots ran deep into the stony soil. If Geordie's did also, how could he be anywhere else?

"Tell me what to do with these wild feelings that fill me," she bade her brother. She had never imagined such a love as the harper had described between her ancestors, those two who seemed to have journeyed together through time from life to life.

Such was but pure fancy, was it not?

CHAPTER FIVE

THE GALLOWGLASS TROOP arrived the next day, bursting upon the keep with such a clatter and furor that Katrin scorned herself for having kept watch all the while, fearing she might miss them. No one could miss so many strapping males at full bore.

They arrived on foot, being in fact a troop of foot soldiers, a group of some thirty in number, all big and heavily armed.

All loud.

From the outset, Katrin knew life at Murtray would never be the same. She hoped Da understood what he had wrought.

She watched from the main door as they passed through the gate and into the bailey where, as she understood, most of them would bivouac until Earl Randolph called them up. Indeed, Da had told Katrin that he meant to send a message to Earl Randolph upon their arrival letting him know he now stood ready with reinforcements.

Katrin had argued with Da about that, before ever he sent for these men. He believed he owed a duty of loyalty and fealty to Randolph, even if it beggared them.

It just might.

Eyeing the soldiers, she wondered what it would take to keep them fed. At the same time, something in her soul responded to the sight of them. She'd always had an attraction to a man fitted for war. And these were definitely warriors, flagrant males to the core. What woman could keep from responding to that?

The officers—three of them, to her understanding—would

require separate accommodation. She would put two of them together. The captain in the harper's former hut.

As the daughter of the house, she needed to go forward, speak to the men and determine which of them was, in fact, the captain.

Unless she could pick him out.

Da had already gone rushing forth greeting the men and providing a hearty welcome. Katrin narrowed her eyes as she watched him. The men all moved with a certain amount of authority. One of them…

He was tall, as were they all, his fair hair long and braided, carrying a touch of red. He wore two long mustaches framing a generous mouth and was clad in armor of leather and mail that fit him like a second skin. He fair bristled with weapons, including a great claymore worn across his back. Pure masculinity, in fact, on the hoof.

Indeed, for an instant Katrin lost her breath. Who was he? He had to be their leader, such a man.

It seemed so, for Da had fallen in at his side. Together they moved toward her.

She went down the steps, paused on the bottom one so that when the men reached her, they were all of a height.

"Katrin, this is Reagan O'Hanlon."

Irish. *He was an Irish warrior.*

For an instant, there in the sun of the yard, Katin's vision blurred. *She saw another man, one with a mane of auburn hair and a steady, hazel gaze. Foremost among the warriors.*

She saw him with his sword in hand aboard a chariot, riding away to battle. Away from her.

This man's sword remained strapped across his back, and at his belt he wore a war axe such as the Norse had been want to carry—or so the old stories such as Finlay gave them told. A knife strapped to one shin. The man was a walking arsenal.

Och, was this what they had come to?

"Master O'Hanlon," she said.

He focused on her, and it felt like being pinned by a wildcat. Tawny eyes he had, with a feline intensity of attention. A cat, tracking its dinner.

"Mistress." A deep, gravelly voice that caused the skin on the back of her neck to prickle.

Refusing to be intimidated by him or anyone, Katrin drew herself up and met his gaze. "I understand your men will bivouac in the bailey."

"That is so. From what I have seen, they should be comfortable enough." The wings of his mustache wiggled as his wide lips curved. "They are not accustomed, ye understand, to soft beds."

"Aye, so. I ha' other accommodations for yoursel' and your commanders. If ye will come wi' me."

He turned and bellowed over his shoulder, "William! Conyer."

Two other men peeled off from the group and, with a certain gravity, O'Hanlon introduced them. William was dark with the devil in his eyes and Conyer brown as a bear.

Sweet heaven, the women of the settlement were going to lose their heads over this lot.

"This is the chief's daughter," O'Hanlon informed the pair, "and mistress o' the house. Ye will make sure the men treat her accordingly."

A surprising thing to say. Did he imagine otherwise?

"Do your men tend to grow impolite, Master O'Hanlon?" she inquired with weighty calm. "We have young lasses about, and children."

His gaze did not flicker from her face. "My men know their jobs and are very good at them. But they do get bored when idle, and therein lies the danger. 'Tis my understanding we will need to tarry here till your father's lord calls us up."

"That is my understanding also," Katrin agreed.

Da had already walked off. Katrin sent a look after him. Ah well, he knew little more than she as to when Laird Randolph would summon them to battle.

"Pray follow me. I will show ye your quarters."

The stone huts seemed smaller than ever with the men inside, but William and Conyer appeared satisfied with the accommodations and made no complaint.

Katrin led O'Hanlon last to the hut where Finlay had passed a night. "I hope this will do, Master O'Hanlon."

"'Twill suit me fine." When she turned to him, she found he looked not at the chamber, but at her. A raw measure of awareness sprang to life in the tiny place.

"If there is aught ye or your men need, ye can ask me or Angus, who is my father's seneschal. I am sure ye saw him there in the bailey, a tall, thin man."

"I did see him, aye."

"I shall send a lad to let ye know when dinner is laid."

"Do not cause yourself any trouble, Mistress Katrin. Ye need not call my lot o' ruffians into your hall. They will be happy enough at their camp."

Oh, and that would be a great relief to her. "Are ye certain? We ha' already set a board for them."

Again, the wings of his mustache twitched. "I thank ye for that, but they would all be happier if they kept to their camp."

"I will tell my father so. But ye—" She could not help but send a glance over him, half inquiry, half wonder. "Will ye and your commanders join us for supper?"

He gazed back at her for a moment before he replied, "'Twould be my pleasure, mistress, to dine with ye."

That was not what she'd meant, precisely. She could scarcely say so.

"Good. We ha' a fine harper wi' us at present. I do no' ken whether ye enjoy a well-told tale, but..." Her voice trailed off. This man routinely beheaded other men with his battle-axe. What did he want with pretty stories?

But he said, "Am I not from Ireland? Did we not invent the art o' the tale?"

Had they?

"Well, then, I shall send a lad to call ye in."

"Do that. I will no' be here, but wi' my men. Is there a field, mistress, we can use for drilling?"

"Aye, there is. To the south o' the keep, where we exercise the ponies."

"Then we shall do well enough. Thank ye for your hospitality."

"Ye are most welcome."

But was he? Katrin asked herself that question as she walked away and back to the hall. The Gallowglass were bound to provide a disruption she did not need.

She liked an ordered life. Things in their places and expectations met. The Gallowglass looked to turn everything on its head in noise and confusion.

Such was war, she reminded herself. They lived in a time of battle and strife. She must do her part even if that was but as the mistress of the house.

Even if she'd rather be marching out herself, with a sword in her hand.

CHAPTER SIX

T HE MOOD OF the settlement had changed, so Finlay decided
when he took his place in the hall that evening. With the
arrival of the Gallowglass troop, the energy had risen along with
the noise level. A squad of tents sprang up in the bailey like rather
grubby toadstools and armed men strode everywhere.

He'd had a look outside when he came down from his chamber, that belonging to Mistress Katrin's brother, and had to admit
his heart quickened. Many and many were the stories he carried
in his head, more than a few of them about such warriors.

Some of the stories were his own.

But he had chosen differently this time on his ride around the
wheel of life, had he not? Chosen as he'd been bidden.

Still and all, something about the clatter of it, the stir and the
banked magnificence, caught at him. His very muscles twitched.

Long ago, long, long ago, he had trained as a warrior. A man
did not forget.

He had to force himself to go inside, set up his harp, and take
his place at the side table where he would sup. Along, so it
seemed, with a new guest.

The man, a strapping figure who could be none other than
the head of the Gallowglass troop, stood speaking with Anders
MacMurtray when Finlay entered. Finlay knew enough of
fighting men to grasp that he had shed much of his weaponry
along with his chain mail cotte. He stood with his arms crossed
on his chest speaking to Anders, the torchlight shining on his

tawny hair.

Finlay's attention was snagged when Mistress Katrin entered the hall. She wore blue tonight, undoubtedly her color, and as it always did, his very breath hitched at the sight of her.

Helpless against the feeling, he was. The feeling of wanting her.

Did she not know? Could she not feel this?

A curious sort of woman she was, a blend of the brisk and the impatient, as if with every word and every step she fought inwardly against who she was. She played the role of the dutiful daughter, but it did not quite fit.

He watched as she walked up to her father and his Gallowglass companion, and began speaking to them. Both men nodded at her. Anders went to his place at the head table.

Katrin led the Gallowglass to Finlay's table.

Last night before beginning to sing and play, he had shared it with a number of Murtray clansmen who had been more than welcoming. The smith and the head man who cared for the ponies, and the healer. Now another place had been laid at the board.

Finlay was to have company.

He stood motionless as Katrin introduced the man, Reagan O'Hanlon. Aye, so, an Irishman, and he looked it, with that indefinable something about him that screamed *Ireland*. A controlled kind of power he had also, and vitality Finlay could feel.

As Katrin stepped away, O'Hanlon nodded at the occupants of the table in a casual and friendly fashion.

"So ye be the harper," he said, focusing last on Finlay. "Mistress Katrin did say ye were wondrously gifted."

That gave Finlay a warm rush. The other occupants of the table jumped in, telling the captain about the stories Finlay had given them, all of which they well remembered.

"Never ha' I heard the like," the healer enthused.

"I am sorry I missed it," O'Hanlon said with a half-smile.

"Whence in Ireland do ye hail?" Finlay asked.

"Meath. Are ye familiar with the green isle?"

"I am, and roamed there in days gone by."

"Aye, so, I imagine a harper such as yourself covers many a league. But ye be Scots?"

"Aye, I am."

"As ye may imagine, I have traveled far also," O'Hanlon said. "Though I do not expect my accolades have been the same as your own."

Finlay reckoned not.

Anders stood at the head table and spoke in welcome of the Gallowglass, telling his gathered folk of their purpose and the debt he owed to Earl Randolph. The platters began to circulate around the hall.

Finlay's table companions plied O'Hanlon with questions. Where had he traveled? What sights had he seen? How many battles had he fought?

To which he replied, "Countless."

Finlay tried to imagine it. Perhaps not so surprisingly, he could. The clash and din of battle. The raw edge of courage in a man's heart. The determination and the narrowing of sight...

O'Hanlon, calmly eating his supper, did not brag on himself, even though those at the table gave him plenty of room for it. A modest man, mayhap. Or one so confident, he had no need to stoke his own pride. Either that or he had become hardened to the glory of what he did to earn his bread.

For there was a certain amount of glory in it. As a storyteller, Finlay both sensed and appreciated that.

Besides, as a young lad, had he not himself began with training at arms? Before he'd realized that could not possibly be his calling...

What began to bother Finlay as the meal moved along was naught about Master O'Hanlon so much as the realization that when Katrin glanced toward their table, it was to the Gallowglass captain her eyes were drawn.

To be sure, she might well be checking to make certain her guest had all he needed. But it was no such mundane concern Finlay saw in her eyes.

Nay, for there he beheld interest. A measure of fascination.

Aware as he was of Katrin's every movement, he knew when she rose and began making the rounds of the hall. Felt it when she approached their table.

She had braided her hair this night. It fell over her shoulder in a thick, ashen plait when she bent down. As did her bosom press forward inside her blue gown.

"I trust ye ha' everything ye need, Master O'Hanlon?"

The Gallowglass looked up. As caught by her pale, clear eyes as was Finlay? For an instant the man looked taken aback, just as Finlay felt.

"Aye, mistress, thank ye."

Finlay got to his feet and Katrin looked at him, startled. Remembering belatedly that he was also there?

"Excuse me, mistress."

He went to his place beside the hearth and took up the harp. As always, he felt better with Brada in his hands.

He nodded toward O'Hanlon's table, where Katrin still stood.

"In honor o' the chief's guest, I will gi' ye some tunes and tales o' Ireland this night, for yer pleasure."

With chagrin he saw Katrin slip into the seat he had just left. Opposite the Gallowglass.

But, as he reminded himself, she would be listening to *him*.

He gave them an old tale indeed of the great warrior, Cuchulain, he who during a grand and terrible battle planted his back against a stone and fought so well that even after he was killed, no enemy dared come near to him. Finlay lost himself in the music. Did he forget the lass who listened?

Not quite.

He had not figured, after winning his way here to her at last, that he would be caught in a competition for her. And he resolved not to be drawn into such. A woman's heart was her own and must be freely given. Else it was worth naught at all.

The trouble was, this woman's heart meant his whole world.

The spell he wove in the hall this evening must have been a strong one. For when he finished, when the guests began to leave for their beds and he took up his harp, O'Hanlon came to him.

"I did enjoy that, Master Finlay. Mistress Katrin was not mistaken—ye be a fine harper. I do not know when I have so relished an evening's entertainment."

"That is generous praise, Master O'Hanlon."

"Naught but the truth. I should like to commission fro' ye a march for our company. Wha' is yer price?"

"I am at the moment under Chief MacMurtray's hospitality, and nay price to one o' his guests."

"Aye, so, I ha' a valiant troop who would appreciate a tune in their honor."

"Would they so? Tell me about them."

"More than half hail from Ireland. The rest are from Scotland and Wales, and two from Brittany that we picked up along the way. Our man Modur, a Welshman, often sings for us on a march, but a tune o' our own would be finer still."

Finlay bowed his head. "I will be honored to provide ye one."

"Come watch us drill in the morning so ye may get a feel for who we are. The bards I knew back home in Ireland went by feel more than aught else."

"As do I." A curious sort of man, this. All warrior, bristling with vital energy, yet with a Celt's understanding. Even after O'Hanlon walked off, Finlay stood where he was, thinking.

It had been a long while since he'd seen a warrior troop in training. A long while, indeed.

CHAPTER SEVEN

N O QUESTION BUT Finlay shared his borrowed chamber with a spirit that night. The fact that it was a borrowed chamber and that Mistress Katrin might well have lent it to him with some reluctance could not explain the conviction that he was not alone.

The feeling came stealing over him as soon as he doused the light and stretched out in the bed. Awareness of a presence, one that moved very softly around the room. One he could almost hear breathing.

A mouse? Ghosts did not breathe.

It might well be Mistress Katrin's brother wondering why Finlay intruded here. Only the presence did not feel hostile, as if it wanted him gone or even as if it noticed him.

It was just *there*.

Still and all, it took him a while to drop off to sleep. And when he did, he dreamed.

A familiar dream, this, and one he'd inhabited before. One that in fact echoed the first song he'd sung in Murtray's hall that night.

He rode in a chariot with a sword clutched fast in his hand.

The air all around him was alive with sound and color—the glitter of light on the edge of a shield, the green of the turf that covered the hills around him. The rattle of wheels and the voices of men.

He was not alone in the chariot. A young man stood fast beside him with the reins in his hands, controlling the ponies. He had fair hair caught up in a number of plaits, and the energy that came off him...

He was excited, aye, and edgy, for they rode into battle. But for all that, his presence provided pure comfort.

Finlay woke on his back in the bed, breathing hard.

Och, by heaven, that had been too real. So much so that, back in the dark chamber, his senses swam. His upheaval was not helped by the sudden knowledge that the energy of the young man who had ridden in the cart with him was the same as that here in this room.

He swore to himself, sat up in the bed, and whispered, "Conall?"

But how could Conall be here? He had lived years away in Ireland. His bones lay beneath the green sod of that isle. Aye, indeed, Finlay knew better than anyone that ghosts could appear. But why here and now?

He said again, more strongly this time, "Conall?" No reply, but the air of the room seemed to ripple around him.

People came and went in life—that, too, Finlay had learned. They brought comfort and left sorrow. They brought love.

"If ye be here," he whispered, "then help me. I do no' ken if, even wi' the aid o' the tales and the songs, she will see me for who I am."

Still no reply. Finlay propped himself against the bolsters, eyes wide, and listened to the silence. He did not sleep again.

DESPITE HOW EARLY Finlay rose, the Gallowglass were up and at work ahead of him, making a clatter at their practice in the field next to the bailey. The hall was still being cleared of last night's supper, so, following the racket, Finlay went out to watch.

The day promised rain, a bank of low clouds spreading in from the sea. He was not the only one drawn by the spectacle in the field. Most those already out of their beds stood around in clusters. Finlay saw Chief MacMurtray among them, arrested like everyone else.

Aye, so, and the troop of men made an impressive sight there against the lush green turf. No wonder they carried such a fierce reputation and commanded so much respect.

They had broken up into groups and had at each other with such violence that one might be forgiven for mistaking it for true battle. Narrowing his eyes, Finlay saw it for a controlled violence, a kind of practiced fury almost beautiful to behold.

No chariots. Those had gone the way of things centuries ago. But the weapons were not so different, nor the skills they demanded. Finlay found himself caught up in it there beneath the tumbling sky.

Someone moved into place beside him. For an instant he thought it the presence from his chamber and he said, "Will ye look at this?"

"Aye." Not his ghost after all, but Chief MacMurtray shifted to his side. "I maun say, I am pleased. I spent a high price for these fellows. Almost beggared us," he added, as perhaps he should not to a wandering bard. "It looks to be worth it."

"It certainly does. Though I am no' the best judge, being nay a warrior."

Anders turned and looked at him. "Ye ha' seen a great deal, though, I do no' doubt. And"—he smiled—"ye tell a damn good tale o' warriors."

"Aye, so," Finlay agreed ruefully.

"That captain o' theirs, now."

Finlay picked O'Hanlon out with ease, the man fighting against two others on the far side of the field, fair hair flying. He moved with a smooth, restrained power that even among these warriors made him stand out.

"Aye, so."

"I shall send a message to Earl Randolph today telling him we stand ready to fulfill our duty—wi' our own men and these— when he calls."

Finlay barely heard the chief. The beginnings of a tune started coming together in his mind. It contained the rhythm of the fight, the stomping of feet, the clash of weapons. But more than that, it heeded the beauty of what he saw. The unflinching courage. The fearlessness.

"O'Hanlon has asked me to make them a song. A march." Forgetting himself, Finlay spoke to Anders as to a friend.

The chief stared at him, his eyes clear blue in the murky light. "Aye, so?"

"So I decided I had best get a feel for how they fight."

"I do no' doubt ye will ha' a good length o' time for it. No telling when Randolph will call upon us. We have already been waiting overlong."

And when he did and they answered the call, not all these men would return. Despite their bright valiance. What folly was such business? Folly and glory all in one.

"I am certain ye will gi' them a grand tune, one more than worthy o' them."

"Chief MacMurtray, if ye would prefer me to leave—" Finlay had to make the offer, loath as he was for it. Having traveled the five kingdoms in search of his heart's need, he did not want to surrender it. "I will."

"Nay, nay, ye are welcome."

"Ye are pressed for room, and I am taking that up."

Anders's face tightened. "Ye tak' only my son's chamber, and that we were no' using." His hand clenched on Finlay's shoulder. "'Tis a joy having ye here. One must leave go of sorrow when one can, aye?"

"Aye." Finlay wanted to ask, *What was your son like? Was he like the friend I knew so long ago?* But that would be tantamount to pouring salt into a wound.

Better perhaps to ask Mistress Katrin. If he could locate her. If he could get her alone.

What if he said to her, *Tell me o' yer brother. I think I shared his chamber wi' him last night?*

He and Anders stood long watching the Gallowglass at practice even after the other watchers recalled their duties and moved off, or went inside. Not until the first drops of rain fell in big, splashing plops that landed first on the sea, and then on the green grass, did Anders pull Finlay within.

"Come, breakfast will be laid by now."

The Gallowglass worked on as if unaware of the rain.

Breakfast was, indeed, set in the hall, and Katrin was there.

That brought a lift to Finlay's heart.

She never appeared wholly comfortable with her domestic duties, this woman. She seemed always as if she would rather be somewhere else, doing somewhat else. But she moved about them anyway, clad this morn in a plain dress with a smock tied over it like any other of the women.

A large job, overseeing so large a house, especially at a time like this. He wondered with sudden and piercing passion why she had never married. Past the age for it now, or so most folk would say. Mayhap she had not desired a domestic life.

Yet here she was.

Look at me, he beseeched her silently, and she did, just a glance that then switched to her father, still beside him.

"Come, Da," she called. "I ha' cleared the head table."

"Sit wi' me," Anders bade Finlay.

They sat one on either side of the board and Katrin served them with her own hands. Better yet, she came and sat with them after, looking not again at Finlay or her father but gazing around the hall as if searching for tasks undone.

That gave Finlay the chance to study her, while striving to seem as if he did not. The clear skin, the ashen hair bundled in a simple knot with apparent haste. She was not a woman to fuss over herself. The strong yet delicate hands that showed the marks of hard work and scrubbing.

He longed to drop kisses upon those hands.

"'Tis raining," Chief MacMurtray remarked to her.

"I can hear that, aye, Da."

"And the Gallowglass are at practice."

Indeed, they still were.

"I can hear that also."

"A grand sight, it is."

Katrin stared at her father, and Finlay wondered at the emotions astir in her eyes. Exasperation. Impatience.

"A fine thing it maun be, to be a man," she commented, "and praised for having a sword in yer hand, though without enough sense to come in out o' the rain."

"Och, Katrin, do no' start wi' all that again."

Anders had no time to finish. Katrin rose from the table and stalked off.

"My daughter," Anders said then, "thinks she should be permitted to go to war like a man."

Finlay said nothing, though wild feelings coursed through him.

"Her brother was foolish enough to begin wi' training her. Before he died. Now she thinks she should step into his place."

"Ye will nay let her?"

"Och, nay. Why d'ye think I went to the great expense o' hiring the Gallowglass, but to remove her obligation? The thing is, master bard"—Anders leaned toward Finlay—"I am no' entirely sure I can stop her, even though I try."

CHAPTER EIGHT

T HE RAIN MOVED off by noontime and the Gallowglass were
  still at work, so Katrin walked out to the field. The grass was
high and very wet, but had been well tramped down in many
places, so she did not bother sparing her skirts.

The men at work there had finally paused for a break. They
stood in small groups talking and laughing. She heard at least
three languages.

O'Hanlon stood on the far side of the field, which meant she
had to wend her way, catching glances. She knew she was not
beautiful, but men—especially men such as these, who took
opportunities where they may—would look at anything in a skirt.

O'Hanlon turned those tawny eyes of his upon her well before she reached him. He was wet to the skin with rain and sweat,
his half-loosed hair like a pelt down his back, mustaches drooping.
He stood with one of his officers, but the man moved off as soon
as Katrin walked up.

"Master O'Hanlon."

"Mistress Katrin." He gave her a slight bow and thrust the
axe, which he gripped in one hand, through the loop in his belt.
"Is somewhat amiss? I hope we have not been making too much
clamor and disturbed your household."

"Ye have, aye, but it is no' that."

He smiled.

"I ha' come"—she sucked in a breath—"to ask ye for a favor."

"Only name it." His gaze moved over her with curiosity and

something more. A very masculine sort of admiration. "I am at your every command."

Och, and was that not a heady proposition?

"I should like the lend of one o' your men."

"One of my men?"

"Only when ye do no' need him, of course."

"Aye, but—" He looked honestly puzzled. His gaze moved to the keep and back again. "Have ye not plenty men of your own?"

"Aye, so. But I should no' like my father to find out."

"Mistress Katrin, ye have me curious."

She sighed. "I am framing my request poorly. I should like help wi' training at arms. Wi'out my father's knowledge."

He actually backed off a step. "It is an odd request."

"Not so. I began training some time ago wi' my brother. My father never approved. Since Geordie's death, my training has fallen off. I merely wish to tak' it up again."

"I see," O'Hanlon said, though clearly he did not.

"I can pay ye," she said, "if I must."

"'Tis not that. Only, I am hired by the chief. If he does not approve—"

"And"—she eyed him up and down deliberately—"are ye afraid o' incurring another man's displeasure? Now ye surprise me."

That made him smile again. "Nay. Though when he holds the purse wi' my pay—"

"I see. I misjudged ye."

"Wait." When she moved to turn away, he put out a hand. His fingers lightly grazed her arm before falling away. "I have not refused."

"It sounded to me like ye had." Her gaze once more met his.

"Might I ask, mistress, why ye wish to train at arms?"

"That I might become proficient."

"And why d'ye wish to be proficient?"

"That I might then go to war." She tipped up her chin. "In my brother's place."

This time it was he who performed an inspection of her, head to foot.

"Ye can see, Master O'Hanlon, I am no delicate flower. I am strong and determined, and I do no' at all see why a man—why my brother—had to die in my place." To her horror, her voice choked on tears. She had not meant for that to happen. He would not be convinced by her emotions.

"'Twas my understanding," O'Hanlon said, "that I was to go to battle in your brother's place."

That struck her. Was it how Da looked at things? She stared.

"Mistress Katrin, have ye ever been in the midst o' a battle?"

"Nay."

"The clamor, the fury—the dying. I do not think ye would like that."

"Does anyone? Do ye?"

He shrugged. "There are men who glory in their abilities."

"But women should no'?"

He shook his head slowly.

"Fine, then." Katrin grew angry now, and embarrassed. "I will ask someone else."

"Mistress Katrin, I still have not refused."

"Och, I think ye have."

"There are practical considerations. There is nowhere here that lessons could be pursued privately, without your father knowing."

"I thought the armory. At night."

His lips twitched. "Because no one could hear swords beating against one another in the armory."

"'Tis a bad plan. Ye ha' made yer feelings clear." Again she turned away.

"Why do ye not just ask your father for training?"

"I have done. He refuses."

"He does not wish to see ye hurt."

"I understand that. But if I had been there on the practice field with Geordie—" She caught herself.

The Gallowglass sighed.

"My quarters," he said.

"Eh?"

"There is not a lot of room, but if I turn the cot against the wall and we bar the door, it may suffice. Any passersby may think I am working on me own."

She stared at him. This time his tawny eyes were full of light. "You will train me? Yersel'?"

"Did I not say I was at your command?"

"Och, but—"

Katrin's thoughts ran swiftly. What had she thought? She had imagined he might assign to her some underling. A junior member of the troop, perhaps. But these men were all hardened warriors.

To go alone to his hut—if she were seen, folk would think only one thing.

"Ye realize," he went on, perhaps assuming her acquiescence, "we may have little time. As soon as your father's laird calls, we will be away to the fight. I will be away."

"Then we had best act quickly. Tonight?" It felt all at once as if she propositioned him—in a way, she had—and her cheeks burned. "I am sorry if this will cost yer sleep."

He gave her another slight bow. "Mistress, some things are worth losin' sleep."

She walked away, again gathering stares, and heard him call his men back to work in a great voice.

Och, what had she done? He was like a bear, a big golden one. She had poked the bear. One never knew what a roused bear might do.

For the rest of that day, she lost herself in chores and duties, or tried to do. Da had sent his messenger off to Earl Randolph. He seemed to be on edge, even though getting any sort of reply could take days.

Once again, only O'Hanlon and his commanders would join them for supper. The rest of the Gallowglass were content to prepare their own food at their makeshift camp. But as Da told her, he had agreed to supply them while they were there. So Katrin met with a member of the troop who acted as their steward.

His name was Daffid, and he was a Welshman, big and brown-haired, with broad hands and dark eyes. He sought her out just before supper and said in a musical voice, "Mistress, I hear ye have supplies for me."

"Aye. Come, tell me what ye require."

He accompanied her to consult with seneschal and then to the larder, still wet from his day's work in the rain. His manner was polite and, for such a big man, gentle. When they finished their business, he stood for a moment outside the storage hut and gazed out to sea.

"'Tis a fine holding, this. It does, just, remind me of home."

That surprised her. Did strapping warriors such as this get homesick? And whyever should she suppose not?

"From whence in Wales d'ye hail, Master Daffid?"

"A place called Angelsea. On the ocean, not unlike this. But you do understand, much more humble. 'Twas a humble life, ours. I could not feed myself. 'Tis why I took up the sword."

"I see. How long since ye went home?"

"Ah—ages now." He pursed his lips. "My mother will be dead. My brothers will have split up our small plot o' land." He let his gaze rove over the sea again, and Katrin felt his longing.

Aye, men such as this grew homesick.

"A fine place, this," he repeated softly, "and something to fight for."

Katrin agreed. She wished suddenly she'd approached this man, who had something gentle inside him, for training. But he would no doubt have had to go to O'Hanlon anyway, for permission. Still and all, she found the prospect of facing the Gallowglass commander…intimidating.

Do not be a fool, she told herself. *Ye be a strong woman, intimidated by no man.*

Yet not until after supper, when Master Finlay took up his harp to play for a much smaller company, did she relax. With his music, her cares seemed to lift and fly away from her, and she remembered other things. The beauty of his stories and the love of which he had sung.

One so brave and strong, it withstood time itself.

She sat listening with her eyes closed and visions in her head, and her heart longed—just a bit—for such a love. But she was not a woman who succumbed to such feelings.

She was a woman who desired the feel of a sword in her hand.

CHAPTER NINE

Though Katrin was not in the habit of creeping about her own holding for any reason, she did so after dark that evening, donning her cloak and secreting beneath it her sword.

Her sword.

The one Geordie had given her long ago.

She remembered that moment all too well. He'd been resting after training—and a braw, sunny afternoon it had been, with high white clouds chased by a fair wind.

The sun had shown full into Geordie's gray eyes when he looked at her.

"Geordie, will ye train me to fight?"

She'd been perhaps thirteen and him not a year older. Indeed, he'd only begun his own training recently. Had he been older, would he have refused her request?

Instead he'd told her to meet him behind the armory, where he would find her a sword—this very sword. He'd presented it to her with the air of a man who knew everything in the settlement would one day be his. Theirs.

Da had found out about those training sessions—and Ma, for she'd still been alive then—and put a stop to them. Which merely meant she and Geordie had been forced to move their sessions anywhere they could. Up the shore. Into the forest.

They had learned together. As his training progressed, so did hers. Only her brother had known how good she was. Or how determined she'd been to stand up in her own defense.

When the time came for him to leave this beloved place and go to serve their laird, he'd gone without her. No one would ever know how she regretted that.

Master O'Hanlon was waiting for her, even though when she slipped into the hut he greeted her with, "Och, I did wonder if ye would come."

He was not clad in his mail or leathers and wore his saffron kilt with a tunic open at the throat. Did he not think he would need armor against her?

When she shrugged off her cloak and he saw she wore leggings and had her hair tightly braided, his eyebrows flew up. "I see ye came prepared."

"I ha' done this before."

"Let me see that sword."

She passed it to his hands, and he examined it with close attention, taking his time.

"Not a bad weapon," he said at last, handing it back.

"'Tis no' a great claymore like yer own," she replied. "But no' too heavy for me either." It took a man and a half to wield a sword the length of his.

He did not wear it now, and turned to the corner, where a number of weapons were stacked. "For our purpose, I will use a sword similar to your own." He eyed her and tossed the long tail of his hair so it slapped his back. "Show me what ye have learned."

The following moments were interesting. Katrin had forgotten none of Geordie's lessons, but it had been many weeks since she'd put in an earnest effort, and she felt it. Her feet remembered the old patterns, but muscles used to lifting no more than a table or crock of milk protested.

O'Hanlon stood and received her blows on his sword, not for the moment striking back. Striking against him felt like trying to move a boulder. He might have been rooted in the stone floor.

She'd begun to sweat before he held up his hand. Not precisely maidenly, she supposed, to be perspiring at every joint, but he would see worse than that of her.

"Not bad," he pronounced. Was that approval in the tawny eyes? "Your brother—"

"Geordie."

"He must have been a fine warrior."

"He was. That is why I canna understand"—to her horror, tears threatened—"how he came to fall. In practice, no less. 'Twas no' even a proper battle."

O'Hanlon told her gravely, "It takes but an instant for even the very best o' fighters to fall. I might. Ye might, if ye persist in this."

Katrin's chin jerked up. "Then mak' me better than the very best. 'Tis why I am here."

"I shall not have to show ye the basics." He glanced around the hut. "I regret now we have not more room. I thought we would have to begin at the beginning."

"I told ye—"

"Please, mistress. I believed ye. But 'tis not every day a woman comes to me and declares she can fight with a sword. We will do the best we may."

They were the last words either of them spoke for some time. Instead, they worked. Katrin's muscles screamed at her, but O'Hanlon was relentless, and she was not about to beg mercy from him after requesting exactly what he dished out.

A strong man and practiced with it, the blows he delivered to her sword had both power and precision behind them. Geordie, as she remembered, had been quicker, with a certain litheness in his movements. O'Hanlon, so she imagined, would go at the enemy like a man reaping grain.

With that great sword of his.

She had lost track of time before he put his weapon up, crossed to his pack, and took out a flask, which he unstopped and passed to her.

"Enough for now."

She examined the flask, which was made of silver with an

embossed pattern of twining knots on the side, since she was not sure she wanted to drink. "This is a bonny thing."

"'Twas a gift from a chief in Ireland."

"Aye, so? He must ha' been gey pleased wi' ye."

"He was. I hunted down and brought to him the man who was lover to his wife, then executed him before the chief's eyes."

Katrin swore softly, and O'Hanlon's mustache twitched in a smile. "Drink."

She drank. Not ale, this, nor mead. It burned as it went down. She passed the flask back to him.

He'd used the time to bring down the cot from the wall and now perched on it. He drank deeply before he said, "Now ye can tell me why ye wish so very badly to be a warrior, besides just a desire to fill your brother's place. For after that session, I can see that ye do."

Some of her discomfort with him forgotten, she sat on the other end of the cot. "Why should I no' want to fight? To defend mysel'?"

"Most women do not even think on it. They are content to let their men go off to that duty and defend them, as some say God intended. To remain at home and see to the equally important duty of raising the next crop o' warriors."

Katrin made a sound that translated to *pffft*. "And if danger comes to her door?"

"Aye, then many a good Celtic woman will fight. Like a she-wolf, in fact."

"Then she had best know how."

"Mistress, forgive me for pointing out that in the current instance, the fight is not likely to come here. When your father's laird calls, it will be an army that marches out."

"And am I no' permitted to desire a free Scotland? To love my country enough that I might also march out and fight for it? As ye may ha' noticed, I ha' nay husband and am no' likely to ha' any crop o' children to raise."

His gaze moved over her. "A wonder, that."

"I am past the age for all o' it."

"Ye are not. How old may ye be? A score and five?"

"Closer to a score and seven."

"Aye, well, me own mother was bearing me brothers and sisters past two score—"

"I am no' interested in doing that." She waved a hand.

"I might ask why, but I scarcely dare." He drank once more from the flask.

"I ha' never met a man worth having." Or had she? There'd always been a part of her, a deeply rooted part, that yearned after a skilled warrior even as she derided the fact that such men risked themselves on a regular basis. That, wed to one, she might have to watch him march off and die.

Just as Geordie had.

O'Hanlon was the consummate warrior, the ultimate fighting man, so she might say. And that pulled at her. It pulled hard.

He eyed her in a much friendlier fashion. "I think I understand. But surely there is somewhat between wedding a man ye do not want, and marching off to war."

She made a face. "My father wants for me to marry so he may ha' a grandson for an heir." She choked up again. "Now that Geordie is gone."

"Aye, so. 'Tis a fine holding, this. I am that surprised there are not men lined up from Inverness and back to marry ye."

"Ye expect me to accept a man who wants only the holding?"

"Nay, mistress, not in the least." He offered her the flask again, but she shook her head and got to her feet.

"I must go. My duties begin early tomorrow morn."

"As do mine."

"Thank ye for this. May we do it again?"

He rose from the cot. "D'ye want to do it again?"

"Aye, so. If ye ha' the patience for it."

"'Twill require nay patience."

She flung her cloak around her and again secreted the sword

in its folds. At the door, she looked back. "As I say, I will repay ye—"

"Nay, mistress. I suspect 'tis a privilege, this, that is beyond price."

CHAPTER TEN

Finlay's day did not truly begin until he saw Mistress Katrin the next morning. Even though he woke in his borrowed chamber with the first of dawn's light trickling in the window, following a mass of confusing dreams, and even though he got up on his feet and dressed himself, it felt as if he did not breathe properly until setting eyes on her.

He hoped he might encounter her in the hallway. Had she not said her chamber was next to her father's and his own? But nay, she must have been astir far too early for that.

Not till he entered the hall with its morning bustle did he spy her among the other women, laying out the breakfast.

She had her hair plaited into a single thick braid and wore a dull-blue gown with a plain, unembroidered overdress. Indeed, for all her lack of ornamentation, she might have been another of the servants.

But he knew far better. He had seen her in a score of dreams, if in various guises, and she drew him irresistibly. Bent over the hearth, she coaxed the fire before straightening to cast her gaze over the hall as if judging its readiness.

Her gaze met his where he stood in the doorway. Would she come to him? Would she speak? Did she see him, rather than just noticing him standing there?

His heart bounded painfully when she did cross the flagstones to him.

"Master harper. Ye be just in time for breakfast. My father is no' here yet, but please tak' a seat at the head table. He may join ye soon enough."

"Will ye no' join me?" he asked humbly.

She hesitated, and he felt sure she would refuse. She had many duties. None to him.

To his surprise, she nodded. "Aye, so. Let me fetch our portions."

He sat at the board, scarcely believing his luck. None of the Gallowglass warriors were present, so they must have risen far earlier. Indeed, he could hear them already drilling, outside.

Katrin came to the table and set a platter in front of him before sitting opposite. Her clear, pale eyes examined him from the beads woven into his hair, to his tunic, to his hands, before she said, "I hope ye slept well."

There is a spirit in yon room. He did not say so, telling her instead, "I had a wealth o' strange dreams."

"Did ye? I sometimes have those also."

Och, and he took that as a hopeful sign. *Do ye dream o' me?*

She smiled, the rueful smile that so often came to her lips. "I do believe those stories ye told ha' got inside my head. 'Tis as if I see snatches o' them disguised as dreams. So talented ye are wi' yer tales and yer tunes, both fair haunt me."

"I should like to mak' a tune for ye." The words were out of him before he could prevent them. When she stared, clearly astonished, he added, "A planxty—for my patron's daughter. 'Tis often done."

"Is it?"

"Och, aye, as a mark of gratitude." How could he tell her it might take a thousand years and every drop of skill he'd ever possessed to make a song worthy of her?

She blinked at him. "I can't imagine what ye could find to celebrate about me."

He could.

"But I would be honored."

"The head o' the Gallowglass troop has asked me to mak'

them a march."

"Has he? O'Hanlon?" A new light entered her eyes.

"Aye, so. He has men from the five kingdoms in his group, and they do appreciate a tune."

"A worthy challenge, I am sure. Marking so much renown. And—and valiance."

Valiance? Did she prize that, then? In spite of all the past losses and pain, and the promise she'd won from him?

Aye, it had been a long road he'd taken to her side. And looked to prove longer even now. There was irony in it. That his story should end at this place where part of it had begun…

"I am certain," she said softly, "ye will do a grand job and give them a fine tune. I ha' never heard anyone play as well as ye do."

"Thank ye, mistress."

"As I ha' said, yer music gets inside my head. Into my heart." As if startled by her own words, she made to rise. "Ye must excuse me. I have many duties."

He held her there simply by touching her hand gently where the knuckles lay upon the table, red and raw. "Ha ye hurt yersel'?"

She flushed. "Och, 'tis naught."

"Those scrapes look sore." And newly acquired.

"I was but clumsy and rapped mysel' when I stirred the fire."

He lifted his brows at her.

She got to her feet. Finlay rose also, in courtesy. "Do no' allow me to hold ye." *Only, allow me to. In my arms, as long ago. In my heart, as always.*

He ached when she left him, and his gaze followed her helplessly as she moved about the hall.

Not long after, Anders entered the room. He spoke for a moment with his daughter and then, spying Finlay, came to join him.

"Good morn, master harper."

"Chief MacMurtray."

A servant brought the man's breakfast. Katrin had left the

hall, which made it easier for Finlay to focus on her father.

"I was hoping for a messenger this morning," Anders said. "Indeed, a man did arrive, but 'twas no' from Laird Randolph." He frowned. "I suppose 'tis too soon for any orders to come down. But," he sighed, "we are all on tenterhooks."

"Indeed, the situation is unsettled. Who was the messenger, if I might ask?"

"A man named Culter. He says there ha' been dispatches from France, and the king is meeting with his advisors." King David of Scotland had an agreement with King Phillip of France, to stand with him if required in war against the English. "I canna think 'twill be long before we do hear the battle call."

"Aye, so."

"And I begin to wonder, Master Finlay"—even though the chief spoke Finlay's name, he more than half spoke to himself—"wha' I should do when the fight does come."

"Ye will send the Gallowglass, will ye no'?"

"Aye, but is that enough? I love my country, Master Finlay. I love it—and my wee portion o' it—to my very bones. Always, an I determined to fight for wha' I believe is its due, the right to self-rule. I did march out in the old days, wi' Bruce. But now…

"Och, I had a braw son to go when I grew too aged. Stout he was, and in my own image. He told me, 'I will tak' up the fight, Da, in yer stead.' For we both believed, aye, in a free Scotland. Now he is gone. Did I do wrong to send him awa' in service to another?"

He did not speak to Finlay at all now but wrestled with his conscience and his regret.

Finlay answered softly, "If he was the man ye describe, wi' so true and devoted a heart, I daresay ye could no' ha' held him."

"Ye be right, ye be right. But I canna help but think, had I been there—"

"The life o' a warrior is a tempestuous thing, Chief Mac-Murtray, like a storm at sea. Ye may no' ha' been able to prevent what happened to him, even had ye been there."

That made Anders give him a rueful look. "Ye speak as if ye know the life ye describe."

Finlay remembered. "I do," he said, "if ye count my stories."

"Aye, to be sure. Did ye never consider becoming a warrior? Ye ha' the build for it."

"I did, and began the training in my youth." The memories and, indeed, the realizations that had come to him, faster and faster as he grew, had stopped him from completing that training. "Then music called."

"'Twould be a sin, aye, to waste those hands o' yours on a sword. A pure waste o' a God-given talent." Anders scowled. "And there has been waste enough."

He hesitated, then said, "D'ye ken my daughter wanted to go off to fight? After Geordie's death—well, to be truthful even before—she came to me. And after he perished, she said, 'Da, let me tak' up his place.' Ha' ye ever heard anything more foolish?"

"She possesses a true heart."

"Aye, so. Is it any more foolish to suppose I should be the one to go, when the king demands, in Geordie's stead?"

A silence fell. Finlay did not know what to say.

Eventually, Anders answered himself. "I ha' no heir. My son is dead and gone fro' me. The closest o' my cousins also. My daughter—my daughter has no' yet given me a grandson, and time flies."

"Would ye be happy to hand over to a grandson?"

"'Tis an old tradition here. As ye did tell in the second o' yer tales."

"Aye." In that instance, the story did attest to the truth.

"Ah, well, time will gi' us the whole o' it, as always. If I go off to die, this place will fall into confusion, and how will that serve the king, or Scotland? 'Twould leave my daughter in a terrible fix."

"So it would."

"Aye, well, master harper, I did no' mean to strain yer ear. Only, after those stories, it feels ye ken our history as well as I do.

Better, mayhap."

"I am always happy to listen to ye, Chief MacMurtray."

"Aye, lad, and I am that glad ye be here. As I say, I would be pleased if ye will stay on till we see what is what."

"I would be pleased for that also."

CHAPTER ELEVEN

AFTER ANDERS WENT off about his business, Finlay walked out into the morning light to watch the Gallowglass at practice.

He told himself he but wanted to get a feel of them, perhaps garner some inspiration to enhance the march already in his head. In truth, part of him felt attracted to the sounds of practice, to the immediacy of it, the ordered crash and clang.

He was still part warrior, so it seemed, deep inside.

How was it that he remembered? He remembered everything, and yet Katrin did not? He'd been sure—or at least he'd hoped—that once she heard his stories, the memories would come flooding to her.

To his dismay, that had not happened. He could tell by the way she looked at him, polite and courteously interested, that she did not recall what they were to each other.

All, and everything.

Watching the Gallowglass at practice, it felt as if his own past lay before his eyes. The future?

Unknowable.

He longed to capture it. But life on this particular turn of the wheel did not look to be so kindly or straightforward.

He took himself off for a walk away from the clamor and down to the sea. A glorious morning it was, with the long combers clawing at the shore and the sky out over the islands reaching for eternity.

Much about the settlement had changed since he'd last

known it—and he did not speak of his visit here as a harper's young apprentice. The keep was larger and better fortified. The huts and cottages had more than doubled in number and now stretched away north to where once there had been a Norse encampment. More cottages and farm plots dotted the higher ground where once had been naught but heather and bracken, and a tracery of drystone walls marked the land like jeweled necklets. But the bones of the place—ah, those could not change.

The coast trail still wended away southward—now, indeed, more a road than the rough path it used to be. He followed it, his feet feeling for the familiarity of the ground, past a few more cottages until the land climbed and became wild again.

When he reached the headland he stood and gazed out, his eyes filling with beauty. Och, his heart had ached for this place almost as much as for her. He doubted he could get his fill of looking.

The wind felt stronger up here. It blew his hair and swirled his cloak back from his sides. It blew away the years. Almost, so it came to him, he might stand so in any time. Any life.

He could not but wonder again—what was the meaning of it? Why did it come about that he remembered it all, to the last detail, but she did not?

He was a man who dealt with words, wove them to entertain, please, and beguile. But if the stories he brought her had failed him, he did not know any other ones that might convince her.

Life after life had been hard in the past, had separated, then joined, and ultimately separated them again. It had taken him near thirty years to find her now. Would it be only to lose her once more?

He closed his eyes for a moment, shutting away all that beauty, and saw her face instead. Her face as she looked now.

The wide, pale eyes. The broad forehead where he longed to plant a kiss. The strength of the chin, the proud nose. The ashen hair. How could she fail to know how lovely she was?

He could not walk away from this. He could not, without her remembering.

Know me, he said to her, to the earth and the sky, and opened his eyes again.

The world wavered before his eyes. He saw not the scene he expected but another, in Ireland.

A wide swath of green turf with a river twining through it, silver beneath a serene sky. A familiar place, well known and well loved, and yet—and yet he carried anxiety in his heart.

And he felt—och, had he the words for it? Aching in his bones. Stiffness in his limbs. The burdens of old age.

He looked down at himself. He wore a kilt of plain gray wool, his limbs well wrapped beneath in leggings made of hide. A tunic and cloak, and a belt from which hung a stout long-knife and a leather pouch, into which he thrust a scarred hand. He drew out a fistful of herbs—bright green—he had collected in the hills.

Enough to save her?

He blinked and the scene vanished, replaced by what should be there. MacMurtray's land, the stretch of shore and the islands. Eternity beyond.

Aye, there were meetings and partings. He needed for the wheel of life to stop turning a wee while.

Long enough for her to know him.

IN THE KITCHENS, situated in the bowels of the keep, all was confusion. Following breakfast, Katrin found herself trapped there, trying to calm Cook, who was shaken by the advent of the Gallowglass, thinking she would eventually be required to cook for all of them.

Katrin did her best to reassure the woman, for her agitation was contagious and she had all her staff in a dither, the girls and lads who worked for her growing clumsy and dropping things.

"How," the woman wailed to Katrin, "am I to manage if I

need to provide for so many—so many great soldiers?"

"I tell ye, ye will no' have to," Katrin reassured her even as she wrapped the hand of wee Philip the spit boy, who had burned it only moments before, in clean linen. "The Gallowglass will feed themsel's. I ha' already arranged for their leader, Master O'Hanlon, to have the supplies they need."

O'Hanlon. She'd regarded him far differently since their training session. How soon would he be willing to work with her again?

Her whole body hurt after last night's session, a constant reminder whenever she moved. And Master Finlay was not the only one who had remarked on the grazing to her hand, where she'd accidentally received a bashing.

Master Finlay. Something—something profound lay in his green eyes. When he looked at her...

But nay. That was pure fancy. She barely knew the man. It merely seemed she did, when she listened to his music. Because of all those tales and the intimacies they contained.

Anyway, she had no time for men of any ilk. Was she not as busy here as she could endure?

No wonder she dreamed of running off to battle.

Cook was complaining at her again. "Och, nay, mistress. The chief has told me, stand ready to feast the entire troop o' them yet, when word comes they are to march out. To gi' them a braw send-off, like. I do no' ken when. And am I to be ready at the drop o' a feather?"

"Aye, so my father said that?"

"He did."

"Well, we shall manage it. We ha' the supplies." She hoped. "We will sit down now and plan a set o' courses that ye may prepare wi'out too much trouble, should the need arise o' a sudden."

Thus she remained trapped in the kitchen long, though her very spirit cried out to up and fly away. A new restlessness had come upon her, not unlike what she'd known in her youth when she'd begged Geordie to train her, or at least run off with her to the hills.

Were her feelings now prompted by working with O'Hanlon? If so, she might be better stopping with the lessons. For she found this hard to bear.

Longing for something one could not have was always hard to bear.

She missed out on a noontime sup while making sure everyone else had what they needed, and then became caught up in a crisis at the laundry, where a leaky tub drenched her from the waist downward. By the time she ran up to her own chamber to change, it was nearly time for her to begin worrying about supper.

Where has the day gone? she wondered as she reached her door. Where did all the days go? She seized the door latch and froze.

The door of the next chamber along the passage, Geordie's chamber that was, stood ajar. The harper was at practice there. Notes spilled through the narrow opening and caught her ear. Caught her.

An old song, it seemed to be, perhaps an ancient one. It twined up and down with beguiling brilliance, the notes like a language understood by her heart alone. The impact nearly sent her to her knees, and she remained so, not moving, barely breathing as emotions tore through her.

She knew that tune.

Aye, surely she did. He had doubtless played it while he told all those tales, for they had been sprinkled with songs, entwined with them. So hearing this now made her feel…

Och, as if she were back, almost, in the midst of those stories.

The man had magic in his hands. Och, aye, he did. What would it be like if he touched her with those hands? For her to lie naked beneath them. At once safe and vulnerable and cherished.

Madness.

She could not possibly feel that kind of desire for the harper.

She tiptoed to his door and stood looking in at him. A shameful thing to do, peeping and spying, since he did not know she was there. She simply could not help herself.

She could just catch sight of him sitting near the window embrasure with his harp on his knee. Such a beautiful instrument it was, but at that moment no more beautiful than the man. He had his head bent to the strings, his hands flowing over them, pricking out those sad, plaintive notes like water dropping. Did he play of a far-off place? A far-off time? He did not see her, for his eyes were closed.

Lost in his own music, which just as surely pulled her in.

She did not want to stir from that place. She could have stood there forever, transported by grief and joy and the edges of memory.

By love.

What would it be, to be loved by such a man as this, who had so much wistful loving in his heart and enchantment at his command? She would never know.

Silent, she tiptoed away to her own chamber.

CHAPTER TWELVE

A CERTAIN MEASURE of unease curled throughout the great hall that night. Finlay felt it as soon as he entered the room and set his harp against one wall. 'Twas as if the arrival of the Gallowglass troop had sparked a different energy—reminded the folks here, perhaps, that war still loomed beyond their jewel of a holding.

Folk seemed restless. They stood in groups and whispered to one another. Anders talked avidly to men Finlay recognized as his advisors. Had he heard from Laird Randolph, then? Nay, not possibly so soon.

Speculation, it must be. An act rarely reassuring to anyone.

O'Hanlon was there and had brought his two officers, the only Gallowglass to be seen. Out of his armor, the man looked larger than ever, his brawny arms crossed, legs planted like tree trunks as he spoke to his men.

Mistress Katrin was there.

Finlay focused on her at once and followed her with his eyes. She appeared discomfited, her hair in some disarray and her color high. She hurried about seeing to details. And she glanced more than once at O'Hanlon where he stood.

Nay. It could not be.

She could not be interested in O'Hanlon. She was his. *His.* The fierceness of that belief flared inside him, near tearing him apart even though he remained standing still and silent, giving no sign.

Anders gestured to him. "Master harper, ye will honor us by joining me at the head table."

Och, and he'd meant to sit off on his own. But nay, how could he refuse?

Anders greeted him heartily when he walked up, almost like—well, a relation. The two advisors nodded and drifted off to other tables. A small enough gathering it was this night, but aye, that uneasy mood persisted.

"I hope," the chief said, motioning Finlay to the place beside him at table, "ye will again play for us this night."

"As ye wish, Chief MacMurtray. I am at your command."

Katrin hurried up, gave her father a distracted look, and shot another at Finlay. For an instant, everything in the room seemed to pause, as their eyes met.

"Master Finlay."

"Mistress." He half rose.

"I hope ye mean to play for us tonight."

"Just what I was telling him!" Anders exclaimed.

Finlay, still holding Katrin's gaze, inclined his head. "If it will please ye."

"It will please me very much."

He lived for that, to please her in any way he might. To love her.

His manner, as he knew very well, was not what it should be. He ought to behave with the well-mannered courtliness folk had come to expect from a wandering bard, smile sweetly and produce some gallant words.

All he could do was continue to gaze at her, his thoughts in riot.

"Sit," she bade him. "The food will be out soon."

"Ye also, daughter," MacMurtray bade her. "Ye ha' been run off yer feet all day long. Did ye think I did no' notice?"

She subsided onto the bench directly opposite Finlay—praise all the powers—where he could look at her. Mark the curl in that disordered tress of hair against her cheek. The scattering of freckles across her nose. The sweep of brown lashes and the way her bosom rose and fell when she breathed. This he could do, without seeming to stare.

Anders went on a bit disagreeably, no doubt picking up the prevalent mood. "Ye do too much, Katrin."

"There is much to do."

"Let Angus see to the rest o' it. He is a competent seneschal."

Katrin settled more resignedly. "Angus is a fine steward but no' good wi' details. If I left all to him, we would ha' cold food and nay pudding."

"A tragedy to miss the pudding," Anders said a bit caustically.

"Father, if ye will assign me to woman's work, ye maun then allow me to do it well."

For a moment they glared at one another. Finlay could see the resemblance between them. He did not know what Geordie MacMurtray had looked like, though after spending two nights in his chamber, he did know the feel of him. But no doubt he'd had the same strength.

"Daughter," Anders said again, sounding edgy, "ye are no' going to begin all that again, are ye? No' before a guest."

"If ye mean Master Finlay, he knows more o' our affairs than we do, I think."

Anders gave a reluctant laugh. "'Tis so. Ah, here is O'Hanlon. Master O'Hanlon"—he half rose—"pray come sit wi' us."

O'Hanlon brought a definite presence to the table. "Ah," he said, eyeing them, "is this not a choice gathering?"

He took the place beside Katrin. Much more casual were things this night—except for that air of discord. He shot a look at her. "Mistress."

"Master O'Hanlon."

Finlay had excellent instincts. They may not be a warrior's instincts—not anymore—but as an itinerant wanderer seeking his living from those he encountered, he must read those he encountered quickly and well. Besides, he was alive to everything about Katrin.

Much as he might want to, he could not deny that something did lie between these two. Something...

Nay, his heart cried again.

The food began its rounds. They made idle conversation, none of them touching upon the subject that no doubt occupied their minds. The state of the country. When those here would be called up to fight.

Finlay kept mostly silent and indulged in the sheer pleasure of having Katrin so near at hand. Watching the color come and go in her face, the light in her eyes.

No matter, he told himself sternly, that it flashed when she looked or spoke to O'Hanlon.

When the meal finished, he rose and took his place at his harp. He gave them an old tale—not a family one this time—of Tristan and Isolde, a love that refused to waver or die. Then he played some of his oldest songs, the ones his fingers knew so well.

When he looked at Katrin, he had the satisfaction of seeing that she sat with her eyes closed, absorbing his music, no longer seeming aware of O'Hanlon, whose scarred hand rested near hers on the table.

Surely, surely, Finlay promised himself, it would come about as it was meant to be. O'Hanlon was but an obstacle, a stumbling block in their path as, in the past, there had been so very many.

Not until he stopped playing did Katrin rise and begin circling the hall again, seeing to their guests. Anders, O'Hanlon, and all the company applauded Finlay heartily.

He took up his harp and left.

Once in his chamber—Geordie's chamber—a sudden longing seized him. He wanted to go out into the darkness, stand above the sea and hear its hiss and thump, like the heartbeat of the world.

He wanted her there beside him. Where was she now?

If she failed to remember, if she did not come to him, how was he to tell her what they had been to each other? What they might be.

He slept but poorly there in his haunted bed. Not until the night moved toward morning did he fall into a deep sleep, and likewise into a dream.

No ordinary dream was it, for he found himself transported to another place, that of his previous dreaming. Into a different time. A different *him*.

He saw again the green swath of turf spread out before him, the sweet sweep of the hill, the settlement below with the lazy smoke from fires rising into the soft air. He came climbing down the hill from the wilder places, his body obedient yet hurting in joint and limb. Aged, he was, and no longer the lithe warrior. Every wound he had ever taken now told in sinew and bone.

But none of that mattered. He'd found more of the leaves to brew for her fever—the ones the healer had failed to search out. She would become well, once she had a draught of this inside her.

The dream flickered and altered in the way they did. He found himself inside a dim hut with night gathered all around. The fretful dance of a low fire at his back, and a cup of the brewed herbs in his hand.

He knelt beside a sleeping bench, having hunkered down there on his reluctant knees. Upon the bench lay a woman.

An aged woman she was, her once-golden hair turned to white, flowing loose over the skins that made her bolster. Her face bore a fine network of wrinkles, and her hands, folded upon the cover, looked frail. Naught but skin over bone.

The most beautiful woman in all the world, to him.

"Liadan," he said to her. "Alanna. My love."

She stirred and opened her eyes to him. Opened her spirit to him. For each time she looked at him, she did precisely that. Faded blue her eyes were, that saw him, as ever, to his very soul.

"I have more of the draught," he told her. "Will ye drink?"

"I am tired, Ardahl. So tired."

"Only drink."

"I canna."

"For me."

She leaned up obediently—would she not do anything for him?—

and he helped her raise her head enough to sip the draught. Naught to the weight of her. Desperation and terror seized his heart.

"There now. Ye must rest and grow well."

She gazed at him, and even before her lips moved, he knew her thoughts.

"Ardahl, I am frightened."

So was he. More than when he'd ridden to battle in his chariot. More than when the druids had passed sentence upon him. This, this he could not face.

She whispered, "I fear I must go from ye."

"Nay. Nay, ye will not." With great emphasis he added, "Ye will drink the rest of your draught and ye will grow strong again."

She merely gazed at him with the deepest of regret.

Two lovely daughters and three stout sons, she had given him. He would have to summon them shortly—if he believed what he saw in her eyes. But this moment, this moment must be for them alone.

As every moment had been.

"I am frightened to go ahead o' ye alone." Her thin fingers tightened on his. "I do not know how to live—or to be dead—without ye."

"Nor I, without ye."

She gave him a weary smile. "I fear we must now find out."

"Nay, Liadan, stay wi' me." He begged now. "Stay wi' me."

"I am so tired." It came on a sigh. "If love could keep me—"

"If love could keep ye, we would be together forever."

He took both her hands in his, lifted them one by one and planted kisses in the palms. Fervent kisses. He kissed each corner of her mouth, both cheeks in turn. He planted a last kiss on her brow. The skin of her forehead burned like fire, consuming the very spirit he adored.

"Liadan, I must go call our children."

"Not yet. Hold me. Ardahl, will ye hold me?"

He crawled onto the sleeping bench with her, his old limbs protesting, and gathered her into his arms. Never had he known the meaning of unbearable till now.

"Ye will not leave me?" she beseeched him.

"Never." It was she who was leaving him.

"Ye will follow after me?"

"I will find ye. Always."

There came no response, only a whisper in his heart.

Finlay awoke to the cold dawn, his face wet with tears, his heart raw.

Love and devotion, joy and loss, all of it possessed him. All of it rode upon the turn of the wheel.

All of it carried in his blood.

※

CHAPTER THIRTEEN

WITH CONSIDERABLE PERSISTENCE, Katrin persuaded Reagan O'Hanlon to move their private sessions out of his quarters and off behind the armory. As her training progressed and what Geordie had taught came back to her, there simply was not enough room in the hut. The area behind the armory—a kind of wasteland containing an ancient forge and cast-off weapons—was deserted after dark, the time when they met.

As a consequence of her dedication, she went through her days nursing a multitude of bruises and one or two sprains—all accidentally acquired—that she sought in various ways to hide. The household undoubtedly considered her inordinately clumsy.

She now thought of the Gallowglass as *Reagan*, for that was what she called him when they sweated and flailed at one another, just as he called her *Katrin*. When they met in the ordinary way, to be sure, she still addressed him as *Master O'Hanlon*.

She had learned much of the man during their time in shared company. Big and unyielding he might be, and fierce on the battlefield—though she'd never yet seen so—but he possessed a dry sense of humor compatible with her own. And more and more, he approved of her.

Just as more and more, she grew comfortable with him.

Yet—it was of the harper she dreamed.

Deep and disturbing dreams they were, brought on, so she first believed, by her exhaustion from the after-supper training sessions. The sort of dreams in which even her sleeping mind had rarely ever indulged. The two of them. Together. Naked and touching one another. Tasting one another.

So frequent grew these dreams that she awoke knowing the pattern of hair that grew on his chest. That he had a tattoo binding one arm, high on his bicep. She awoke still quivering, the flavor of him on her lips, and cursed herself.

It got so she could scarcely gaze into the man's green eyes for fear he would see those dreams. For when he looked at her…

It seemed he could see everything. More of her than there was.

The days both dragged by and spun so swiftly that she could scarcely number them. The Gallowglass drilled eternally. A message from John Randolph did not arrive.

Father and the head of his guard, Robran, drilled their own men also, for when the call did come they would go with the Gallowglass in answer. Katrin watched those sessions with critical eyes, knowing she could match many of these men who ordinarily spent their days tilling the soil or farming the sea. Wondering how to approach her father on the subject.

One evening, behind the armory, she challenged Reagan over it. "How d'ye think I am doing, Master Gallowglass?"

He wiped the sweat from his brow with an equally damp forearm and she grinned to herself, pleased she had made this consummate warrior work so hard.

"Ye do well." Even in the low light, aye, she once more caught the gleam of approval in his eyes. Or was that admiration?

"D'ye think me ready to accompany my father's men?"

"Off to fight, d'ye mean?"

She took up an aggressive stance. "O' course I mean off to fight."

He turned away from her rather than answer and put up his sword. His muscles rippled when he moved, and Katrin experienced that now-familiar, purely feminine thrill. The man had scars. They detracted naught from him.

Yet it was of the harper she dreamed, and awoke with his tunes playing in her head.

When Reagan did not speak, she pressed, "I did hope ye might speak wi' my father on my behalf. Persuade him I am fit and ready."

"Katrin, I cannot do that."

"What?" She'd been more than half counting on it. Da respected the Gallowglass's opinion. He might at last listen. "Ye know full well I am as skilled as many o' Da's men—who will surely march off to die. Ye ha' seen them training." She'd noticed him watching, just like her. "They are clumsy and inept, and handle their swords like reaping hooks."

"I do know it full well."

"Then—"

"Katrin." He turned and approached her, looming up out of the gloom. "Ye be a woman."

That sent her reeling back a step. The last thing she'd expected from him. "Aye. So?"

"A beautiful woman. Ye cannot expect me to persuade your da to let ye go and die."

Suddenly he was right there on top of her, his hands coming up to capture her elbows. He touched her but rarely in training, and then mostly by accident. Oh, he might adjust her grip or lift an arm to a better angle. None of that meant anything.

Now he *touched* her, his hands warm against her skin. His tawny gaze grew intent with a look she'd never received from him before. Not just appeal.

"Ye be beautiful," he repeated, and bent his head.

His lips—twice as warm as his hands—had time to slip across hers, mainly because she was not expecting it. In the next moment, she stepped back from him, tearing away.

"What—"

They stared at each other. She knew *what*. He did not have to say.

His lips curled ruefully between the wings of his mustache.

The mustache she had just felt so very intimately.

"Forgive me."

She did not know if she could. Not the kiss or even the desire for it, but the violation of the trust she had found in him.

She said, speaking to herself as much as him, "We are friends."

"And is it forbidden for a man to feel desire for a lass who is his friend?"

"Nay. No' truly." Most of the clan's young people knew each other from birth. Those who grew up as friends or even while annoying each other might suddenly begin to see with new eyes and then to love.

"Ye cannot blame me," he said, using a touch of that humor he usually kept under wraps. "I am but a man. And ye are"—he inspected her from head to toe—"desirable."

Was she? Rarely in her life had she felt so. And it took a strapping Gallowglass warrior to tell her.

"I am flattered. Truly. But I am no'—"

"Interested? Most wise o' ye, mistress. I am no' the sort o' man upon whom a young woman should center her interest. As ye have so clearly stated, I go off to fight. Maybe to die."

A sudden pain, nearly overwhelming, gripped Katrin's heart. She did not want this man to die. An old, old worry that seemed on some level to continually haunt her.

"Ye be a warrior," she stated softly, again almost to herself.

"A path I have chosen knowing full well where it leads." He did not attempt to touch her now, having also backed off a few steps. "As a youth in Ireland, I was not good for much. I had nay aptitude for letters, for learning. But I grew as ye see me, and I did ha' an aptitude for warfare. A lad turned man does as he must."

She narrowed her eyes at him. Difficult to imagine him as a young boy struggling to learn aught. He seemed to have appeared as a warrior fully defined. Foolishness, to be sure. Did they not all struggle toward what they must be?

"I am sorry," she said, not quite sure why. Was she sorry

about his past? For the choices he had made? For what his future held?

For telling him she did not desire him.

Well, that was not quite true.

Part of her did feel a pull toward all that this man was. Strong and unflinching, relentless in his word given—for he was that. Hired or not, his sword would belong where he promised it, to the end.

Once, as a girl, she might have swooned at the feet of such a man. Leaned into his kiss rather than pulled away. That was before the fear had grown in her.

She said it aloud. "What is loved may be lost."

He blinked at her. Backed off another step and sat on a stump, there in the yard. "That is so. Indeed, everything loved will be lost one way or another."

A stark, cold truth. One they shared?

"My mother taught me that when she died."

"And mine," he agreed.

"And then my brother. There are risks."

"Life is all risks, mistress."

"A man who takes up a sword increases those risks."

"As does a woman. Yet ye ask me to help ye do just that."

That made her flare. "Ye who go out to fight, can ye imagine how it feels to ha' a man put himsel' forward to die on yer behalf? A man ye love?"

He shrugged. "So. Ye will marry some staid fellow who perhaps spends his time sitting sewing shoes or training ponies and never, never takes up a sword?"

"I do no' mean to marry at all."

She could barely glimpse his face now for the gloom, but she felt him eye her again, up and down.

"That would be a terrible shame."

"I do no' see why."

"Mayhap that is because ye cannot see yourself."

"You are permitted to choose the course of yer life. Why

can't I?" She leaned toward him now. "That is the heart of it, aye? Why am I no' allowed to follow the same course in life as Geordie did?"

"Mayhap," he said starkly, "because Geordie is dead. And 'tis the instinct o' those who love ye to protect ye."

She gave a derisive puff of breath, even though she knew his words made sense. "Does this mean ye will no longer train me?" It might be best, withal. Now that she'd been made aware of the desire, she was not sure she would feel quite so easy in his company.

But he answered equably, "Nay. It but means I will not speak with your father on your behalf, to send ye off the war."

She grunted. "Well then, I do no' ken how I am to persuade him."

"Nor do I."

"I might dress mysel' as a lad, mayhap. Run awa' and enlist my sword in Earl Randolph's army."

"What good would that do? Whom would it serve?" He laughed softly. "Comfort yourself, Katrin, with the knowledge that if, by some terrible twist o' fate, the armies in the south are overrun and the English bring the fight here, ye shall be well prepared. Ye may stand upon the ramparts and defend yer home like the Celtic women o' old."

"'Tis a comfort, aye."

He got to his feet. "Well, then. The hour grows late and I am off to me bed. We do not know what the morrow may bring."

"Aye."

He slanted a look at her. "Still friends?"

"To be sure," she said readily.

They clasped arms as two warriors might. His smile was rueful. "A good night to ye, Katrin."

She doubted she would sleep at all, with so many feelings astir inside. She did not say so.

CHAPTER FOURTEEN

ON THE FOLLOWING morning, after Katrin had taken care of a slew of duties, including making sure breakfast was underway in the kitchen, she stepped away from it all. She had no appetite herself for breakfast, with a welter of thoughts still possessing her. All that had happened last night.

All that might have happened.

What if she had stood still and let Reagan O'Hanlon kiss her?

It would, no doubt, have been a pleasant experience. More than pleasant.

She took the steep path down to the sea, returning greetings to those she passed, and headed south along the sea toward the headland. Away. She most assuredly needed some time on her own.

Only belatedly did she realize she was barely presentable, having failed to confine her hair following her sleepless night. She wore her oldest clothing and shoes so aged the sides had split. Och, and who cared? She sought none but her own company.

The wind would have wreaked havoc with her hair anyway, for it was a glorious morning with a strong breeze off the water. Long, deep blue combers edged with white foam raked the shore, and off southwestward, toward Ireland, banks of white clouds flew high. Early light trembled in the air. The world seemed almost too beautiful.

The path was an old one that she had trodden many times. Pleased now to find herself alone, she drew great breaths of air.

Far too long had she been confined to the keep. This was what she wanted.

Deliberately, she let the wind blow the thoughts from her mind. *Do not think of Reagan. Do not think about persuading Da to let ye go with their troops. Leave go of these feelings making a weight on yer heart.*

When she reached the rise of the headland, she caught sight of a figure already there ahead of her, silhouetted against the bright morning. Annoyance flared. That was the place, the very place where she wanted to stand alone with the world spread before her. All that she loved.

She very nearly turned back, retraced her steps and returned to her life. A strong streak of rebellion kept her there.

If it were a clansman—for as she kept walking, she could recognize the figure for male—he would likely excuse himself upon her arrival. She need only be patient.

Something toward which she was poorly suited.

When she reached the place where the path petered out and the land rose, she realized who it was standing on the height. Him. *The harper.*

Och, and had she sought to escape her thoughts only to run smack into them? For the harper was in her head. In some indefinable way, always he was.

He turned from his contemplation of the sea and sighted her. She could do naught else but walk on then, for the sake of courtesy.

"Mistress Katrin, good morn."

"Good morn, master harper." The wind had been at him also, at his glorious, colorful garb, and had put its fingers in his hair, making it stream out.

Because it somehow hurt to look at him, she took the place at his shoulder and gazed out to sea.

"I gather," he said, raising that beautiful voice of his above the wind, "I am no' the only one seeking some solitude this morning. I will go and leave ye to it."

Aye, it would be best that he should go. She did not need him here.

Only she did.

Suddenly, that need arose and swamped her. Deep, wide, powerful. It near brought tears to her eyes.

She reached out and seized his sleeve. "Nay. Do no' go."

She had no explanation for her action. Fortunately, he did not ask for one. They stood so, she clutching his sleeve while the wind rocked them.

Alone. Not alone.

Katrin did not understand what was happening to her life. For a woman desiring to be in control, that was disquieting.

Without her own permission she said, "One o' your tunes has been occupying my head. I canna seem to prevent it."

"Which one?"

"'Tis one o' those ye played during the tale ye told o' Deathan and Darlei. The one ye said was playing just before she had to go awa' to her marriage, when they were—"

She'd almost said *making love*.

"Aye, an ancient song, that one."

"Where did ye learn it?" She still held his sleeve as if anchoring him to her. It made her feel a fool, but she could not quite let go.

"I canna answer that, mistress. It seems I ha' always known it."

"How curious."

"Aye, is it no'?"

"Now I come to think on it, it seems ye played that song— that tune—during each o' yer stories. Mayhap that is how it got so deep in my head."

"Mayhap so."

He turned to face her. She moved likewise, since it seemed she could do nothing else.

His eyes were very green in the strong light. He looked like a figure out of one of his own stories, almost too beautiful.

She released his sleeve, but her hands—both of them now—continued to reach out. He clasped them.

It felt the most natural thing in all the world.

"Mistress," he began.

She interrupted him. "Ye will no' leave Murtray, will ye? Ye will no' go awa' too soon?"

"Yer father has asked me to stay."

"That is well. Because—well, things are so uncertain just now. I feel as if my life is being torn up by the roots. And your music does serve to soothe me. I do no' think I could manage wi'out it."

"I am glad of that."

"It brings peace. And in a time of upheaval, a woman does need peace."

"So she does."

There was a certainty about this man, she thought. A serenity. A strength. Why had she ever thought strength came only behind a sword?

"Mistress," he began again.

"I suppose"—her tongue tripped over itself now—"'tis madness for me to ask it o' ye. That ye should stay, I mean. Be—be there for me. I scarce know ye."

"Do ye no'?" Something bright and magical stirred in his eyes.

"Well—" She did know him, did she not? Somehow.

Madness.

His hands tightened on hers. "Rest easy in yer mind. I will be here for ye." *Always.* Did she hear that word tacked on? Did he speak it? Did it sound only in her head?

He then did a curious thing. He lifted each of her hands in turn to his lips. Kissed not the backs of them but the palms. Deep, warm, fervent kisses. He leaned in and lightly—so lightly she could not object—kissed each corner of her mouth, both cheeks in turn. He dropped a last kiss onto her brow.

Katrin came apart inside. She could describe it no other way. It felt as if her very soul shattered and left her reaching—reaching for something she could barely see but needed most desperately.

If she did not hold to him, she could hold to naught.

Blindly, she clutched his arms. Gazed into his eyes. The world tilted and she saw…

His soul.

But nay, that was just the wind blowing, making her feel she'd been knocked off her feet. Or mayhap an effect of her emotions run rampant.

"What—" She wanted to ask him what that was for, the beautiful gesture of seven kisses, like a blessing. She did not want to spoil it with a question. And anyway, she knew. A part of her *knew*.

She wanted to throw herself into his arms. Cling to him. Kiss him until neither of them could remember aught else besides kissing one another.

She took a careful step away. "I must go back."

"Must ye?"

"Aye, och aye. I have duties to which I should attend, tasks that wait for me." She was babbling.

"As ye say. Ye be a busy woman." Was that amusement in his eyes? Amusement and something more, far more.

"Thank ye—thank ye for saying ye will stay on. And for the blessing."

"Blessing?"

"The—the kisses."

"Mine to give."

Hers to receive.

She fled then. Fled what she saw in his eyes and the words she wanted to say, and how badly she wanted to hold him. How she ached for his lips on hers.

She tripped over her own feet on her way down the slope. The wind blew her hair into her eyes so she could not see, but she paused to look back.

Looked back at him.

He stood where she'd left him with the red hair streaming

out on the wind and his gaze upon her.

He made her ache.

Why? He was but a wandering harper, one who had chanced to stop at their keep, at this place and time. A talented man whose music attracted her.

Aye, surely it was the music. Nothing more.

CHAPTER FIFTEEN

FINLAY MUST INDEED be going mad, for he'd begun speaking to the presence in his chamber. Baring his soul to it as if it were an old friend.

"She came to me this morning, up on the height overlooking the sea. 'Twas as if my longing summoned her, almost. And she *saw* me. I think she truly saw me for the first time."

The presence in the room stirred but did not answer. To be sure, it did not. Finlay glanced at the bed. It was as if he could almost see the form of a young man stretched out there.

"She maun remember in time, must she no'? How can she fail to remember, when I recall everything?" Each detail, nearly. Every time she'd looked at him. Each kiss.

Throughout time. They had both traveled in time, apart and together.

He'd spent this lifetime searching for her. Because he did remember, had done so almost from the beginning of his life. It had come to him in bits and pieces, in memories, in random longings. He'd put them together into stories, into songs. He had found names for them in the world.

He had realized who she must be.

After all that, after so many miles traveled and so many wishes made, how could it end badly?

"The wheel turns," he told his silent companion. "No' always to our benefit."

And what would he do if, ultimately, she failed to remember?

For he could not help but feel in some way it was up to Katrin. Their shared past was all there inside her.

She must choose it.

She carried a barrier of fear, did his love, his *alanna*. She must be given leave to face that, or flee.

If she refused him—refused them—he supposed he would wander the world until he grew too frail to tread the roads and his fingers could no longer dance over the strings. He thought of the dream when he'd gathered herbs on the hill, how stiff and old he had felt. The wheel did indeed turn. Age would find him again.

He finished preparing for supper and said to his companion, "Wish me luck."

Luck. The word seemed to float after him as he went out the chamber door. Or was that only an echo of his own voice?

SEVEN KISSES. KATRIN could not reason out why those two words remained stuck in her mind. But the instant the harper entered the hall she felt it, and swung around to look at him.

His gaze found her. He smiled.

Something settled inside her, beneath her heart. He was here. She could continue with her tasks. With her world. With her life.

Swiftly, she turned back to her work, setting cups at the places along the boards. What she could not do was stand gazing at him. Much as she might wish to.

But she found that very soon she must steal another glance.

He looked very fine, this night. He wore his cloak of green with the embroidered tunic beneath, and the brown skin leggings and boots. The beads woven through his hair were, many of them, green also.

Yet none of that mattered. It was the way he moved that drew her. That smooth, somehow powerful grace.

He carried his harp—well, that was not surprising, but it

made her heart leap. It meant he intended to play for them. She would soon hear his music. Fall under its spell.

Anticipation sizzled inside her, almost like that a child felt for a promised reward. She could be patient, could she not?

"Mistress Katrin?"

She jumped violently when someone spoke beside her, so near they almost touched. Reagan. How could she have missed his approach?

"Master O'Hanlon! Ye did startle me." She was not a small woman, yet had to look up, up to meet his tawny gaze, which held a rueful light. One of his eyebrows quirked.

"Forgive me. I am not usually so easy to overlook."

"I did no' overlook ye, just—"

He shot a deliberate look at Finlay before returning his gaze to her face, not without a tinge of irony.

"I see that ye are distracted."

"Just eager to make certain each of our guests has what he desires."

That made both Reagan's brows fly up. Only then did she realize the words might sound—well, not as she'd meant.

What did Finlay want? For he did want somewhat, on that she would bet her life. Why had he given her those kisses? The ones that even now refused to leave go of her heart.

She needed to speak with him.

"I wanted to speak with ye," Reagan said, and she started again.

"I beg your pardon?"

He edged still closer and lowered his voice to a rumble. "I did not know if ye wanted still to meet tonight." He hesitated. "Given what happened, I mean."

The kiss. The attempted kiss. Och, what had befallen her life?

She was not the sort of woman who strove for male attention. She rarely fussed with her appearance and had long ago given up on any idea of a romantic marriage. She owned precisely one fine gown that she seldom wore, save for formal occasions, which, given the current state of affairs, were few.

Now she had two men giving her notice. To both of whom she was attracted, if in vastly differing ways.

She gazed at Reagan. Since the arrival of the Gallowglass, the young women of the clan had been looking after them, and especially after their commander. A whole lot of man was he. And she had heard lasses sighing after Finlay also.

Finlay.

She ached for another glance at him. Instead she gazed into Reagan's eyes.

"I am willing to continue the training, if ye be."

"Aye, so." Something stirred in his eyes. "With what objective, if I may ask? Have your thoughts about going to war changed?"

"They have not."

He disliked that. His expression settled into a frown.

She added blithely, "When I am ready, I shall speak to my father mysel'."

That made his lips quirk between the wings of his mustache. "And who shall deem ye ready?"

"I shall, to be certain. Do I no' mak' all my own decisions?"

He shook his head. Before he could reply, however, the harper stepped up to them.

"Mistress Katrin, Master O'Hanlon."

Katrin's entire body sprang to life. She could explain it no other way. She became aware of everything about Finlay—his height, his warmth, his presence. Even the scent of him. All her senses leaped.

"Master harper." She could do naught but look at him then. Remember the feel of his lips pressing kisses into her palms.

Her fingers involuntarily curled into fists as if trying to keep those kisses in.

But it was to Reagan he turned, not to her.

"Master O'Hanlon, I wished to let ye know I ha' fashioned the march ye requested."

"Have ye?" Reagan's gaze took light.

"Aye, I would play it for the first time tonight, that ye might hear."

"That will be grand."

What was this, then? The harper making tunes for the Gallowglass? She'd known naught of it.

"A march, ye say?" she asked.

Reagan smiled at her. "So struck was I with Master Finlay's playing, I petitioned it. I daresay, Master Finlay, ye have never before had a patron who is also a Gallowglass."

"That is so, Master O'Hanlon, though many and many ha' my patrons been."

"I can believe it." Reagan raised a hand to Finlay's shoulder. "I shall look forward much to hearing."

Finlay bowed and stepped away.

Reagan gave Katrin a searching look. Before he could speak, she did. "That was an unusual request—a tune from the harper."

"A march," he emphasized, "as befits a company such as we. Fierce and indestructible, we are, and hard to kill."

She hoped so. She tossed her head. "And modest, above all."

"Let me tell ye a wee secret, mistress." He bent to whisper into her ear. "When ye have somewhat to boast about, there is no need to keep silent."

Ah, Katrin thought as he too walked away toward the head table where her da waited for him—if she'd met Reagan O'Hanlon ten years ago, or even five, things might have ended far differently.

But Geordie had been alive then, and she was sure he would marry—just as soon as all the fighting was done, as he'd insisted it was unfair to leave a wife with young bairns to go off to war, and the succession secured.

She might well have tumbled head over heels for Reagan.

And then what? What, when the harper turned up? Ah, well, she was too old for all that nonsense now, was she not?

She spent the better part of supper on edge, for Finlay joined them at the head table and she remained so aware of his every word and every gesture, she could not relax.

Not until after the meal, when he took up his harp, did the tension flow away from her, as she surrendered to the beauty. To the magic.

He played and sang several songs of love, which tugged at her heart. He followed those with the promised march, a tune so bright and strong that at its finish everyone applauded spontaneously and Reagan rose to his feet to bellow his approval.

"A man of great talent, the harper," Reagan rumbled to Katrin after he sat back down.

He certainly was.

The training session that took place later, behind the armory, started off awkwardly, some discomfort lingering from their last meeting. It soon wore off, for Reagan worked Katrin hard, only telling her when she protested, "If ye insist upon bein' battle ready, I will make sure o' it."

He made no attempt to touch her again, nor to approach her in any way that was not part of the instruction. All business, was the Gallowglass this night.

The harper, though, remained on Katrin's mind. Perhaps that was why, when they parted, she asked, "What do ye think, then, o' the harper's march?"

"A grand tune. I was much pleased." Reagan crooked a brow at her. "What do ye think o' the harper?"

Katrin went away without answering.

CHAPTER SIXTEEN

INLAY PACED HIS bedchamber that night and once more spoke to the spirit that inhabited it, albeit in a distracted fashion.

"Wha' does it mean? Wha' for me? For her. For the turning o' the wheel."

He had not meant to follow Katrin when she left the hall at the end of the night. Indeed, he'd come up to his chamber and put away the harp, then decided on impulse to take the air before attempting to sleep. For all he'd known, Katrin was in her own chamber by then. But descending the stairs, he'd glimpsed her clad in her long cloak, leaving the hall and proceeding out into the dark. He had seen who it was waited for her there, inside the gate.

The two of them had come together, naught more than shadows. Katrin had touched O'Hanlon on the arm. They had walked off together quickly and silently.

The emotions that struck Finaly at that moment could not be described. A patient man, and one not often prey to anger, he usually proved able to master unwieldy emotions.

Not this time.

Jealousy, hot and raw and entirely violent, assailed him without mercy. The two of them looked like a pair headed for an assignation.

Was she lying with him? With O'Hanlon? *A warrior.*

He'd noticed her attraction to the man. He could scarcely miss it. He'd striven to understand. O'Hanlon was the kind of man to whom any woman might feel drawn. Not just a warrior, but the consummate warrior. Confident. Handsome.

Finlay had not imagined that could come before what lay between him and Katrin. And given their encounter on the heights this morning…

It felt like a punch to the gut. Like a thrashing.

He might have followed them, he supposed. They would not have been able to see him in the dark. But he would not so lower himself. Was this not about Katrin's choice?

Perhaps she had chosen. A warrior. Something she knew. Something she trusted.

Something she had forbidden him to be.

If so, he did not want to know. He certainly did not want to see her in the Gallowglass's arms.

Instead of following them, he returned to his chamber and raged at his unseen companion. Terrible thoughts beset him. A storm of loss and longing.

He did not attempt to sleep, fearing his dreams. Instead he paced the floor until all but one candle snuffed out.

Only then did he hear a knock at his door. Who could it be, in the midst of the night?

He swung the panel open and his heart leaped painfully. Katrin it was who stood there. Katrin, in her nightclothes, a look of concern on her face.

"Master harper? Is all well?"

She did not wait for an answer but slipped past him into the dim chamber. She glanced around as if she too expected to see her brother, before she turned to face Finlay.

"Are ye ill?"

He shut the door very carefully, scarcely believing she was here with him.

"Nay, mistress. Why should ye think so?"

"I could hear ye. Walking and walking about." She jerked her head. "I am right next door."

"Och, by heaven. I am that sorry."

She narrowed her eyes at him, as if trying to plumb the depths of his feelings. She wore a gown of white with her feet bare, and her hair hung loose in a glorious fall of ashen blonde over her back and shoulders that made Finlay ache to touch.

He fisted his hands. She may have just come from O'Hanlon. From lying with him.

Hoarsely, he said, "I did no' mean to disturb ye."

She sat on the bench that faced the fire, which, neglected, had nearly gone out. With visible irritation, she took the poker and assaulted the embers.

"Ye are usually such a quiet guest, I scarcely ken ye are here. That was why I thought—" She caught herself and returned her gaze to his. "I could feel somewhat amiss."

Finlay spread his fisted hands, forcing himself to ease. "I am but restless, mistress."

"Ah. I suspect we shall soon lose ye after all."

"Lose me?"

"Men such as yoursel' do no' stay in one place long. Ye will ha' the itch, no doubt."

"I do no' ha' the itch." Except to take her in his arms, kiss her until she begged him to carry her to the bed—ghost or no. To make her one with him and be damned to the world.

But she might already have made her choice.

"Come." She patted the bench beside her. "Sit and tell me wha' it would take to persuade ye to stay a while longer."

He perched on the bench. "I ha' told yer father—and ye—I will stay." Could he bear to, though? If she and O'Hanlon began a courtship—

"Aye, yet I feared ye had changed yer mind. I am glad. We are in need of peace, and ye can provide it." In defiance of her words, she sprang to her feet as if she were now the one beset by restlessness. She prowled the room, picking up and setting down the possessions that had been her brother's.

Finlay watched her, helplessly admiring the strength and beauty of her movements in the thin white gown.

She paused at his harp, which he had set beside the wall, and reached to touch the strings reverently. A shimmer of sound came to life in the air.

"I ha' always wanted to play," she confessed, "like Bradana, in your story."

"It is your story—o' your own people," he told her, his heart beginning to bang hard and high.

She turned suddenly to smile at him, a brilliant smile. "Bradana—and Brada. Is that why ye named your harp Brada?"

"Aye, so."

That made her blink at him, a host of thoughts tumbling in her eyes.

"I could teach ye to play," he said, "if ye like." His arms around her, guiding her fingers on the strings. The music enwrapping the both of them.

"I would like that," she said.

He had to work hard then to disguise the extent of his joy. He smiled. "Mayhap no' in the middle of the night."

"I do no' mind your playing here in your chamber. I can hear ye sometimes through the wall. It helps me to sleep." She hesitated. "If I go back now, will ye play?"

He did not want her to leave. He wanted to keep her here with him, to pour his love into her ears, his kisses to her lips. But he could give only what she would accept.

"Ye might play a while," she suggested, "since ye canna sleep."

"I will be happy to play for ye."

She nodded and went to the door, where she paused and looked back at him. He was on his feet by then, straining after her. Not moving.

"Thank ye, master harper. Good night."

"I hope ye find yer peace." *Alanna.* Whether it was with him, or otherwise.

She went out so softly that he did not hear the door close. He brought his harp to the bench by the fire, sat down, and played.

The old songs, he gave to her. The ones that had accompanied the tales he had told.

Mayhap they would help her remember.

He imagined her hearing his music, there in her bed. Imagined her dreaming.

Of him.

CHAPTER SEVENTEEN

WHAT BEGAN FOR Katrin then was the strangest of times, when she seemed to live her life on two divergent paths, both of which beckoned her to follow. The paths possessed their similarities. On both did she oversee her father's house, work with his seneschal, look after his guests, and fulfill ordinary duties. But in the afternoons, when it grew quiet, she took lessons on the harp from Finlay. And evenings after supper, she continued to work with the Gallowglass commander.

It felt almost as if she were two women. One who dealt in beauty and dreams woven across the strings of a harp. One who perfected the most effective way to remove a man's head.

Which was she, in truth?

She'd always been aware on some level that Da was disappointed in her—and Ma too, while she was alive—for not fulfilling her expected role in life, marrying early, and producing a herd of children. It would have taken care of Da's current difficulties. She'd heard him call her stubborn when he thought she could not hear. But she'd never found the man to whom she could give herself entirely.

Now there were two of them. Both so different it made her head spin. Both of whom she admired and sincerely liked in vastly different ways.

Reagan brought out something inside her, a fierceness she'd always known was there and that she sought almost instinctively to cultivate. An ability to look after herself and so be her own woman. An assurance that no one would ever have to go off to die on her behalf.

But it was more than that. She liked Reagan's sense of humor and his great and boundless energy, and the fact that he respected her. It came to be that she enjoyed the work itself.

The trouble was, ever since he'd attempted to kiss her, she'd looked at him differently. Now, although he said nothing of it and never attempted to press himself upon her again, she saw more than approval in his tawny eyes.

There was desire.

She dealt with it by telling herself she could have him, if she chose. Why not? She was a spinster and the head of the household, promised to no one. She could have the Gallowglass commander, which would unquestionably be an experience like no other. He would then go away. Naught permanent and naught lost.

He would go away perhaps to die.

That was the trouble with warriors. They lived life on the edge of a blade, and that terrified her.

Still, she did not think of loving him, of giving him her heart. She thought on physical gratification.

Then there was Finlay. Och, Finlay. They met in the hall when it was deserted or sometimes, when the weather favored it, out on the hillside for the lessons he provided on his harp. A privilege it was to hold the beautiful Brada in her hands. And Katrin proved to have an aptitude, the same fingers that could grip a sword—Reagan said she was particularly skillful with a long knife—agile enough to coax delicate notes from the strings.

Ye might ha' been a harper, Finlay told her. *Just like Bradana.*

She remembered it then. Had Adair not given his Bradana seven kisses—two in the palms of her hands, two at the corners of her mouth, on her cheeks, and one upon her brow? Had, in fact, Ardahl not also done so for his Liadan? All the times the two lovers from Finlay's tales had met through the ages, it had been so. Over and over again.

Was that why Finlay had treated her to those seven kisses, what she'd called a blessing? Had he been trying to suggest something?

Nay, and nay, that was far too fanciful. For what might he have been trying to suggest? And why did she crave that he might so bless her again?

Despite her confusion, she enjoyed the lessons she shared with him, aye, as much as the instruction at arms, if not more. The true joy of it, though, was spending time with Finlay. Being in his company. Merely absorbing the feel of him.

There was an ease in that, and a fierce temptation. Whereas she spent her time with Reagan hoping he would not try to kiss her, she spent that with Finlay praying he might.

He did not. He conducted their time together with perfect propriety as if anyone might walk in upon them. Sometimes, folks did.

Yet during that time she became intensely aware of him. The depth of patience he possessed and the quicksilver ability of his mind that could retain a host of stories and tunes to the smallest detail, yet could leap also to laughter.

The music of his voice so often in her ear when he instructed her. The grace with which he moved. The light that came and went in his eyes.

She could not possibly be falling in love with the harper.

Why not?

Because it was a thing she did not do, and anyway, growing feelings for Finlay would be just as inappropriate as for Reagan. For Finlay, too, would move on eventually, leaving her.

Leaving her.

To be sure, he gave no signs of it yet. Every time she brought up the subject, and she surely brought it up more often than she should, he said only that he had accepted Da's invitation, and hers, to stay as long as he wished.

The question then became, how long would he wish?

She had a feeling when the word came from Earl Randolph to

muster, Finlay would take up his harp and move on. Sail to Ireland, mayhap, where there was less war and strife. Free as the wind, he could go anywhere he chose.

Meanwhile, she learned his songs. The ones he had made, like the Gallowglass march, and some far older. She did not play them with any skill approaching his, to be sure. But it satisfied a need inside her, almost as bright as that to take up a sword.

While they worked, she spoke to him. She became so comfortable doing so, it felt like speaking to herself rather than another person. He took in her words the way the sea accepted raindrops, without fuss or exception, and said little enough in return.

He did not have to. She could so often see his thoughts in his eyes.

Wondrous eyes, the harper had. Deep and yet bright, caught like living gems between dark-brown lashes, intelligent and often full of laughter and—well, she did not possess sufficient words to describe them. Sometimes when he looked at her, she saw the whole world there.

Mayhap, after all, she was falling in love with the harper. Which made a good enough reason to stop with the lessons.

Only she could not.

Occasionally she asked him direct questions just to hear him speak, most often the question she had asked before without receiving what she considered a satisfactory explanation. *How and why did ye learn those stories o' us?* Because that question haunted her, so it did.

Mistress, a bard learns many stories.

Aye, but why us, and no' some other clan? Some other family. Are ye certain what ye told us of our ancestors is true?

Every word.

How could he know? Not the general history of her ancestors, nay—that he might well have picked up somewhere in their world. But how could he tell in such detail how Liadan had felt standing in the sun, watching her Ardahl strip down to wash himself? How did he understand the fear in Bradana's heart when she crouched in the bottom of a tiny boat with her hound, knowing they returned to Alba only to fight? How to so well describe the agony of Darlei, the Caledonian princess, traded away from the man she adored, or the fierce resolve of Hulda, the Norse maiden, set upon fighting her own battles?

All the things Katrin felt.

It must be some mysterious magic, for Finlay did know these things. He but rarely spoke of it. He asked her few personal questions, merely answered those she asked with brief yet boundless courtesy.

One afternoon they moved out to the grove of rowan trees that grew at some distance from the keep. A glorious afternoon it was, with a limitless sky of deep blue above and a light breeze that brought to them the scents of the hills. Too lovely, as Finlay had commented, to stay indoors.

Katrin could hear the sea from down at the shore. She could also, distantly, hear the Gallowglass at practice. A strangely divergent combination.

Something about it made her restless. Or perhaps it was Finlay's calm that did. Like a small child seeking attention, she wanted a reaction from him. At last she put aside his harp—with great care, for she never treated it any other way—and got to her feet.

"Are we finished, mistress?" He had grown used to her moods, as she had to his. Not that he had moods, as such. The man merely flickered quietly.

"Nay," she said. If he thought they had finished, he would leave. She was not ready to part with him. "I am merely feeling unsettled. Ye must play for me. Please."

She knew no greater pleasure than listening to him. She wondered if kissing him would be a still greater pleasure.

"The point o' us meeting is for ye to practice," he told her. "Ye may hear me play anytime." He slanted her a gleaming look. "Through the wall, of a night."

Aye, he continued to do that for her, oft times. A kind of lullaby it was, and good of him.

She said, "I can ne'er get enough."

Their eyes met and held. The breath hitched in Katrin's throat.

He smiled. "Ye flatter me, mistress."

"Call me Katrin, for God's sake."

"Katrin."

"And nay of flattery. Ye maun ken ye be a magician with Brada in your hands. Is it too much for me to ask that ye might play for me?"

"Naught ye might ask would be too much."

Then lie with me. Let us strip off our clothing here in the warm sun beneath the rowan branches and touch one another skin to skin, so I might memorize the feel o' ye, and we might forever become one.

She did not say that. Instead she kept her wanton thoughts in her head and stretched out in the fragrant grass to watch him while he played.

His fingers wove enchantment upon the strings. What, she wondered, if he wrought a new song, only their own?

Breath caught, she listened. She admired.

Whereas she might be unable to do aught but watch when beads of sweat gathered upon Reagan's brow as they worked together, and ran sliding down over the muscles of his broad chest, she now marked the many colors the sun found in the harper's hair. Not just rich red but threads of gold also, and copper, and brown. The way the tiny hairs grew along his jaw. He did have a fine jaw, the harper. And the glint of hair at the open throat of his tunic.

How would he look naked? No warrior, the harper, but not a soft man either. She'd learned that much when he sat behind her and reached around to direct her fingers on Brada's strings. He had tramped all over the Highlands, and other lands, in all weather.

She could almost see him stripped of his clothing. She could almost taste him.

Those fingers that moved so deftly over the strings, how would they feel upon her body?

She wanted to give herself to him as she never had to any man. She saw herself rising, going to him, taking the harp from his hands and kissing him so she'd know how he tasted. So he'd know how she felt.

She did not, merely lay there listening, her mind and body alive with desire.

He finished the song he was playing and let his fingers rest on his knee, asked softly, "Ye remember that tune?"

To be sure, she did, and he knew it, for had she not mentioned it to him before? It was the tune the old harper, Coll, had played while Darlei and Deathan made love for what they'd believed would be the last time, in the alcove behind the great hall. Desperate and unendingly devoted love.

"I do. Do ye, Finlay, believe in the wheel o' destiny that ye describe in your tales? That we are caught upon it and return to this lifetime after time to mayhap find one another?"

"I do," he told her in turn.

"Do ye suppose we—ye and I—might ha' known each other before?"

He seemed to catch his breath for an instant before his lips—those mobile, beautiful lips—curved in a funny, canny little smile. He ran his fingers down the strings, producing a shower of bright notes. "I think we might."

"As friends?" *As lovers.*

He said nothing.

Katrin sat up in the grass. "Let us go sailing."

"Eh?" Seldom did she surprise him. She did so now.

"As Darlei and Deathan did, in your tale. As Bradana and Adair did, for all that."

"To Ireland?" Now it was his eyes that smiled.

"Aye, why not? 'Twill be a rare adventure."

He dragged his gaze from her and looked toward the sea, as if considering it.

Say aye, she bade him silently. Because out there upon the sea, away from everything that anchored her life, she could kiss him even as Darlei and Deathan had kissed for the first time.

"Say aye," she pressed aloud.

"Can I e'er deny ye anything?"

CHAPTER EIGHTEEN

FINLAY WANTED TO smile. He wanted to dance. Chief Anders's staid daughter, so it seemed, seldom did anything unconsidered or impulsive. That much became obvious when Katrin, towing Finlay behind her, went down to the shore and demanded a boat from the men who were at work there.

They stared at her as if she had grown two heads. "A boat, mistress? Now?"

"Aye, so." She became impatient, did Finlay's princess, eager to be obeyed. "Is it so much to ask?"

It appeared so. The men dithered and suggested someone should clear the loan with the chief, which half enraged her. She pointed to a small tub at hand, overturned on the shingle. "That one will do."

"Aye, mistress."

The men gazed at Finlay questioningly. "Are ye puttin' out wi' Mistress Katrin, master? Mistress, are ye taking the harper?" one asked.

"I am."

Finlay met the puzzled gazes of the men, keeping a lid on his emotions.

"Pray, right that boat for me and find some oars."

In the experience of these men, Mistress Katrin rarely gave orders. She gave instructions and suggestions. She made requests using her father's authority. No one ever questioned that. So now they scrambled to obey.

Though sailing off for no reason with the harper seemed uncommonly strange.

Katrin looked at Finlay. "Can ye row? If no', I am perfectly capable."

Aye, so she was, his independent lass.

He said, unable now to hide his amusement, "I can row."

They had stopped by the keep on their way down from the rowan grove so he could stow his harp and she could change her shoes. Naught else to be done.

The men held the tiny craft for them as they climbed in and pushed them off. Finlay, half bemused by this unexpected turn, took up the oars.

"Where?"

"Ye will no' harm yer hands wi' rowing, will ye?" she asked him. "Ye ha' such wonderful hands."

Did he?

He held them out for her inspection, one after the other. "Nearly all calluses, as ye can see."

"Still and all, perhaps we should trade places."

"Mistress, allow me."

He wanted this, now that the thing had begun. Wanted to row her out from this selfsame shore, to relive it all again at the stirring of two hearts.

She fell silent. He pulled hard against the inshore combers. All the men stood watching.

He could feel Katrin looking at him. Och, aye, her gaze, steady and serious, inspected him. Hair by hair, so it seemed, and blemish by blemish. Could he tell what she was thinking? Nay. But she wanted this adventure with him. That was enough.

Not till they were far out and tacking to skirt the small isle—the same where the Norsewoman Hulda had once hidden her longboat—did she say, "I wonder how they felt, Bradana and Adair, when they set out for Ireland."

"Uncertain," he told her. "She was distraught at leaving the place she loved. To her, Alba was home."

"She loved him more."

"She did."

Their eyes met.

"Can ye imagine such a love?"

He could.

"Och, list to me. To be sure, ye can. Did ye no' tell tales o' it?"

She fell silent, the only sound to be heard the swish of water along the hull and the trickle of water from the oars.

"Master Finlay, ha' ye ever been in love?"

"I have."

That made her blink at him with those pale eyes of hers. She pondered it, calculating where and when. "Mayhap that is how ye can speak o' it so convincingly, as ye do."

"Mayhap it is."

"Wha' happened—if ye do no' mind me asking—to your love?"

"We had to part, the way people do."

"And it broke your heart?"

It had done that, had shattered him completely. *Every single time.* But the wheel of the years held hope. Did she not sit here with him as she had twice before?

"I do no' believe I ha' ever been in love," she said, confiding in him as completely as if they were linked at the soul.

"Ye must ha' been."

She shook her head. "I ha' been too busy for all that. Too preoccupied wi' duty." She studied him thoughtfully. "Let us drift for a while. Talk."

They had very nearly lost sight of land. As alone as two people could be.

"Wha' is it, Katrin? Ye ha' somewhat on your mind." Did she begin to remember? More than the details of the tales he'd told. He wanted her to *remember.*

"We are friends, are we no', Finlay?"

"I hope so."

"I would hate to ruin a friendship. Still and all—"

She leaned forward and kissed him. She did it with blind intent and yet somehow also with a simple innocence, diving in to place her mouth over his. Since they sat facing each other, she did not have to reach far.

Sensation poured through him, and a wall of emotions he no longer had any hope of controlling. He had wanted this so long. He had wanted it endlessly.

A thousand images flickered through his mind. *Liadan, standing in the sun. Bradana, half starved, crouching beside a meager fire, pulling him into her arms. Darlei, offering her lips to him, silver eyes bright. Hulda, claiming him with equal parts offer and demand.*

All of that narrowed to one thing, one point in time. Katrin, here in his arms.

The taste of her was the same—all woman, all strength, all belonging. He could not keep from drawing her closer, of letting his fingers twine into her hair. Drawing her into alignment with him so he could kiss her deeper, and deeper.

Time stood still. Or perhaps, there on the eternal water, it began moving in its own, everlasting rhythm. Finlay did not think. He did not even wonder or hope. He merely felt.

Wild and sweet she was, and warm in his arms. She had not kissed many men, nay—her tentative manner betrayed that. But her lips clove to his and parted. He could as soon stop breathing as keep from diving in.

When he felt her draw away, he let her go at once, dropping his hands to his knees, trying to remind himself: just because he remembered it all, did not mean she would.

Wide-eyed, she gazed at him, emotions flickering like light and shadow, like a reflection from the water. She had not retreated far, and she must be able to see every detail of him, from the beard that curled along his jaw to the scar on his cheekbone he'd taken when he was ten. Could she see the love?

She blinked at him, long ash-brown lashes sweeping up and down. "I suppose I should apologize for that."

Robbed of all words, Finlay said nothing. But his soul cried, *Kiss me again, alanna.*

Her gaze turned rueful. "I hope I ha' no' spoiled our friendship, 'Twas impulse, just. Which is odd, for I am a woman but rarely prone to impulse. Something about being out here on the water must ha' overtaken me. But I hope—"

"Ye ha' ruined naught." His voice did not sound like his own. "Nothing ye might do could spoil wha' lies between us."

"Nothing?"

He shook his head. Because he wanted so badly to touch her, he took up the oars and began once more to row. Back the way they had come.

She quieted, and yet she did not. So violently did her heart pound, he could see the tremble at her bodice, and color lay high on her cheekbones. "Ye be taking me back?"

"Do ye no' think I should?"

"We are no' running awa' to Ireland, then."

He stopped rowing. "Would ye run awa' wi' me, Katrin? Abandon yer father and yer home and all yer duties? Live the life o' a wandering bard's wife, carrying my harp behind me?"

"Wife?" Their eyes met again, near blinding him.

"Wha' else?"

The light and darkness flickered in her eyes more brightly. "Ye would trust me to carry Brada?"

He smiled despite himself. "I would."

"'Tis a rare compliment, that. And I am…tempted."

Was she?

He wanted to say, *Come wi' me and I will hold ye. Cherish ye. Worship ye with my heart and my body, and my soul. With every bit o' me that has ever been or ever will be.*

But he could say none of that. Instead he told her, "But ye canna come awa' wi' me."

"I do no' suppose I can. Duties, as ye say. I belong here." She made an effort to speak lightly as if striving to relegate what had just happened between them to unimportance. "I could no' break my father's heart."

"To be sure, no."

"And—and a wandering bard canna stay at one hall forever."

Finlay pulled on the oars. "Else, he would no' be a *wandering* bard."

Dare he tell her he would give up all that for her? Put down roots in the rocky soil. Sacrifice whatever she asked. Change his way of life.

He had been wandering their world, aye, for but one reason—to find her. Having done so, why would he stir?

Lest she bade him.

She it was who must choose. Who must remember.

He rowed slowly and steadily, the way he'd once rowed to Erin, and back again to fight for Alba. As he'd once rowed his princess, showing her the place he loved. He rowed them back from the depths of time.

The people on the shore pretended not to watch. But they scrambled when the wee boat came in, laid hands on the hull and drew them onto the shingle.

An older fellow, mayhap one of her father's friends, was there and gazed at Katrin in concern.

"Mistress, are ye quite well?"

"Aye, so." She leaped from the boat with alacrity. "I wanted only to show the master harper our holding fro' the sea. Before he moves on fro' us, I mean."

"Aye, so." The man looked uncertain.

"Come, master harper," she called to Finlay. "I do no' doubt we shall be late for supper."

He followed her, as he had forever vowed to do.

CHAPTER NINETEEN

As Katrin soon discovered, the men on the shore, or at least Robran, who was sworn to his chief at the heart, must have run to Da and told him what she had been about. Taking a boat out to sea for no good reason. With the harper, no less.

As a consequence, Da attempted to speak with her several times before supper. She avoided him by pretending she had duties to which she must attend, hurrying around the hall. She did not feel like making explanations and moreover did not like feeling required to provide them.

The experience out on the water had affected her deeply. Shaken her profoundly. She was a woman who liked to keep her tasks in a line and her world under her thumb. The time on the water had challenged all that.

No matter. She could beat it all into submission again. Be the strong woman she was.

But och, she did not expect her reaction when next she saw the harper. They had gone their separate ways after climbing up from the shore, he to his chamber and she to the kitchens. He entered the hall quietly, as was his way, while still she saw to the preparations. When she turned and beheld him—it felt like being struck hard beneath the breastbone, and it cost her all her breath.

He wore his green cloak, the one that matched his eyes, and had braided the silver sigils back into his hair. He looked composed and self-effacing and—

She wanted to kiss him again. She wanted it so much she

ached.

What had come over her? Had she indeed gone mad out there on the sea?

It just went to show her that giving in to impulse was never wise. No wonder she so seldom did that. She wanted to blame him, or rather his stories. For giving her such ideas.

But nay, she was woman enough to fault no one except herself.

Curse it all, though. Every time she so much as glanced at him, she craved the taste of him. She wanted the feeling that had assailed her when she was in his arms, all over again.

Good thing he was a man of such discretion, for he sat with her and Da and Reagan, at table. And if the time spent with him was all she could think of, he did not in any way reveal he thought about it also.

Mayhap he did not. It had been but a kiss. A man who looked like him and who possessed such talent must garner many such. He would as soon forget it.

Not until Finlay rose from the board after supper and moved away to his harp did Da succeed in bringing up the matter. Indeed, Katrin had meant to move off also but, lost in watching Finlay, failed to do so.

"Daughter, wha' is this I hear about ye and the harper going sailing?"

"I suppose Robran told ye." Katrin focused on her father.

"Nay less than five people told me." Da scowled. "It seems a daft thing to do."

It *was* a daft thing to do.

"'Twas no' sailing. It was but rowing."

Reagan, who sat by listening, raised a brow and his lips twitched. "Does it make a difference?" he wondered aloud.

"I think it does." She sought to quell him with a glare.

"Still and all," Da continued, "why should ye go wi' the harper out on the water?"

"Did yer spies no' tell ye that also?"

"Nay spies." Da looked taken aback. "They merely had some concerns, since ye are no' in the habit o'—"

"By all that is holy, Da. I am nearly a score and ten years old. May I no' tak' a boat out on the water when I choose?"

"Ye are no' even a score and seven."

"Same difference."

"I hope not." Da glanced at Reagan. "Since ye are my one hope left for an heir."

Katrin flushed—with annoyance, so she told herself. "Must we discuss that here?" She spoke in a hushed voice that did nothing to disguise how upset she felt, but heads were beginning to turn. "The harper is about to play."

"Aye, and," Reagan murmured, "we would not wish to interrupt that."

Not until later, when Katrin met Reagan behind the armory, was the matter reintroduced. Reagan was limbering up, swinging the sword he used for practice, since he did not use his grand claymore against her, when he said, "Wha' is all this about the harper, then? D'ye fancy him after all?"

The question stopped Katrin cold. She lowered her own sword and eyed her companion. "Fancy him? I told ye before, I did not."

One of Reagan's mobile eyebrows rose. "*Did* not. I supposed ye might have changed your mind. Women do, so I understand. The lasses I have known oft spoke of *fancy*. Men have other terms for it, with which I will not insult your ears."

"The lasses," she repeated in disgust.

"The fair sex. The gentle beauties."

"I am neither gentle nor a beauty."

He made no answer to that, but when she glanced at him, she caught something in his eyes.

"I do no' go about *fancying* men."

"To my sorrow. Ye may not warrant it, but I have myself been fancied a time or two and consider it a grand compliment."

She could warrant it. Seeing him standing there as he was,

clad in no more than tunic and leggings with his sheen of tawny hair hanging down and every muscle on display, she herself felt a tug.

She snorted.

He gave a bark of laughter. "Well, then. What possessed ye to take a very wee boat and the harper and go out for a row?"

"He is teaching me to play the harp."

"Is he, then?"

"Aye, just as ye are teaching me at arms."

"And that must be done out on the water?"

"Do no' be a fool."

"Och, what a blinding contrast between the harp and the sword! Me, I love irony."

She smiled reluctantly. "Me too. But"—she fixed him with a challenging stare—"there is naught between me and ye, is there? Why should there be anything between me and the harper?"

"I shall tell ye, shall I?" Reagan twirled his sword in the air. "It is in the looks ye steal at him when ye think no one can see. And the stillness that comes to yer face when he plays."

"Stillness?"

"Like—like ye be hearing something holy. Now, I will admit, the man has a rare talent, but, well, personally I have only ever put that sort o' look on a woman's face after I—"

"Pray, say no more.'"

"And so, what has Finlay giving ye lessons at the harp to do with ye taking him out in a wee boat?"

"I wanted to thank him by showing him somewhat of the settlement. 'Twas a treat."

"A treat," Reagan repeated. Then suddenly he guffawed. "I should call that by another name also!"

Och, men, Katrin thought in exasperation. An age-old cry. "He has never seen Murtray fro' the sea."

"D'ye say so? And can ye be certain? He is a wandering minstrel. He will have been all up and down these coasts by boat."

"That is no' the point."

"Nay, it is not." Reagan took a step closer to her and a wry smile twitched his mustaches. "I should rather say the point is, ye wanted to be alone wi' him."

Katrin lifted a brow, emulating him. "And this concerns ye—how?"

"Naught at all, mistress. Does he know ye fancy him?"

Katrin thought of that kiss, the one she had bestowed upon Finlay. He knew. He must.

"'Tis neither here nor there," she told the Gallowglass. "Up wi' your sword."

She fought well that night. She would say even Reagan would admit so, for she caught him a few times very nearly off his guard. A great energy flowed through her, and her muscles hummed, her reflexes sang.

"Ye grow fearfully good," Reagan noted when they parted. "Ye, Katrin MacMurtray, be a woman in a thousand."

"I am certain there are women all over the Highlands willing to take up weapons to defend their families—and their land."

"Aye, mistress, but not all are so terrible good at it."

CHAPTER TWENTY

S INCE THE WEATHER remained fine the next day, Finlay carried
his harp out to the gardens where he and Katrin often met for
her lessons. *Gardens* was a fairly inapt term for the place. The
western coast of Scotland was not hospitable to much more than
sturdy wildflowers. Even though a wall surrounded the place and
trapped the sun, the season for flowers was short. But there was a
kale yard and beds of herbs holding up their rangy heads and, of
course, the rowans.

He felt a bit uneasy when he set up beneath one of the rowans within sight of the kitchen doorway. He'd been subject to
dreams all last night. Or not so much dreams as snatches of scenes
from the past, set on bedeviling him.

Yesterday had felt like an extension of those dreams. Had it
truly happened? Katrin getting a wildness in her head and taking
him out in the wee boat. Almost as if she remembered.

Or did she but recall his tales? The romance of them.

He cursed himself. In telling the tales, he'd intended to spark
her memories. But now he could not be certain what that kiss
meant.

Would she feel awkward being here with him again? Had
things altered irrevocably between them?

Upon the thought, she exited the kitchen door, moving in
that self-controlled way she had, all gathered power. Just the way
Hulda had moved, he recalled with a tug on his heart, so long
ago.

As if she did not carry his whole world.

She had not bothered to dress herself in finery for their sessions, and he wondered what that meant. Was it insult, or compliment? Did it mean she did not care to look well for him, or that she respected him enough to believe he was not the man to focus on appearances?

So he was not. It was all about her presence. For the very feel of the gardens changed when she entered them. Something within him eased. And tensed.

She looked as if she'd just come from some arduous household chore—the laundry, perhaps, or the weaving shed. A plain dress frayed at the hem. Hair bundled loosely at the nape of her neck.

So beautiful.

Though he'd wondered what her attitude would be, she began as if naught of yesterday had ever happened, joining him and saying breathlessly, "I am that sorry I am late. I was delayed in the stables."

"The stables?" He had not imagined that.

"Aye—a great fuss. One o' the stable lads got kicked right in the basket."

"The basket?"

"Aye, ye ken." She swept him with a look. "He refused to see the healer, but all the wind was knocked out o' him. God knows why he agreed to see me."

Because she was the center of this place, its backbone, and its spirit. If she did not see that, he could not tell her.

"Ye ha' no need, mistress, to apologize to me. As ye ken, I am at your service."

Her gaze flew to his. And just like that, he could taste her again. Smell the salt air, the scent of sunshine on her skin, and feel the movement of the little boat.

"Where were we?" He fought to steady himself. "Grace notes, was it no'?"

She sat beside him with a groan. "Ye play them so effortlessly,

I so clumsily."

"No' all harpers play the same. If ye keep up wi' it, ye will no doubt find yer own style and be the better for doing."

"If I keep up wi' it?"

"Once I am gone."

That drew her gaze to his again. "I thought ye said ye would stay. Have ye changed your mind? Do ye ha' plans to leave?"

"Nay plans yet. But I can scarce stay forever."

He gestured, and she took the harp onto her knee. It pleased him beyond expression to see the instrument in her hands.

She said, "I do no' see why not. Why ye canna stay forever, that is. Are there no' lairds who keep a harper in their hall?"

"Aye, so, but I ha' never been one o' those harpers."

"Would ye no' consider staying in one place?"

She does not want me to go. His heart bounded. "I might."

"Ye might stay here?"

"Who can tell what the future holds? The past is easier to know, as we can sometimes remember it."

"And sometimes no'."

He had to acknowledge it. "And sometimes no'." He wondered again at the meaning behind his remembering all they had been to one another, and her failing to. After all the trials they had endured in the past in order to be together, was not this—the recapturing of her heart—the most challenging?

"Now let us begin with the queen's lament." That was full of grace notes.

"Let us not. Let us play again the march ye made for the Gallowglass."

The Gallowglass. That very nearly made him wince. He remembered having seen the two of them slipping off together through the dark, her and Reagan O'Hanlon. Was there something between them? Was it the Gallowglass she truly desired?

If so, then what had been the meaning behind that kiss she'd bestowed on him?

He said a bit sternly, "There is nary a grace note in that march."

And she tossed her head. "Why d'ye think I asked?"

He would love to know the true meaning behind the request.

They worked together there in the quiet yard, amid sunlight dappled by the rowan branches overhead. She already knew the fundamentals of O'Hanlon's march and learned to embellish it before she put up the harp.

"I am that clumsy today," she said in disgust.

"Give it time." It was all about time.

"There should be words."

"I beg yer pardon?"

"To the march. Brave and valiant ones to be sung along." She looked at him, her gaze lingering at his lips before finding his eyes. "I love to hear ye sing."

He stopped breathing. *Love.*

"There is magic in it," said this most practical of women earnestly. "It seems to flow up, does that magic, out o' the past when I hear ye, and—and overtake me." She asked impulsively, "Why d'ye no' mak' words for the march? To—to immortalize the Gallowglass. Reagan would be ever so pleased."

Reagan.

"Why d'ye no' mak' the words," he suggested with lightness he did not feel, "since the idea came into yer head?"

"Och, I ha' no skill wi' any o' that."

"Try, and we will work together on it."

"Aye, so. Come walking." Her gaze grew rueful. "No' now—I will have to go and see to supper full soon. But tomorrow. Ye will come walking wi' me tomorrow?"

His heart bounded again, painfully. "I will."

"Good, then. I—" She handed Brada back to him carefully and sprang to her feet. Stood for a moment looking at him as if she would say more. Leaned a bit closer.

Would she kiss him again? He ached for her lips on his. As they had been in the sun outside the roundhouse. As they had been while in flight through Alba. Up the trail on the headland. Down the path to the Norse encampment.

But she said only, "I will see ye at supper. Ye will play for me after?" Mischief kindled in her eyes. "Somewhat wi' grace notes, since ye manage them so well."

He would play for her life long.

She had only to choose.

Supper was quiet and intimate that night. Folk had grown used to the presence of the Gallowglass and not many were in attendance. The fare was simple and those there left off their casual conversing to hear Finlay play.

Indeed, Finlay thought Reagan O'Hanlon dozed in his seat, head tipped onto one great fist, when the interruption occurred. A ruckus at the front door that intruded into the song Finlay sang. Raised voices and a servant putting his head in apologetically, seeking Anders MacMurtray's eye.

"My chief, apologies, but there is a messenger. He says it is important."

Anders sprang to his feet.

A heavily armored man strode into the hall and directly to the head table. He did not pause until he faced Anders.

"I come from Earl John Randolph," he said then, loud enough for all to hear. "He bids ye call up your clan for war."

CHAPTER TWENTY-ONE

"**B**UT DA," KATRIN said, not without a measure of desperation, "ye are being unreasonable. It makes perfectly good sense for me to go."

They were alone, Katrin and her father, in the small chamber off the great hall that served him as a den, a refuge, and a meeting place. No refuge now. He had been busy without cease since daybreak, calling up the clan and organizing for departure in a mere matter of days, seeing to more details than even Katrin could number.

She knew all too well he did not want or need her to pester him. But she had not much time. They were to muster in order to meet up with others of Earl Randolph's forces as they moved south from the Western Highlands.

He waved a hand at her. "Lass, do no' bother me now."

"If no' now, when? List to me. I ha' been training wi' Reagan—"

"Reagan?"

"O'Hanlon. He says I am ready." She set herself. "To go to war."

That made him stop and stare at her as if seeing her there for the first time. "Wha'?"

Patiently she repeated it all. "Master O'Hanlon has been training me even as—as Geordie did. He says I am better prepared than many o' the men who shall lay aside their hoes and pick up pikes."

"Ye be my daughter."

"Aye, so." She tipped up her chin. "Ye are going, are ye no'?" That little detail had filtered through to her after they heard out the messenger last night. Da had not marched out since, well, since Geordie had taken up the responsibility and gone in his place.

Da said, "I will go at the head o' my men."

"Then I will go wi' ye. Ye should ha' one o' your blood at your side. Da"—her voice caught—"I love ye. That is why I will no' let ye march off alone, to die for my sake."

"I love ye also, lass. And that is why I will no' give my permission for somewhat so daft. I will scarce be alone, will I? Our men and the Gallowglass go wi' me."

Fear, deep and terrible, stirred in Katrin's heart. "Forgive me, Da, but I am twenty and seven years old and do no' need your permission. I am my own woman."

"I ken ye be. But lass, if this fight goes badly, as well it might, ye will be the only surviving member o' this family. Aye? Ye can do yer best for me by staying back. Marry a good man. Carry on the line."

"Da—I had to stand and watch Geordie go off, no' to return to me. Do no' ask me to do the same for ye."

"'Tis a woman's fate to stand. 'Tis the way she fights. Now leave off and let me think."

It felt like getting dashed with a basin of cold water. Da did not mean to hurt her. To disregard her feelings. He no doubt felt overwhelmed and, aye, pressed for time, and mayhap a wee bit worried himself that he might not return. This possibility of battle had been so long promised and so slow in coming.

And to march into England—aye, it was a daunting prospect.

But for her to be swept aside as a mere woman, well, it stung.

She possessed wisdom enough, though, to leave him then. To leave it then. Hands shaking, she went back out into the hall, where there was still a score of tasks to accomplish. Mundane yet necessary things.

The female servants stood in groups talking and expressing their fears. What she must do was go to her chamber. Gather her own things now, while she had the chance. A pack with spare clothing. Things she had borrowed and now appropriated from Geordie, like the padded leather jerkin and light armor.

She must be ready to leave without delay when the others did.

Still, she paused at her chamber door, unable quite to open it. How many more times would she walk through this doorway? She had lived here all her life. Seldom left. Oh, there had been a few trips of short distances to visit relations. Naught approaching a march to England.

She—just like Geordie, like Da—might not return.

The panel beside hers swung open, Geordie's door. The harper stood there.

They gazed at one another in the gloom and silence of the hallway. Katrin could still hear commotion from the hall, and from outside also. Reagan would be preparing his men there.

"Mistress," Finlay whispered. His gaze flicked over her swiftly. "Are ye well?"

"Aye." *Nay.* She gestured to her chamber. "I must—I must prepare."

He cocked an eyebrow.

All at once, she needed to speak to someone. He was here.

"Come in. Pray shut the door."

He followed her into the room, though not far, and stood regarding her. "Your hands are trembling."

So they were, still. Not just her hands, but in truth her whole body.

She stepped past him and shut the door firmly. Began talking.

"I have to prepare to leave, and I have no' much time, only a matter o' days. I am going wi' my father. To meet up with Earl Randolph's forces. To—to fight. Da has bade me nay, but I shall no' listen to him. How can I listen to him? Am I a child that he might order to do as he wishes? I am seven and twenty. I have a right—a right to mak' my own choices. There will be an argument when he learns I mean to accompany him. No doubt a grand one, and before all the men. But he canna stop me, can he?"

Speaking to Finlay felt almost like talking to herself. But his hands came up and lightly caught her shoulders.

"Wait," he said. "What is this ye're saying?"

"I am going wi' my father when he leaves. For war."

Finlay's grasp tightened convulsively before gentling again. He stared into her eyes and she gazed back at him. A thousand thoughts, she saw moving there. As if he would say a hundred things but thought better of each one.

He drew a deep breath. "You wish to be a—a camp follower?"

"Nay. I mean to fight. Like Hulda, in yon story ye told." Katrin tipped her head to one side. "I am no' so unlike her, am I?"

Now a tremor passed through him, one she felt. "Nay, ye are no' unlike her."

"Was she no' my ancestress, and a woman in her own right?"

"Katrin. Katrin, Hulda was trained for war."

She tossed her head. "As am I. Geordie did train me, and I ha' been working wi' Reagan since, in the evenings. After supper."

"I saw ye wi' him," Finlay said. "I thought—"

"What did ye think?"

"That, mayhap, ye grew feelings for him."

"I do ha' feelings for him. He is a good friend. He and his men will be a vital part o' this fight. The fight I mean to join."

Finlay said naught. Katrin stepped away from him, farther into the room. Had Finlay thought she loved the Gallowglass? Then what had he supposed that kiss she'd given him meant?

It meant naught now, she told herself grimly. It might all end here. Her life might end.

"I ha' much to do," she said, still to herself more than him. "If I do no' pack up my belongings now in readiness, I will no' be able to join the company when they meet wi' Earl Randolph's men on their way south. And I maun mak' certain the household will continue to run wi'out me. I will speak wi' my father's seneschal. He it is who should take over."

"Would it no' be better for ye to continue on wi' that duty? In case war comes to Murtray." She could hear the desperation in his voice. Just like the other men, he wanted her to stay back.

"Here? 'Twill no'. We are too far north. We march a great distance south to England." She spun to face him. "I thought better o' ye, Finlay. I thought ye would understand."

He did not speak.

"Ye understand the impulses that moved Liadan's heart when she took up a sword, do ye no'? Bradana's agony when she had to stand and watch her man risk himself against their enemies. The impulses that moved the Caledonian princess, Darlei, to seize responsibility for her own life. And Hulda—Hulda, a warrior in her own stead. Am I any different?"

"Nay, ye are no' different." Emotions now burned in his eyes.

"I ha' a right. To stand up for myself. More, to stand up for those I love. Can ye imagine—aye, ye must, because ye described it so well—the agony of watching those ye love go off wi'out ye, to die?"

"I can imagine it."

"'Tis like ye told in yer tales. Life is a wheel. Mine turns now, for me."

"'Tis a braw and a brave declaration, Katrin. And aye, 'tis yer right to choose. Still and all, I would beg ye—do no' go."

He did not wait for an answer. Instead he stepped up and took her in his arms, his grasp hard and compelling, then harder. Before she could draw a breath, his mouth came down upon hers.

Everything went still. For an instant it did, before all that was inside Katrin came to life. Leaping. Glorying. Triumphant.

Was this the gentle harper? The same man she had kissed in the wee boat? Nay, for this time he kissed her, and with passion. She could feel every part of him, body, heart, spirit. He burned. He burned only for her.

That kiss said what words could not. It shook her, claimed

her, enlightened her. By the end of it, she clung to him, her one mooring in a sea of time.

His lips traveled from her lips across her cheek to her jaw, shedding fervent kisses.

"Tell me—tell me I did no' convince ye to do this mad thing wi' my stories."

"Mad thing?'"

"It is madness for ye to risk yoursel'. I do understand wha' drives ye to it, but och, Katrin, 'twill pull the very heart fro' me."

"That is how a woman feels. D'ye no' ken? Every single time." She reached up and captured his face between her hands. Looked into his eyes. "I canna do that again."

"Aye, but Katrin, lass, whom d'ye hope to protect by spending yer precious life?"

"My da, mayhap. Mine might be the sword to save him, wi' Geordie gone." To her dismay, she felt tears flood her eyes. "This place I love more than my life. You."

"Me?"

"Your way o' life. Mayhap your life itself."

Now she kissed him. Telling, telling him how she cherished all he was. How she would defend it. Bonny, beautiful man.

Her beautiful man.

Impulses came, images flickering behind her eyes. A man, a man who felt like him, in firelight, more than half naked somewhere in the wilds of Alba. Him, wetted down by the rain. Her, opening herself to him completely and him filling her.

Claiming and holding the place she'd kept always for him.

"Ye should leave Murtray," she told him when she could again speak. "Go now while yet ye can travel, before all this begins. For I ken—aye, I do understand—the cost o' watching someone off, someone for whom ye care."

"Care?" He croaked out the word, all he seemed able to say. In truth, he did not need to say more. She could see it all in his eyes. Feel it in his kiss.

Something grave and wonderful connected her and the harper. But…

"Spare yoursel'," she urged.

"Ye expect me to leave here, no' knowing—no' knowing wha' may become o' ye?"

"Ye will no'?"

"I canno'."

"Then…" Katrin spoke softly, her gaze clinging to his. Her heart had never been more certain, nor any choice more assured. "I suppose there is but one thing to be done."

"What is that?" Finlay asked hoarsely.

A tremendous force gathered inside Katrin and flowed outward. "Before I must go, before we need bid farewell to one another"—mayhap forever—"ye had better spend the night wi' me."

CHAPTER TWENTY-TWO

Having left Katrin's chamber—with the promise to later return—Finlay went first to search out Reagan O'Hanlon. Not an easy task in itself, as the entire keep had been thrown into confusion by the order to muster. Aye, it had been expected. One might even say greatly anticipated. Still and all, chaos reigned.

He ran O'Hanlon to ground not in the bailey with his troop but at the armory, helping Robran, the head of Chief Mac-Murtray's guard, sort through the supply of weapons. Panic filled Master Robran's eyes. O'Hanlon looked steady and resigned and just a mite impatient.

The latter emotion filled his eyes when he glanced at Finlay. "Harper? What be ye doin' here?"

"I need to speak wi' ye."

"Now is not a good time."

Aye, he was naught to the warrior, was he? Not in this life, nay. But he remembered. Remembered the hum that ran over a man's skin when he picked up his weapons. The way resolve made a knot inside him, and the narrowing of vision.

He knew what would fill O'Hanlon now—the deliberate setting aside of ordinary life to take up sword and shield.

And, in the Gallowglass's case, axe.

"'Twill no' tak' long," he told O'Hanlon. "And 'tis important."

O'Hanlon looked at him, seemed about to brush him off, but reconsidered. "Very well. Talk."

"No' here."

That made the Gallowglass's eyebrows lift. With a gesture, he stepped away to the open area behind the armory. Finlay followed.

"What is it? I've a hundred things to do. We move out in a matter o' days. My men are ready, but despite the time they've been given, Chief MacMurtray's troops are woefully unprepared."

Everyone had things to do, running headlong to destruction.

"Mistress Katrin," Finlay said.

The Gallowglass's gaze quickened. A frown flitted across his face. "Wha' of her?"

"She intends to accompany her father, and ye, on this campaign."

New thoughts appeared in O'Hanlon's eyes. "How do ye know this?"

"She told me."

"Och—" O'Hanlon looked like he wanted to spit or throw something.

"She says, Master O'Hanlon, that ye ha' been working wi' her. Training her at arms."

"At her request."

"She seems to think"—Finlay's heart pounded—"she is fit to go off and fight. Ye and I ken full well she is not."

O'Hanlon eyed him slowly, up and down. "What d'ye ken o' war?"

"Enough."

"To be honest about it, harper, she is likely better prepared than most o' the men who will march awa' out o' here under her father's banner. Not like to my troops, of course. But these men are farmers. Fishers. Builders." He hesitated. "Fodder for English swords. I hate to think how many will die. Mistress Katrin trained wi' her brother before he died, and 'twas she who came to me asking to continue that training. She is no' bad wi' a sword."

"Be that as it may, she is no' prepared for wha' is to come, the sights she will see. The sounds and the stench o' battle. Ye maun talk to her, O'Hanlon. Convince her she is no' fit to go. She will listen to ye."

"Will she? This is as stubborn a young woman as I have met. Stubborn and strong-willed." O'Hanlon narrowed his eyes at Finlay. "What is her safety to ye, by any road?"

"Everything."

That seemed to knock O'Hanlon back on his heels. He blinked before he said, "*You* talk to her, then."

"I have. She will no' listen."

"Then I suggest ye let her go."

It felt like a blow. "I canna."

"Look. From all I have heard, this invasion—if such it may be called—will be an easy enough task and any battles should fall in our favor. The English are engaged in war, in France. How many men can they spare to beat back a horde o' wild Scots? The way I understand it, King David—who's been hard pressed by the French king to act—will put on a show and come back home again. It may no' be a bad way for the lass to cut her teeth, be she so insistent upon it. Let her watch some o' her clansmen die in the skirmishes. Learn what battle truly is and whether she be the warrior she thinks, before she returns home."

"And if she does no' return home?"

O'Hanlon did not answer.

Finlay tossed his head, a rare anger rising inside him. "Ye do no' care, d'ye? War is naught to ye, or loss—"

"War is my way o' life, harper, and my living. I have long since found a way to deal with it. I admire Mistress Katrin a great deal. She is a grand woman, one in a thousand. But her choices are hers to make. I would not try to tell her what to do. Will ye?"

Finlay thought of Bradana making her way through the wild Alban forest. Of Hulda facing down their enemies at sea. In an ordinary way, he would not. This was not ordinary.

"I am no' asking ye to tell her what to do. Merely tak' her aside and advise her, as someone for whom she has respect."

Again, O'Hanlon hesitated. "Aye, so. If I have time."

"Make time," Finlay told him, warrior to warrior, if O'Hanlon but knew it.

O'Hanlon said nothing. Finlay turned away, only for the Gallowglass to catch him back.

"Harper—have ye ever held a sword?"

"Och, aye," Finlay answered him softly. "Long, long ago."

He remembered…

Mornings working hard in the cool mist, and long afternoons sweating in the sun. The all-too-familiar feel of a sword hilt in his hand. A body that near instinctively knew the back-and-forth steps of warfare's dance.

All that lay deep inside Finlay still. Nay, he had not hefted more than a long knife since the age of fifteen or so, when he'd laid all that aside for the harp.

She had bidden him lay it aside. Begged for it.

Nay, not in this life. They had not known each other then, in this life. But she had asked.

And he would give up even what he was, for her sake. It stung a bit that she was not willing to do the same.

But—she did not know. She did not yet remember all they had been to each other. Och, aye, she had heard the stories. Like the others in her father's hall, she had listened, rapt, to them.

She did not believe.

Mayhap once he made love to her. He still could not believe she had bidden him join her in her chamber this night. Had he heard her aright? Had he been mistaken in what she meant? To lie with her. To hold her in his arms after so very many long years. To make her his own.

The afternoon swiftly flew, all in a welter of activity and confusion. Night would soon be here. If she'd meant what she said, Katrin would become one with him, heart to heart and soul to soul, as it had always and ever been.

He would convince her then that she was too precious to him to risk her life. That she should stay here, and if she did, so would he.

REAGAN CAME TO Katrin just at nightfall following what should have been supper, had a formal supper existed. It had not, no one having time to sit down to eat and listen to entertainments. The women had set out food, and folk had taken it as they might, in passing, so to speak.

Had she eaten? Katrin could not remember. She felt hollow and frightened and—

Her emotions overflowed. Had she truly invited Finlay to lie with her this night? What had come over her to do such a thing? It had been an act of impulse that had come from beyond her, and also somehow from deep within. All she had been able to think was, if she went away to battle and he left and returned to his life on the road, she might never have the chance.

Unbearable, that was. Untenable. Unacceptable. But…she must be going mad.

Yet—the way he had kissed her there in her chamber… There had been a wealth of unspoken words in that, an aching, and a demand. There had been music. A promise she could not refuse.

If she did this thing, marched off to war in Geordie's place and did not come home again, she must have Finlay first. Experience what it meant to lie with him. Explore the deep well she sensed existed between the two of them.

For once in her life she would have what she wanted. Nay, needed.

Reagan found her there in the hall as she directed the women. He came striding swiftly, looking huge and not too clean, and glanced around, his tawny gaze setting on her.

"Katrin, a word."

Her brows flew up. Usually, in front of others, he called her *mistress*. She stepped away with him, followed by the curious glances of the women.

He swept her with a hard glance before he said, "I hope ye do not suppose ye are coming with us when we leave to rendezvous with Earl Randolph."

She drew a breath while protest and a measure of disappointment filled her. She had dared think she might count on Reagan for support. It seemed he, like all the other men, would betray her.

Instead of answering him directly, she asked, "When do we leave, do ye ken?"

"Four days, if we are to be ready. Yer father's men seem woefully ill prepared, still."

"Four days?" Her heart leaped. "Ye be certain 'twill be then?"

"Nay, I am not. But if we are to make the meeting place, it cannot be long after."

Katrin considered that. "Ye will notice I asked when do *we* leave. To be sure, I will be coming."

"I think ye should not."

She narrowed her gaze on him. "Ye? Of all people, I thought ye would be the last to try to thwart me."

He sighed. Rarely did this man of great energy appear tired. A hint of weariness showed in his face now. "I do not say ye are incapable—"

"Well, then."

"But I do not wish to see ye come to harm."

Well, that was stark! "Wha' makes ye think ye will? Have ye so little faith in me?"

"I have great and splendid faith in ye. But the fact is, if we meet enemy forces or even fall into a skirmish, some o' us will die. As your brother did at practice. Death on the field is heedless and random. Why not ye?"

"If I do no' go, it may be my da who falls."

"I will look after your da for ye. Trust me."

Surprised, she said nothing.

"Stay back home this time."

"Wait." As he began to step away, she called to him. "Did he—my da—bid ye speak to me?"

"Nay, the harper," Reagan said.

Finlay.

A thousand emotions tangled in Katrin's heart. How could he? To go behind her back that way…

It made her angry enough to deny him after all. And, in so doing, deny herself.

Almost.

CHAPTER TWENTY-THREE

A HUNDRED TIMES during the course of that evening did Finlay question himself. Wondering over and over if he'd mistaken what had passed between him and Katrin in her chamber earlier. Whether it had been wishful thinking on his part.

Many lifetimes' worth of wishful thinking.

Or, if he had not mistaken the invitation to spend the night with her, whether mayhap she had since reconsidered. Thought better of it.

Perhaps she'd reexamined the wisdom of leaving with her father's men and decided she need not act in haste. That they had all the time in the world to come together, if she so wished.

He did not know. He repaired to his chamber late, wondering, wondering, and played upon his harp, listening all the while for footsteps in the corridor. For the sound of her chamber door opening and closing.

At last he did hear her come up the passageway to her door. She went in, and naught more happened. Had she indeed changed her plans, changed her mind? Had O'Hanlon convinced her? Or did she even now continue working at packing up her belongings?

He played on, his fingers moving across the strings even though his thoughts remained stuttered and frozen. Not until the latch on his door lifted did he cease.

There she stood, still in the wrinkled and soiled gown she'd worn this day long and with her hair half tumbled down. Gazing with a world of emotions in her eyes.

"I should be angry wi' ye," she said.

"Should ye?"

"Aye. Ye went behind my back and talked wi' Reagan. Bade him dissuade me fro' going wi' my da."

Finlay's heart sank violently. He could not deny it. They would not be together after all.

"But I find—" She shook her head, her gaze holding his. "I find I canna be angry, at least no' angry enough. No' when there is so little time to spare."

He set Brada aside and got to his feet, his heart—so he very much feared—in his eyes. He held his breath to hear what more she might say.

She glanced around the chamber before speaking in a whisper. "No' here. Come wi' me to mine."

He slipped behind her, moving surely even though he could not feel his feet on the floor. At the door of her chamber, she caught his hand in hers, the touch warm and so much more than just the contact of skin on skin. She towed him inside and shut the door carefully behind him.

Her gaze met his, wide and pale blue, clear in the soft light of the candles.

"Here is your chance, Finlay, to tell me nay. Do ye still want to be wi' me?"

Still. Always. Eternally. He had no words, so he stepped up and pulled her into his arms.

He wanted to kiss her, every separate part of her, he did. Instead he tipped her chin up gently and sought to determine what lay in her eyes.

His voice sounded choked when he returned her words. "Do ye still want to be wi' me?"

"Aye. Och, aye, Finlay. We are fast running out o' chances. If no' this night, tomorrow, or the next, then mayhap never at all in this world."

She still planned on going, leaving here. Leaving him. His

heart sank again and then bounded. O'Hanlon had not been able to persuade her. "Katrin." *Alanna.* "I would ha' ye be certain this is wha' ye want. That I am wha' ye want."

"My heart wants," she told him gravely. "And somewhat even more fundamental to my being than my heart. My spirit, mayhap." She smiled tremulously. "Parts o' me I never knew existed seem to want ye."

"Well, then." It was not remembering. Not quite. Or mayhap it was as close as he would get, in this life.

"Ye will no' tell me nay?"

"I will no'." He had never been able to deny her.

"Then let us ha' what time we may together—here, now, on this turn o' the wheel, as my ancestors might ha' said. To begin, let me see ye. My imagination has been running riot. Is that too bold a request?"

"Naught ye can say or do this night is too bold." He shed his clothing for her as he had—how many times in the past? Remembered how she had looked at him then. With desire, with longing, with lazy possessiveness. He wondered what she would see now and if she would be disappointed. He was what he was and who he was, but as a man he wanted very badly for her to desire what she saw.

"No warrior," he told her when he stood bared. "As ye see."

Thoughts moved in her eyes. She examined him from the length of his limbs to the tattoos he bore, and must have found nothing lacking, for she came forward into his arms and kissed him, unleashing a tumult of sensation. Fully clothed still, she clung to him, parted his lips with her tongue, and tasted him. Moaned deep in her throat.

"Ye be as perfect, Finlay, as I imagined ye. I find naught wanting."

He laughed unsteadily. "No' fair for ye to stand clothed while I—"

"Stand unclothed? Aye, ye are upstanding, so I see." She breathed it into his mouth. "So I feel."

Aye, so he was.

She backed off from him but a half step. Removed her garments with deliberation, all the while letting her gaze caress him.

She was bonny, as ever she had been. Long, long legs and flared hips. Breasts high and proud, rosy-tipped to his gaze. Strong, aye, and graceful. Everything she had ever been and would ever be. All, to him.

"Come," he bade her. "To the bed."

"No' yet."

She dropped to her knees, reached up, and ran her hands through the swirl of hair on his chest before sweeping them downward, ever downward. Across his stomach, which flexed to her touch. Up and down his thighs before she wrapped her fingers around him.

"I just ha' to know how ye taste. It has been a thing much on my mind. Since the boat, when we kissed."

Had it? *By holy, sweet heaven—*

He stood trembling violently while she leaned into him. Parted her lips, took him in, and indulged herself, for indulge herself she did. He buried his hands in her half-tumbled hair—for she'd neglected to take the bulk of it down—and gave himself up to her, as ever. To sensation, and the sheer rightness of it.

Fate, he decided, was a strange and wonderful thing. That they should be together here this way, as so often they had been in the past. That it should be so wondrously new, and yet so much the same.

She slid up his body, skin against skin, and wrapped her arms around his neck. "Now, ye may come to the bed."

Finlay tasted just the way she knew he would, like every desire she'd ever had, all her dreams rolled into one. The taste of pure man. He possessed a whipcord-strong body beneath the bard's robes, not a spare bit of fat on him, but no lack of muscle either. A body in its prime, honed by years spent traveling over hill and stream.

Not that Katrin would have cared, had he been far less beautiful. It was Finlay that she wanted. The fire of him and the gentleness. The patience and the wit. The man inside.

The fact that he pleased her so, that he was just as she best liked a man to be, with a trail of hair down his chest leading to what stood so proud for her, with long, graceful limbs, and freckled skin, just added to her heady pleasure.

At her bed, she threw aside the covers, tumbled down, and, with what might have been a breathless laugh, pulled him atop her.

They kissed. It might have been for hours; she could not tell. Better than breathing, it was. Something they had done a thousand times, yet never, never before. She could feel the hot weight of him nestled and pressing between her thighs.

She scarce knew herself, who she was, where she was. When she ceased kissing him, it was only to say, "Now. Please."

Aye, surely this had happened before. Her demanding him this way. Begging to have him inside her. It was wild and desperate, the need to have him inside her. To hold him.

"Now, lass? But—"

"Only the first o' times," she said against his lips. "We ha' all night."

He plunged into her, and it was as if her entire world fell into place. As if all the pieces of who she was formed a pattern always meant to be. He began to move in a rhythm as ancient as his songs, too beautiful almost to bear.

Joined at the mouth and below, they rocked and rocked until she could not remember that anything but this existed. Him, a part of her. Her, part of him.

When he would have withdrawn, she locked her heels at his back and he came inside her, both of them climaxing in a storm too powerful to be denied.

"Lass," he breathed into her ear. "Alanna."

"Call me that again."

"Alanna. Darling."

She drew his face up from where it burrowed in her neck and gazed into his eyes. Green eyes, deep as eternity.

"List to me, Finlay. This time together we have for certain. Aught ye want o' me. Understand? There is nothing I will withhold."

"Nor I."

When she left here, her beloved home, when she left *him*, she wanted to carry at least a part of him with her.

If only she could make time cease to pass upon this night.

They did their best. In truth, the hours they spent together did make time stand still, rendered it at once eternal and immediate. Long before dawn, Katrin knew it would not be enough. Forever with this man might not be enough. Had she given her heart to the harper?

Nay, not her heart so much as her soul. If it had ever been hers to give…

They lay quiet for a while. They spoke in intimate whispers of the pleasure they shared. They made love again with tender eagerness. Katrin slept, slept and dreamed.

It seemed she was back in one of Finlay's tales, the first that he had told. Aye, and she had shared in the story as he told it, but now she found herself there in truth, her feet upon the green turf of Erin. She stood on a hillside, the sun moving through the sky to set, and a soft wind bringing the far scents of thyme and heather. Should she be able to sense so much of a dream?

She walked down the hillside into a settlement made of roundhouses with a larger structure at its center. Her heart lifted and sped as she went. He would be there. Her mother was away helping with a birthing, and he would be there alone.

Stolen time they might have together, before the wheel turned and perhaps parted them.

She entered a tiny roundhouse, one that looked no different from the others, though she knew it for home. The scent of it, the fire burning low in the center of the floor. The sleeping benches beyond.

He was there, back from his practicing at arms, and turned to regard her when she went in. Tall he was, with broad shoulders and a graceful, limber frame. Not the harper. And yet, and yet…

Helpless against what she felt for him, she went forward. They linked hands. His eyes, bright hazel, met hers and asked a question.

"Come," she whispered.

Was there aught more to be wanted or had in the world than the feel of his arms around her? Ah, but how had she ended up in Finlay's tale? Was this real, or imagining? Filled with him, filled with his love, she lay curled in his arms on the sleeping bench, and wondered. She could feel the stars moving overhead, way up above the roof of the roundhouse, and even those stars slowed in their courses to afford them this time. It was not enough. By heaven, it would never be enough.

Katrin awoke in her own chamber, in Finlay's arms, knowing one night would not be enough. Perhaps not many nights, or many lifetimes.

She lay listening to him breathe, a sound she seemed to know deep within, like the coming and going of waves on the shore. Their night must have passed. Light filtered in through the window and she could hear that activity began outside the walls, and down in the house. A pit of dread opened in her stomach. She did not want morning to come.

Finlay lay sprawled beside her, his lips still at her cheek. She wondered, with the coming of the day, what would happen between them, even as she stroked her fingers through his red hair. What could happen between them? In a mere matter of days, she must go, and he stay.

By the time she returned from this battle, if she returned, he would likely have moved on. She had no right to ask him to wait for her, while making the choice she did.

One with which he disagreed.

"I maun rise," she murmured to him with heavy reluctance. "We have another hard day afore us."

His eyes opened, magically green in the dim morning light. Many things, he might say. He could once more attempt to dissuade her from her plan, ask her to stay. His words carried much more weight with her now. Being the man he was, he did not ask. Nor did he speak of love.

Ah, and could what had been born between them go by so ordinary a name?

Instead, he requested, "Kiss me."

She did, putting the whole of her soul into it. He accepted the gift and breathed in deep.

Should she tell him about the curious dream? Confess that in his arms she had slipped off to the place in the past he'd described to the company so well?

Instead she said, "Tonight."

"Eh?" Curiosity—or was it wonder?—sparked in those incredible eyes, and moved in his face.

"We have—we have a few more days." She stumbled over the words. "A few more nights. If I ask to ha' ye again—?"

"Lass, och lass, has there ever been aught I've been able to deny ye?"

CHAPTER TWENTY-FOUR

K ATRIN WAS NOT herself that day, nor anything approaching the self she knew. Though she kept busy with tasks aplenty, both helping with preparations for the Murtray army to move out and providing for the families of the men who would go, a part of her remained in her own chamber with Finlay. Lost in the heat of him, the safe harbor of his arms, the thrill of blending her very being with his. Who would ever imagine such a thing could occur? That she might lose so great a part of herself to any man, and in so doing gain so very much?

She ached all day long to see him. But by accident or design, he kept away from her and her agitation grew along with his absence. Och, but this was the very reason she'd long determined never to fall in love. Who would want to surrender a portion of her well-being and self-determination, subject to whether or not a man was in sight?

Unless that man was Finlay.

His tunes haunted her head all day long—it seemed she'd heard them even when he made love to her. She told herself she would not meet with him again that night—though had she not promised? And then she decided she could not live, possibly could not continue to breathe, if she did not lie with him again.

Somewhere around midday, Reagan came to her. He had been working hard, not with his own men now but with Da's, trying to get them all armed and in possession of some sort of armor, and looked impatient. He snagged Katrin's attention in the great hall, where she was helping to set out a meal, by standing in front of her till she regarded him.

He made a very large barrier.

"Have ye spoken to the harper?" he asked abruptly.

Spoken to him? Aye, she had tumbled words right into his ear. Run her hands all over his body. Had her tongue in his mouth. Felt his eyelashes against her skin as he suckled at her breast. She knew the taste of him. The weight and the heat, inside her.

"Why?" she asked.

Reagan scowled. "Somewhat is not right."

"No' right wi' the harper?" That made her stop what she was doing. "How d'ye mean?"

"I do not know." Reagan gave himself a shake. "I have seen him here and there all about the settlement today. And I think—"

"What?" Katrin knew Reagan for the consummate warrior, and knew how good his instincts were. If he had noticed something about Finlay…

"Is he gettin' ready to leave?"

"Leave? Here? Leave Murtray?" She sounded like a madwoman, but those were the last words she wanted to hear. Dread stirred within her, all mixed up with desire. He would not. Had Finlay not promised to be with her again tonight?

Had he? Had he actually promised?

Ah, perhaps he was still annoyed with her for saying she meant to accompany her father off to fight—though 'twas she, in truth, who should be annoyed. She needed to see him, talk to him.

"Where is he?" she asked Reagan.

"Now? I just saw him headed toward the armory."

The armory? A harper?

"I maun go," she said distractedly. She had to run Finlay to ground. Reassure herself that he would be here as long as she needed him.

And how selfish was that? Was that what she had become in

her determination to direct her own life? Selfish?

"Katrin." Reagan seized her arm. He touched her so seldom, save when they were at practice, that it made her narrow her eyes at him. "Did the harper not persuade ye to stay back from the mustering?"

"Is that what ye thought he meant to do?"

"Let us say I still had some hope."

She lifted her head. "Finlay knows me for a woman who possesses a mind o' her own. That is no' likely to change."

Reagan let go of her and gave a careless shrug. "Mayhap that is why he is planning to leave. Not much reason for him to stay here, with ye gone."

And why should a man not stay and wait for a woman? How many women, over the scores upon scores of years, had done just that?

She glared at him. "No call for ye to speculate over the harper's decisions."

"Nay, none at all. I just thought it odd, and supposed ye would want to know."

So she did, and mayhap she should thank him.

Instead, she ran from the room, out of the keep proper and down the stone stairs to the bailey. When had it become so late in the afternoon? The light had already begun to fade, and if she was to be with Finlay this night, they needed to get the matter settled.

The bailey, overflowing with Gallowglass warriors and Da's men at practice, hindered her progress. She kept trying to see past heads and shoulders for a dark-red mane of hair or the edges of a green cloak. Men there were out here in plenty. None that was the harper.

Katrin went suddenly breathless, as if a weight had descended upon her. As if a number of heavy clouds weighted by grief had come down. What if she could not find him? What if he had already gone? Off across the hills and glens. Away from her.

He would not do so, not without telling her. Not after last night.

She ducked around the side of the keep and headed for the armory.

FINLAY COULD NOT think of a good excuse for a bard to go seeking a sword.

The bailey was overflowing with men. Many of those who would be required to march out at their chief's command seemed to have flooded in, perhaps from outlying places, perhaps to get their orders and weapons. Some had brought their women, or probably more accurately their women had come along, eager to learn how risky this venture would be. Women worried for their men, as ever. Just as men worried for their women.

It was, as he had learned over the many, many years, one of the prices of love.

He had been shaken to his core by what passed between him and Katrin last night. Holding her in his arms again, tasting her sweetness, claiming her for his own just as in the long-ago. But he did not fool himself—she was not yet his own, at least not in this life. Succumbing to passion did not mean she remembered all they had been to one another. All they were.

He stood for a while outside the crowded armory, lurking in a manner unbefitting a bard. No one paid much attention to him, not even Chief MacMurtray, who was very much in evidence, talking to his clansmen and lending any who wanted it a patient ear. A good chief, was Anders MacMurtray, and worthy of his name.

The chief of his guard, Robran, seemed to be in charge of passing out weapons. Quite evidently, there were not enough to go around. Men were showing up with implements of their own, everything from hoes to scythes, and many did not seem to want to trade them for more traditional arms. Perhaps the tools with which they were familiar felt more comfortable in their hands, and no question a scythe could make a formidable weapon.

But against a mounted English knight, if that was what King David's army would ultimately face?

Finlay might argue that far less than these others did he warrant a sword in his hand. But if Katrin thought he would let her march off without him, she was very much mistaken.

"Here ye be! Och, I ha' been all over the place, high and low, looking for ye."

He whirled to find Katrin behind him, looking harried and clearly out of breath. Finlay suffered an immediate flashback to last night, and the sight of her sinking to her knees in front of him. The glorious sensations that had come after.

"Wha' are ye doing here?" she asked, narrowing her eyes at him.

He could scarce tell her the truth. It had been well over ten years since he'd held a sword in his hand with any real intent.

Fortunately, she did not wait for his reply. Instead, she clamped her fingers to his forearm. "Are ye planning to leave?"

"What?"

"Are ye intending to leave Murtray? Take off down the road, just, wi' Brada on your back? Because I refuse to stay at home, I mean."

"Lass, alanna, I would no' do that." He meant to leave here, aye, but only at her side.

"Are ye certain? Reagan said ye are acting strangely." Her fingers tightened.

"Reagan, is it?"

"I wondered—I wondered if ye meant to strike back at me."

"I would no' do that either." Love did not strike back.

"Or if I had done somewhat last night"—here she lowered her voice, even though no one could possibly hear them in the racket of the yard—"to displease ye."

"Displease me?" He had to close his eyes for an instant, the emotions came so strong. "Nay, and nay."

"Then come."

"Where?"

She bent a look on him. "Just come."

People did stare when she led him away. Finlay supposed it made a strange enough sight for the chief's daughter to be hauling off the harper. Katrin hissed between her teeth and let go of him.

"Go to yer chamber. I will be right up."

"Eh?"

She bent a look upon him that left nothing to the imagination.

"Now?" he asked. In the midst of the day. Broad daylight.

She stepped closer, so close he could see the dark ring around the pale iris in her eyes. "I mean to ha' ye again. Will ye argue wi' it?"

"Nay, mistress." His whole body came alight. "No' me."

She marched off away from him, her hips swinging with confidence. A spear of delight pierced him. Och, and she was today as she had ever been, if only she knew it. So far, she did not. She had not remembered. Mayhap if they lay together again?

It would take much less than that to persuade him.

She was waiting when he reached the corridor outside his chamber, and her door swung open before he could touch his. She reached out and seized him, towed him in.

Her lips were on his before the door finished closing. Aye, this was the woman he remembered. The one eternally his own.

KATRIN DID NOT care that it was still daylight. Dark would fall soon enough, though she had not the patience to wait for it. She could not say what had got into her. The effects of that which had passed between herself and Finlay last night, mayhap. Or the way the stories he had told kept sneaking up to capture her. The dream she'd had while in his arms. The man himself.

All she knew was, they had not many days left between them. She wanted all the nights with him. And if the night was to begin early, then well enough.

She leaned up and kissed him. He tasted wonderful, did the harper, sweet as honey mead, his mouth warm and somehow instantly her undoing. If she'd had any resistance left, it would have deserted her then.

She had none.

"We will no' be ready to leave tomorrow," she said as she tore her lips from his and began to undress. "It will be a few days yet, for naught is ready. No' the house, as we maun leave it, nor the men. We have at least this night together."

"Aye, so." He stood there watching her as she shed her clothes, a thing she could not seem to do fast enough. "Ye said, *we*. Ye are still planning to accompany yer father, then?"

"I am." She paused with the front of her dress undone, aching for his touch. *Aching*. "Does that matter? Does that change aught between us? Finlay, are ye angry wi' me for no' heeding ye and staying back, as Reagan says?"

"Reagan said that?"

"He implied it."

"I am no' angry wi' ye. Fearful for ye. Worried half out o' my mind. But that is nay the same thing."

"Do no' worry." Half naked, she pressed against him. "I am strong. I am able."

"Aye, so I ken. But Katrin…" He put his hands in her hair, and his touch affected her so strongly, the pleasure was nearly pain. "Life is made up meetings and partings. I would no' part wi' ye so soon."

"Do no' worry about it." She kissed him again, putting all her passion into it. Why could he—this one man in all the world—not believe in her? Have faith that she was strong enough? To take Geordie's place at her father's side. To come back alive.

Strong enough, it seemed, to do aught except resist lying with him again.

"Touch me," she begged when the kiss ended.

He swept her up in his arms and carried her to the bed. Once again, time—perhaps even life itself—seemed to slow down as she lost herself in the sheer need to be with him, and the rightness of it.

He finished undressing her and shed his own clothing without regard. He began kissing her, starting with the palms of her hands, working his way up her arms, down to her breasts and further, across her stomach, down her legs and up again. She surrendered herself to the sensation, knowing that, just like last night, she would be able to deny him nothing.

She yielded, as she would not ever to any other man. She lay in a haze with her eyes narrowed, watching the beauty of him as he kissed her, and when he nudged her thighs apart she did not resist. Whatever he wanted of her, she would give.

It was as he was bringing her to the pinnacle of delight, his tongue inside her, that the room altered. In fact, it ceased to remain a room at all.

Instead, they were outside with a sky full of stars stretching overhead and tall trees all around. Firelight flickered nearby and the man she loved—the man she adored—knelt between her legs, his warm mouth a searing caress.

Naught more for which she might live than this. To be sure, they were hungry, desperate, in danger and on the run. But so long as she remained in his company, she would ask no more of life.

"Adair," she whispered as she shattered, and he took her in his arms and held her close before plunging into her, even while the stars sang overhead, an ancient song.

Ah, Katrin thought as she came to herself. She must have slipped into another of Finlay's tales, the second one he had told, when Bradana and Adair fled across Alba together, the very spirit of the land helping to hide them. A curious thing…

But all she cared for now was the feel of Finlay inside her, and the warmth of his touch. The way he tasted when she pressed her mouth to his. Be they in her bed, or out on the breast of Scotland, she wanted only to be in this man's arms.

Dark found them, the light draining from her chamber as the daylight died outside. Katrin wondered if anyone was looking for her downstairs, if they would come searching. She was always on duty in the hall or the kitchens. But this, this was time apart.

"Finlay." She turned to him and rubbed her lips across his. "Will ye spend each night wi' me? Until I maun leave to meet up with Earl Randolph?"

At first she thought he would not answer. His hand lay upon her naked breast, the calluses earned by contact with the harp strings a wondrous abrasion. But he kissed her deeply and said, "Aught ye ask, alanna. Aught ye ask o' me."

CHAPTER TWENTY-FIVE

ONE NIGHT, ONE glorious night, and then two. Would they have more together before the Murtray troops were formed up and ready to depart? Katrin could not say, and had little time for it with a hundred thousand details to which she must attend. People looking for her, aye, and seeking her advice, her direction on every hand. Yet, following her second night with Finlay, she could barely focus on any of it.

Finlay.

Had it been a kind of waking dream that she'd experienced when he made love to her? Had she been half asleep, or had she merely imagined she'd been back in one of his stories? Had it been his voice, whispering and crooning to her that had taken her into the tale he had told of Adair and Bradana? Was she merely losing her mind?

She must be, since she remained intent upon spending the last two nights with the harper, as she had the first two. To be truthful, though, the time in his arms remained all she could think about. Even as the clan's folk, troubled and worried, came to her. As she worked with Angus to verify the details that would keep the homestead running well while she was away.

For she still did mean to go away. To be sure, she did. She could not let the harper's sweet kisses, or the places to which they took her, alter her plans. Was she not a woman determined to make her own decisions?

And Finlay—Finlay did not question or badger her about it.

He did not once ask her again to stay, to hold back, even though what Reagan had said haunted her. Finlay did not want her to go off to fight.

Seldom in this world could a person, man or woman, have what he or she wanted.

But when they were not alone and losing themselves in one another, Finlay seemed intent upon avoiding her. During the days so full to bursting, she barely caught sight of him. He did not show himself in the bailey and did not come to the hall for his meals. Heaven alone knew what he did with himself.

And since there were no suppers at eventide for entertainment, she did not get to hear him play. Except in her head. In her heart.

He haunted her, did the harper, and it was with her own mind that she argued.

If she did not go off with her da, if she did what Finlay, Reagan, and likely every other man in existence wanted her to and stayed home, she could prevent him from leaving and would therefore have more time with him. Nights uncounted to lie in his arms. To feel the magnificent, depthless sense of belonging that came to her, unexplained, when she was with him. The emptiness inside her that she had not even realized existed, filled.

But if she did go off to fight… Well, she feared, she feared he would not be here when she returned. If she returned.

Why go off, then? one half of her head—or perhaps it was her heart—argued. Why take a chance on losing him, and never seeing him again? Why not claim this strong, wondrous, and yet somehow fragile thing that existed between them, while she could?

Duty, or perhaps sheer female stubbornness, argued back. She could not betray herself or her loyalty to her da, not even for the sake of… Was it love she felt for Finlay? Nay, and nay, she still did not believe it could go by so ordinary a name.

As evening fell on the third day, she panicked. She had not seen hide nor hair of Finlay since they had parted at dawn that morning, he arising from her bed and slipping off to his own chamber, and the need inside her, that great and undeniable need, began to nudge her harder and harder. She paused in the act of helping the women clean up from the rough-and-ready meal that had been laid out—for the benefit of clansmen and Gallowglass soldiers alike, for the latter had already mostly packed up their camp—on a sudden flash of fear.

What if he had changed his mind and gone? What if, knowing the parting between them would be hard, he had already slipped away and up the track, over the brae?

He had said he would not. He had promised it. Would he break a promise to her?

Her heart said nay. Her fear… Well, it spoke differently.

Leaving the women to finish the task, she went up to his chamber, but he was not there. His belongings were piled neatly against one wall, the pack he wore on his back and Brada, already in her wrappings. Ready for travel.

He had not gone, not yet. But he did intend to go.

She flew on feet made clumsy by haste. Ran down to search the hall again, praying for sight of a dark-red head, a tall, graceful figure. Seeing none. The bailey next, still crowded with people. Fear rose up inside her more fiercely than before.

The garden, the kale yard, the stable, the armory, now very nearly empty of weapons. Sweat beaded on her brow. She must find him.

It was Reagan who found her instead. He stepped in front of her when she left the armory, a deep scowl on his face.

"Katrin? What is wrong with ye? Are ye ill?"

"Me? Nay."

"Well, ye do not look—"

"Ha' ye seen Finlay?"

Reagan's eyes narrowed. "The harper?"

"To be sure, the harper."

"What would he be doing out here in this tangle?"

Katrin pressed the heel of her hand to her forehead. "I do no' ken."

Reagan took hold of her by the shoulders and backed her up to a stone bench that stood outside the armory. "Sit. When is the last time ye took anything to eat?"

"No' long since. I just came fro' the great hall."

"When is the last time ye took a rest?"

Lying in Finlay's arms. But she could not share that. She shook her head.

"Then go up to your chamber and lie down for a wee while."

"I cannot. Too much yet to be done." She searched Reagan's tawny eyes. "Do ye know for certain when we leave?"

"Day after tomorrow, at dawn."

Only two more nights, then.

His frown deepened. "Katrin, do ye still mean to accompany your father away?"

"Of course I do." Would he start with his persuading all over again?

"Then ye must take better care o' yourself. By God, woman, look at ye! A headless chicken would appear more sensible."

"Insult me as ye will. It means naught."

"I do not insult ye. Katrin. Katrin"—he snagged her gaze, which once more wandered across the yard—"I am concerned for ye. Can ye not see that?"

"Aye, so." She puffed out a breath. "Ye ha' been a good friend to me."

"Friend. Aye." He raised one eyebrow. "Even if I might have wished to be something more? It is for the harper ye search like a lost child."

"I am no' lost. I ha' never been lost. I can make my own—"

"Choices and decisions, aye. And so it seems ye have done."

Sudden, foolish, and quite unacceptable tears came to Katrin's eyes. "There are but two more days."

"Ye think he will not be here, when ye get back."

"I know he will not."

"Have ye asked him to stay?"

"I ha', even though I ha' no right to do so. No more than he has the right to ask me no' to go south with the army."

"Ye be a mad lass, do ye not know that? Any man would hurry to make ye promises, I do not doubt."

"Stop wi' yer foolishness."

He heaved a sigh. "Get to your bed. 'Tis the best place for ye."

Katrin could only agree.

FINLAY PAUSED ON the rise of land above the keep and let his eyes wander, taking in all the details of this place he loved. Evening fell swiftly, already gathered across the graveyard at his back and in the forest high above. He had tramped long this day, unable to linger in the settlement, to watch Katrin make her preparations to—as she thought—leave him. He knew he could ride her no further on the matter. He above all men understood her heart, knew that ever since she'd been a Caledonian princess, if not before, the best way to make her stubborn was to keep berating her about anything. A man could only use reason, or cajole, or apply kisses.

He had tried that last course of action, for the past two nights he had. He'd not changed her mind, only lost himself to her more surely. Surpassing even their past four lives together.

He could not come out and tell her what they had been to one another. She would never believe it. She had to remember for herself.

There had been moments during their time together when he believed she had come close. Yet still she carried on with her plans as if naught had changed. As if he, and what lay between them, did not matter. It stung.

He let his eyes roam over the keep below him, the clusters of stone huts all around, and the sea beyond. Emotions that felt very like homesickness stirred inside him. She knew if she went away from him—she might well not return. Aye, and a fitting enough answer to him might that be. How many times had he gone from her with a sword in his hand, and she not knowing if he would return to her? Once right here, at this very setting.

It was the reason she had asked him to be what he now was, not what he had always been. But did the ancient warrior not still linger inside him, like the remnants of a song? Did he still possess a warrior's heart?

Mayhap, after all, they were not meant to be together in this lifetime.

A figure stirred on the path below him, the one that led up to the graveyard. She wore a dusty blue dress and her hair trailed over her shoulders, having fallen from the careless bun she had no doubt tied up this morning. His longing stirred, the way the music so often did in him. He felt the wheel of life turn.

She came to him. Weariness rode her shoulders, but when she caught sight of him standing there motionless on the path above her, that fled. Her step quickened and she skipped over the stones. Fleet of foot, if not light of heart.

"I ha' been looking for ye all day!" she cried, breathless, when she reached him. "Where ha' ye been?"

"Walking. Thinking." He took both her hands in his and felt something—some terrible fear or restlessness in her—ease.

"I thought ye had gone. Off on the road wi' your harp on your back. Then I looked in your chamber and saw Brada still there." Her gaze searched his. "But wrapped. For traveling."

"Aye."

She drew in a great gulp of air. "So if I hold to my truth and accompany my da, ye will go also?"

"Aye."

With an edge of desperation in her voice, she said, "But ye promised to stay."

"While ye were here, aye."

"That is no' fair. I ha' told ye, Da loves your music. He would gladly gi' ye a place here for good. Ye might stay, wait—"

"Nay, Katrin." He need not tell her he had no such intention, that even if he did, he could never go. He must hold firm. She it was who had to choose. To love him because she remembered, or just *to love him*.

"Reagan says we leave the day after tomorrow, at sunrise. That gives us two more nights together. Come."

She tugged at his hand. He did not move.

"Finlay?"

Two nights. Only two more, possibly, in all the world. In all his life.

When she spoke again, she sounded impatient, but he caught the glint of tears in her eyes. "Will ye no' come to my chamber wi' me? Nay? Then let us lie out here beneath the stars. In the forest."

"Katrin—"

"I maun ha' ye."

She must.

CHAPTER TWENTY-SIX

I N THE MOMENTS before Katrin opened her eyes, she struggled to determine where she was. *When* she was. Not her bed in the keep or anywhere she at once recognized. But that did not matter.

She lay in the arms of the man she loved.

The familiar warmth of him wrapped around her. The well-loved scent of him teased, and satisfied, and lent an inestimable sense of security. Wherever she might be was exactly where she needed to be.

She lay with her cheek against the naked skin of his chest and could hear his heartbeat. Slow and steady as the rhythm of the world. She wondered, with a tentative sort of marveling, in which of Finlay's stories she had landed now. For surely, in one of those she did lie.

"Darlei," he whispered, and kissed her.

She opened her eyes to darkness.

They lay outdoors in the forest, for surely those were trees swaying gently above her against a backdrop of eternal stars. And the man in whose arms she lay was not Deathan, but Finlay, the bard.

It came to her then. How she'd towed him up the slope away from the sea and across the graveyard where lay her ancestors, sleeping. Into the trees beyond. They had spread his cloak out on the ground and lain down to make love.

Once had not been enough. Nor twice. He had fallen asleep before she had, and she'd lain there wondering—wondering what he made of her life. Even now, she was only half certain whether this be the truth of that life, or dreaming.

"Finlay. Finlay?"

He stirred. All his movements were beautiful. Those of his hands at her breast. The way his body bowed when he came inside her. Even now, he reached those graceful fingers to her cheek before he opened his eyes.

"Katrin?"

"Call me alanna."

"Alanna."

"Am I Katrin, or am I someone else? Someone out of your stories."

He said nothing, but she could feel him watching her.

"I dreamed I was caught back in one of those stories, I did. Dreamed it while I lay in your arms."

"Which tale?"

"Ye were Deathan. I, Darlei."

"The Caledonian princess."

"With the heart o' a wild woman, so ye said."

"Aye. Och, aye." He stroked the hair back from her temple. She ached for him to kiss her again. But if they kissed, they would make love, and she had something to say first.

"Deathan was wise enough to know better than to try to change his Darlei. Would ye change me, Finlay?"

"Never."

"Then ye will ha' to let me go, day after tomorrow."

"I canna' stay ye or hold ye. Only your own heart can do that." Was that grief she heard in his voice?

"Then mak' love to me again. Just in case we do no' get the chance tomorrow night."

She did not have to ask him twice.

THEY GARNERED NO more sleep there in the forest. Instead, once they had again made love, when Finlay had felt the wheel of his life turn beneath him, Katrin rose and caught up his cloak, held it out to him.

"I maun go back. If Da is looking for me, he will be frantic."

"Aye." Finlay swirled the cloak around him. It was damp from the ground and smelled of her. Of their lovemaking. The two of them entwined.

She said, "I would no' cause Da the kind o' worry ye caused me today."

"I had no intention to grieve ye."

She reached up and laid the palms of her hands on either side of his face, kissed him deeply. For an instant he felt certain she would tell him she loved him. For surely she did? No such words came. Instead she said, "If ye would no' cause me grief, then promise ye will wait here at Murtray while I am gone."

"Katrin, I canna mak' that promise."

"Verra well. It seems that neither o' us will gi' the other what he or she wants."

"It seems no'."

SHE LONGED TO tell him to remain in her sight. But he had not offered that reassurance. He refused to give her the assurance that if and when she came back from the long march south, she would find him here.

He wanted something from her too.

Katrin could not be sure what, or why her heart knew that. It just did.

A man in ten thousand, was the harper. And she maun leave him.

The following day—that before they were to leave shortly after dawn—flew by. Katrin wanted a thousand times to seize hold of it, make the spinning of life's wheel halt for just a few moments so she might catch her breath. But there were Da's things to pack up, Angus being far too busy with other matters to tend to it. There were last-minute arrangements to make. And people wanting her attention on every hand. With each passing moment, her grief and her desperation grew.

She did see Finlay throughout that day. He stopped in the hall when she was there at midday to take a meal, standing within her sight while he ate, though she had not the time to talk with him. She saw him also out in the bailey while she ran errands. He did not approach her, and she determined—tried to determine—that neither would she approach him this night, much as she wanted their last night together. Desperately, achingly wanted it.

A glimmer of red hair, a flash from the hem of the green cloak—they had lain together upon the softness of that—and little more did she catch of him. When night began to close in, she retreated to her own chamber to make sure all she would need was packed up for morning. Very little time would there be to spare, then.

She did not admit to herself that she was waiting. But her ear strained for his step in the chamber next door, a whisper of his movement in the passageway. The sound of notes loosed from his harp if he were there, and had unwrapped Brada for one last session.

She tried to imagine it—the morning with its rush and clamor. His leaving in one direction, and her taking another. What could she say to him? Would there be an opportunity for a leave taking? Would it be better without one?

When she'd packed up everything that she thought she would need, had Geordie's leather armor ready along with the sword he had given her, all in a pack she should be able to carry on her own, she curled up tight in her bed.

He was not going to come. He would not approach her. She would be cursed if she would go out searching and pull him back with her again. Even if it did half kill her to go without the hours she'd thought to have with him.

There were hundreds of men in the world, besides Finlay. Many and many of them would accompany her away tomorrow, including Reagan O'Hanlon—one of the finest she'd ever known. Why should she lie and ache for Finlay?

She closed her eyes as weariness took her, drowsing.

She dreamed she sailed aboard a long, narrow vessel, a craft built with a high prow in the shape of a dragon's head that, like a living beast, crested the waves. She could smell the sea, the salt in her hair, and could feel her own strength as she clung to the dragon's neck, gazing hard in the direction they sailed.

She returned to her lover, a man named Quarrie MacMurtray. She went with a sword in her hand. And if she had to fight battles for his sake, to win a place beside him, then this thing she would do. For she belonged but one place in the world, and that was at his side.

She awoke to find her chamber dark, and a fire burning within her. She had been caught up in another of Finlay's stories, the last one he had told. But she'd fallen from the story too soon, before she'd been able to reach the man she loved…

The man she would love eternally.

A creaking told her that the door of her chamber had edged open. She raised her head from the bolster and peered through the gloom, not at all sure whom she would see. Ardahl, the Irish warrior? Adair, the prodigal son? Deathan, who had loved a princess? Quarrie, who'd possessed the strength to love a warrior? Why should she think it might be any of them?

A figure stood dimly silhouetted in the open doorway. Graceful, with long hair streaming over his shoulders, his body edged in green.

It was none of those men from the glorious stories Finlay had told, but the man himself.

She rose and welcomed him with eager gladness, all her pride forgotten. Closed the door firmly and undressed him with her own hands. Tasted him. *Tasted him.*

If that night had lasted forever, it would not have been long enough, and it did not last forever. She awoke in the cold dawn to find Finlay already stirring beside her, ready to rise and leave.

But which of them left the other?

"Nay," she said. "No' yet."

She would be late going down to join the company. Already she could hear them out in the bailey, making a clatter. She did not care.

They made love quickly and desperately, just as Deathan and Darlei once had in the tiny alcove behind the great hall. She wanted to remember this, the taste of him on her tongue. All she could think of was his belongings all packed up in the chamber next door, and her heart bled.

She lay upon his chest, for in this, their last lovemaking, she had taken the upper hand. Peering into his beautiful face, she said, "I maun go. I can tarry nae longer."

"Aye, so." He raised his head from the bolster. "I will go gather my things."

Her heart fell like a stone. "Ye mean to leave Murtray at once?"

Emotions flickered through his eyes. A rueful smile touched his lips. Those lips she'd kissed, that had been everywhere on her body.

"I will leave when ye do."

Disappointment touched her. But nay, she had no right to ask him to stay, if she was not willing also to hold back at his request.

"Where will ye go?" Could she find him, if she returned home?

He slid out from under her and rose from the bed, moving with that wonderful, supple grace. Helpless, she could not keep from following him with her eyes.

He said, "Wherever ye do."

"What?"

He stood looking at her where she still sprawled, his skin turned golden by the first light spilling through the window.

"I am coming wi' ye."

She sat up abruptly. "Wha'—"

"I will join the fighting men. Yer da's troops."

"But—nay." Her heart sank so violently, she thought she would be sick. "Ye canna—"

He cocked an eyebrow at her. "Why no'?"

"Ye are nay a warrior."

"Troops frequently tak' pipers and such wi' them."

"Pipers. Drummers. Nay—"

"Katrin." He fixed her with a look like green obsidian. "If ye go, I go also. Given wha' we ha' shared these past four nights, ye canna expect me to do otherwise."

"Och." Horrified, she tossed her hands into the air. "Ye canna mean it. Ye say this only in a last bid to—to convince me to stay back."

"I do no'. I ken better."

"I canna stay back."

"I ken that fine. And so, neither can I."

She scrambled out of the bed and laid hold of him. "Finlay, be reasonable."

"Am I ever unreasonable?"

"I should ha' said nay."

"Is there ever aught reasonable in war, when it comes to it?"

"'Tis a thing called up by duty o' the heart."

"Ye see that now, do ye?"

On some level she had always seen it, always known it. A man fought to defend what he loved. Geordie had. She felt compelled to. And he? "Aye."

He shook his head. "Men—as well as women—who go to war know that as there are winners, there must also be losers, and men die."

"No' ye."

"Why no'?"

"I will no' see ye die." Her greatest fear, one that had now opened like a bottomless black chasm beneath her heart. It had appeared, that terrible pit, right along with the feelings she seemed to have found for him.

She tightened her grip on his forearms. "I will beg if I ha' to." Tears flooded her eyes. "Stay here till I return."

"Do no' weep." He drew her hard against him, her face to his shoulder. "I canna bear seeing ye weep."

She was too angry to weep, too stunned by dismay. Near paralyzed at the prospect of him risking himself.

A great and visceral fear.

"Please, Finlay." The same words she'd given to him during the night when she'd needed him inside her. Now she needed to push him away.

He took both her hands in his, lifted them one after the other and dropped kisses into the palms. Gifted either side of her mouth with a soft kiss, and both cheeks, before placing a final kiss on her brow. "Katrin, alanna, go see to your duties. I will gather my things."

Feeling helpless, she said, "I do no' ken wha' my father will say about taking a harper off to war."

"Nor do I. I am going, all the same."

Katrin drew away out of his arms and bent to gather her clothing. She would not look at him. Could not look at him.

"Do as ye wish, since ye will no' stay for any asking o' mine."

He donned his clothes swiftly and left the chamber.

CHAPTER TWENTY-SEVEN

KATRIN DID NOT approach Finlay as the company prepared to leave. Angry with him, as he knew full well. It proved easy enough for her to avoid him, as great confusion filled the bailey. She hurried here and there, consulting with female servants and her father's seneschal. With her father, and the head of the guard, Robran.

She had dressed herself, after he left her chamber, in men's clothing. Her long legs clad in leggings, a tunic and leather jerkin, a kilt. Given her height and the fact that she had her hair tightly braided, she might almost pass for a young man.

Finlay knew better. He had touched every part of what lay beneath that clothing. Had his lips to it. The feel and fragrance of her fair haunted him.

He himself wore his plainest clothing, his robe packed away into his bundle and the sigils removed from his hair. He had wrapped Brada most carefully, as he did for his sojourns upon the roads, but she still made a bulky bundle upon his back.

They mustered in the bailey, and apart from the Gallowglass, who stood in strong formation, it was far from orderly. A brisk, cool autumn morning it was, with mist still gathered on the headland and far out to sea. Men called to one another; women and bairns wailed, bidding farewell to their men.

A madness, was war. On some level, he had always known that, even when he was a warrior.

Someone—a man Finlay had never seen before, possibly

assistant to the armorer—came up to the group in which he stood, looking distracted. "Sword or bow?"

"Eh?"

"Ye be unarmed. D'ye fight wi' a bow or a sword?"

The man did not recognize him, nay, any more than Finlay knew him. Finlay looked far different in rough clothing and with his hair tamed.

He'd been unsuccessful in finding a weapon at the almost-empty armory, so he took this as a good sign. He could shoot a bow, aye, and had trained at it in his youth, as with the sword. A long time ago.

A long time.

"Sword," he chose instinctively, and the armorer turned to a lad, heavily laden, who followed him, then thrust a blade and belt into Finlay's hands and moved on before Finlay could speak.

He buckled it on with suddenly clumsy fingers. Did this make him once more into what she had forbidden him to be?

The wheel of destiny spun, came round to the place it had started over and over again. He was where he had begun.

Someone shouted—a voice of command. The painful level of noise in the bailey fell. O'Hanlon, so it sounded. Had he been placed in charge of the mass of men? Not a bad choice.

"Form up! We march out. For now, keep together."

They would head south, that much Finlay had gleaned, and meet up with other troops mustered at Earl John Randolph's command.

They filtered out through the gate, and the sea spread before them, great and limitless and eternal. Love of Scotland seized Finlay's heart. He undertook this for love of a woman, aye, but this place lay anchored almost as deep within him.

An ironic smile twisted his lips and words appeared in his mind.

The minstrel boy to war has gone,
In the ranks of death ye will find him.

His father's sword he has girded on
And his wild harp slung behind him.

Nay, he was not the first to take this path, nor would he be the last.

They moved out so slowly, it seemed impossible they could ever march so far as England. Women and old men followed them, the women wanting last words with their men. The clinging of hands.

He had no idea where Katrin might be. He had lost track of her. Somewhere near the front, he did not doubt.

I will find ye. I will find ye always.

"Wha' are ye doin' here? Are ye no' the harper?"

The man marching next to Finlay had light-brown hair and brown eyes. He carried a spear.

"Aye, so. I am going to war now."

"Are no' we all? D'ye ken how to fight?"

"I used to."

A bright picture flashed into his mind. *A far-off green land. An Erin chief declaring him first among his warriors. The unwanted glory and responsibility of it. His skill, inborn, came from the gods. He had never exercised it for gain.*

He would not now, save for the gain of Katrin's heart.

"Aye, well, I am more farmer than fighter, me, though they ha' given us training, all o' us fro' a young age. I am hoping when we get to England there will be so many o' us wild Scots, the English will turn butts and run. Aye? We will soon be home again."

Finlay could not help but grin. "Aye."

"Gregor is the name." The fellow stuck out a broad hand.

"Finlay."

"I ha' heard o' ye and the stories ye tell, though I was no' there to hear them. Mayhap ye can tell some on the road, eh, to lighten the way?" Gregor's face clouded. "I ha' stayed much at home of late. My Kerra is to birth our first anytime. It has no' gone well."

An agony, to leave. The man could be no older than Finlay, quite likely younger.

"I hope for her sake and yours, we do come back soon."

"We are to march south o' Inverness first, so I hear, where Earl Randolph or his captains will collect us."

It was more than Finlay knew.

Aye, well, anything could happen before they reached there. Those in high places could well change their minds. He prayed so.

That day, though, proved a slog. The mist lifted and a cool breeze chased them from the north. They walked and paused and moved on again while a sense of unreality rose to Finlay's head.

Where was Katrin? He'd still had no glimpse of her. Did he occupy her thoughts even as she did his?

He hoped O'Hanlon would look out for her.

When they rested, they conversed. Everyone who encountered Finlay stared at him before they either did or did not recognize him. Those who recognized him always exclaimed, "Harper! Wha' be ye doing here?"

He and Gregor, like two strangers flung over the side of a sinking ship, stayed together as if for comfort.

During one such pause, late in the day, they sat while food was distributed.

"Ye ha' nay tired yet," Gregor observed. "I am impressed."

"I am used to walking great distances fro' house to house, seeking to perform. This is no' great feat for me."

"As I am used to walking great distances behind a plow. But I am beginning to feel it."

Not till nightfall, when they were instructed to make camp, did Katrin find him. Indeed, by then Finlay half imagined she was naught but an illusion, and the past four nights had most assuredly been a dream.

Then, all at once, she was there at his elbow.

"Och! I ha' hoped at the last ye'd ha' the sense to reconsider and stay behind."

She was still angry with him, then. Nay, mayhap not merely angry, for he could see fear in her eyes.

Had she been looking for him? Moving back through the admittedly ragged troops thinking to see him? Hoping, as she said, that she would not?

Her gaze touched him up and down with frank surprise. Had she expected him to go marching in his green robe?

"There is still time, Finlay, for ye to turn back."

"And for ye," he said pleasantly. "Let us go together."

"I march at my father's side. In Geordie's place."

"And I follow."

She growled in frustration. Gregor gave her a startled look, shot Finlay another, and moved off.

"Ye be no' a warrior," she said through gritted teeth.

"And ye be no' Geordie. Yet here we are."

"Are ye punishing me?"

"Och, alanna, nay. I would no' do that. Just—as ye follow yer heart, so do I follow mine."

"But ye *do* punish me." Her eyes flashed. Aye, anger still had a part in the emotions that filled her. "Have I no' enough to worry me, wi'out fretting for ye?"

"Do no' fret for me, then."

"Och!" She examined him again, head to toe. "Ye are wearing a sword."

"So I am."

"Come wi' me. I will find ye a place to sleep."

He was tempted. Och, he was tempted. But he said, "Nay, I will bide here where I belong, among the ranks."

She went off in a visible huff. Gregor edged back and eyed Finlay but said nothing.

It did not take long for Chief MacMurtray to come moving through. Just at nightfall it was, and he gave encouragement to his men, pausing often to speak with them.

He paused before Finlay and lifted shaggy brows. "Harper, ye here?"

"Aye, laird."

"'Tis nay called for, ye ken. Ye be no' sworn in fealty to me."

Not to him, no. Finlay followed a far older demand.

"How is a bard to make braw songs o' battles if he is no' there to see them?"

Anders scowled. "There is time for ye to go back. No' now, when we ha' made camp. But in the morning, perhaps."

"Aye, laird, I will consider it."

"Will ye turn back?" asked Gregor after Anders had moved on.

"Nay."

"I did no' think so. There is a tale in it, I am thinking."

"Best get some sleep. I do no' doubt we will be marching again by dawn."

Gregor, wrapped in his own thoughts, either slept or did not. Finlay did not even try, but instead lay reliving each of the previous nights, touch by touch and kiss by kiss.

CHAPTER TWENTY-EIGHT

ROLLED IN HER blanket and far too upset to have a hope of slumber, Katrin worried her way through the night. The encampment, if it could be called such, was far from quiet. Men shuffled about and mumbled in their sleep. Despite orders, they spoke to one another. They got up and went off up the hill to relieve themselves. They snored and farted and…

If their army's safety ever relied upon silence, they were doomed.

Somewhere back in that seething mass of men lay Finlay. Frustration swamped Katrin every time she thought of him. Frustration and anger and—och, helpless longing. Terror so bright it set her heart to pounding.

Nay, she had no hope of sleep.

After they'd paused for the night, she'd moved back through the troops, hoping not to see him, dismayed at finding him clad like an ordinary clansman with a bundle that could only be his harp on his back.

The man was mad.

After she'd failed at convincing him to turn for home, she'd gone to her father. "Mayhap ye can persuade him, Da. He does no' belong here."

Da had given her a long look. She could almost hear him thinking, *Nor do ye.* But he had gone on a round of their forces, speaking encouraging words to all the men, only shaking his head at her after.

So she'd gone to Reagan.

His troops alone had camped in marvelous order, each man seeming to know his tasks and none making a fuss about it. Katrin found him speaking to one of his captains and drew him aside.

"He is here," she said.

He fixed her with a tawny eye.

"The harper. He is back among the footmen." She swallowed hard. "He has a sword. And his harp."

Emotions flickered across Reagan's face. He asked, "Wha' am I to do about it, lass?"

"Speak to him. Go and tell him he has time to turn back."

He sighed. "We ha' already spoken o' this. He is not under my command, any more than ye be. I ha' no cause to tell him anything."

"As a friend, ye do. Ye know war. He does no'."

Reagan shifted his weight. "How about this? I will bid him go, if ye will go wi' him."

Katrin set her jaw.

"Ye be a stubborn woman, Katrin MacMurtray. D'ye want your way more than ye want his safety?"

"This is no' about me having my way."

"Is it not?"

"Nay. And if ye canna see that, though I ha' tried and tried to explain—"

"I cannot see it, nay. Ye say ye are here for the sake o' yer brother and your father, but neither o' them would want ye here, and it would ease your da's mind hugely for ye to go. And mine."

Katrin said nothing.

"None o' us, lass, needs the distraction o' having to protect ye."

"I need no one to protect me!" Did he not see that was the point?

War was loss, and loss was unbearable. Loss on her behalf, that she might prevent, worst of all.

She marched off, angry now with both men.

The next morning, she did not see Finlay at all. They were on the move early and she could not take the time to go back through the ranks. But she swore she could feel him back among the men, his presence a spark of light in her mind.

Or in her heart.

That day, they began to feel the forced pace. Not the Gallowglass troop at their head—they, so it seemed, might have marched on forever. But the rest of them began to struggle, the long miles being covered with weapons and packs upon their backs.

Katrin eyed her da with concern. He marched by her side, at the head of the men, having refused to take a pony if his clansmen could not ride, and she noticed when he began to flag.

There was a reason Geordie had offered to face battle in his place. She distinctly remembered her brother talking him into it. *Let me, Da. I am ready and 'tis my place.*

Did Da feel guilt as she herself did, for letting Geordie go away without him, only to fall? Did he too wonder if his presence might have kept his beloved son alive?

She didn't know, and she could not ask. She watched helplessly as he began visibly to tire, and she thought of all the rough and lengthy miles ahead. To the meeting place with Earl Randolph and thence across most of Scotland and on to England. By God, after all that, would these men have the strength to fight? Would her da?

Her mind numbed beneath the weight of it, and she concentrated on putting one foot in front of the other, on easing Da's journey in whatever way she might, making certain he had water during the stops, which Reagan called as he thought best.

Reagan O'Hanlon had unquestionably taken charge of their party. Katrin had no doubt his troop could have moved with much greater speed and ease. Strong men all, and she could see they made little of this journey that began to tell on the rest of them.

Frequently, he glanced back over his charges. Sometimes his

eyes met hers with what might be a glint of reassurance.

Yet there was little true reassurance to be found. Rather than calming as they went, the fear in Katrin's belly grew claws and raked at her. Not for herself so much, though mayhap she should fear for herself. But for those she loved.

Love. Did she love Finlay?

Nay, and nay. It was not love but something else that lay between them. Something powerful, aye, possibly more powerful even than love. After those nights they'd spent together, every detail of which her mind insisted upon reliving until her poor body throbbed, she could not deny that desire made up a component of what she felt for him. But nay, not all.

She loved her father. She had loved her brother and did still. What drew her to Finlay was of a different order. Fundamental, as if it had always been there and merely reawakened when she encountered him, spoke to him, learned of him.

Lay with him. *Deep, and ancient.*

It terrified her, did that feeling. Because it was tied to her soul and to the possibility of loss. And because they marched toward a perfect opportunity for just that.

For that reason, she avoided going back among the men to find him, even though she longed to. She ached to set eyes on him, touch his hand, hear his voice. Da did frequently circle back, and she asked him at every opportunity, "Did ye see the harper?" Trying to sound careless about it and, in reality, aching. *Aching.*

"Aye," Da would say. "He seemed to be in good spirits."

Did he?

He'd followed her. It became an agony and a reassurance.

After days of hard journeying, they reached Rannoch Moor, where they were to meet not only Earl Randolph's troops but those from much of Western Scotland. Campbells from Argyll, MacLeods from the islands, and MacDonalds from a wealth of places, all loyal hearts sworn to King David and willing to fight for Scotland's freedom, waiting to be collected.

Many other troops were there before them. Indeed, the

Murtray warriors, who had seemed so many on the move, now appeared a mere drop in a vast bucket as they trickled in. Much confusion reigned, and Murtray's men stood staring about stupidly as if dazed, like people coming out of darkness to broad daylight.

Da sent Robran forward to find instructions as to how they would be disposed. Katrin noticed that Reagan moved forward also. It took an inordinate amount of time before anyone returned. Katrin was left to see her da settled and to move back among the men, who had all gone down to sit where they stood, without direction.

She thus, after working diligently to avoid him, came upon Finlay face to face.

He was one of the few marchers still on his feet, still in the act of unloading his pack from his back, when she came upon him. He looked around and their eyes met.

Everything within Katrin's body leaped. She could explain it no other way. Emotions swamped her, relief that he had managed the journey and looked well. A deep and fervent level of longing for his presence, for the scent of him. For his smile. And aye, desire. A desire not of the flesh so much as the soul.

A hundred things she might say to him. Fully half of them fluttered through her mind. Instead, she nodded at the harp. "How is Brada standing the journey? Is she all right?"

"Aye." He gave her his rare smile, the one that warmed her so wondrously. "She is used to bouncing along on my back o'er track and brae."

All too much like the tale he had told of Adair and the defiant, determined Bradana at loose in the wilds of Scotland—called Alba then—with her deerhound at her side. Love had been enough for them.

Or had that also been more than mere love?

In that moment, standing facing Finlay there upon the breast of the land, her heart yearned to inhabit the tale. She wanted to be bold and fearless, to be Bradana to his Adair, the man she adored. Only, the way Finlay told it, Bradana had not been entirely fearless. More than anything else, she had feared losing the man she loved and had attempted more than once to sacrifice herself for his sake.

Katrin's mind stuttered there and tried to shut down. Concern flickered in Finlay's eyes.

"Katrin. Wha' is it?"

Katrin. The sound of his voice, the music of it flitting into her ear while she lay in his arms. As he became one with her. *Bradana.*

She shook her head. Most definitely, she was not all right. Something grave and terrible moved in her life. This was no time for it.

She stepped up to him, close enough that she could see the freckles marking his skin, golden in the autumn light.

"Be safe," she whispered, and never had she uttered so heartfelt a plea.

CHAPTER TWENTY-NINE

Reagan and Robran came back together and told Da that Earl Randolph wanted to see him. Randolph had summoned all the chiefs to the center of the swarm where flew his standard, a banner of red showing three cushions.

Katrin brushed Da down as best she could, ridding him of as much trail dust as possible, straightening his bonnet, and repinning the plaid at his shoulder. New lines had appeared in his face, and to her eyes, he appeared exhausted.

"Go wi' him," she bade Robran, and watched the two men move off together.

Not till she turned back did she realize Reagan still occupied the place at her side.

"Where are we to camp?" she asked.

He shrugged. "Where we stand. There are no facilities for so many men, and we will not be here long. As soon as all the clans arrive, we will be movin' on."

Katrin glanced around at the rough, barren hillside and prayed rain would not come. So far they had been fortunate in that regard, enduring little more than brief showers warded off by the men's plaids. In the west of Scotland in autumn, that could not possibly last.

She turned her gaze back to Reagan. "So many men to move south. It defies imagining." Surely, surely the English would not have a force to match them? Da said the English king spent his men on the war in France.

This must all be over soon.

Reagan gave her a crooked smile. "Sorry ye came, yet?"

"Nay," she said. Did she lie?

"Ye will be."

He began to walk away. She snagged his arm. "Wait. How many more men do ye suppose will gather yet?" Laird Robert Stewart, whom they were yet to meet, would have his own army. "How great will be the force that moves to England?"

"Who can say? I heard up there"—he jerked his head toward the standard—"King David himself is to lead the armies."

"Och, aye?"

The wings of Reagan's mustache twitched. "'Twill make an impressive sight."

"We still ha' a long way to go. I am concerned for my da."

"Try no' to be. An army this size will not move very quickly."

"Aye, but—he tires."

"At least 'twill be the earl's business now to feed all this lot."

When Da returned a goodly amount of time later, he looked worried. Reagan was gone from Katrin's side by then. She hunkered down beside her father, who had quickly seated himself, and said, "Wha' is it, Da?"

"We are to wait here till the other western troops arrive and then move on eastward."

"Aye, so. Let me find ye somewhat to drink."

Did it surprise her that even here among naught but warriors, and a supposed warrior herself, she took on the role of caretaker? Of looking after not only her da, in truth, but all of them. She ventured off to collar one of the men she saw circling, who proved to be Earl Randolph's servant, and demanded rations for her father's men.

He stared at her in surprise when she spoke, having at first glance taken her for just another fighting man.

"Aye—mistress," he said a bit uncertainly. "We are doin' the best we can to reach everyone."

"Our men ha' marched far and are in need o' drink."

"There is a stream." He waved a hand vaguely. "I suggest ye avail yoursel's o' it."

She did, going back for a flask, now empty, and bringing it full to her father, advising all of their men she met to do the same. She made sure Da ate from the last of their own rations, took none for herself. An empty belly was the least of what she would likely endure.

Earl Randolph's servants did come round eventually, but provisions were pitifully few. Dark fell and a chill crept in with it. They camped where they stood—or, more accurately, sat.

Such a vast force could not possibly be silent. Indeed, as they settled for the night, sound undulated like the sea on the shore back home. Rising and falling. A *shush* of being.

When the music began, she could scarce believe her ears. It seemed so small and delicate amid that other sweep of sound. Yet it drew her inexorably.

She rose from her place beside Da, who opened one eye and asked, "Is that the harper? Our harper?"

Our harper.

"I believe so."

She moved back through Murtray's troops, only some of whom slept and most of whom sat in clusters. Around Finlay, the cluster was dense. They leaned to him as to one of the fires, for comfort, for enchantment.

He had unwrapped Brada and had her on his knee. Hands caressing the strings, magic in his eyes.

He did not play soft and soothing songs for them now, despite their need for comfort. Nay, for these were bright and jaunty tunes that sprang from his hands, strong and speaking of valiance. Music meant to lift the heart.

Katrin went to her knees beside him. He shot her one glance of gladness and acknowledgment, and played on.

Ducked down there, so close, she could feel the music spin out with him as its center in an ever-widening circle. Like a wheel turning, carrying both fate and time.

Only he was not upon the wheel. He was its hub.

It lifted her beyond herself and somehow, at the same time, took her deep within. When he broke into O'Hanlon's march, she lifted her voice in song, matching to it the words they had made together.

She did it without true intention, the impulse drawn up from her heart. Finlay approved it with his gaze upon her face, a thousand emotions resting in his eyes.

Come all ye who would valiant be
Who would follow the train o' bright glory.
Where battle brings us gory fates
We follow them both soon and late.
The Gallowglass gang to die!

For fight they will wi' sword or spear,
With blade and axe, their numbers dear.
The heart o' courage lingers here.
We follow them wi' strength o' eye.
They lead us on to victory,
May the Gallowglass never die!

After the second or third time through, the men around them took it up. The song grew—so very much like the swell of that ocean to which she'd likened it. In this time of the unknowable and the unbearable, the Gallowglass were, to these soldiers, a guiding star. And aye, to their fates would they follow them.

At length, some of the men wandered off to sleep. Others lingered, perhaps valuing a high heart more than rest. When many had taken themselves off or rolled into their plaids where they sat, Katrin found herself with Finlay, the two of them as good as alone.

Even the fires had died down. Finlay set Brada aside and wrapped her carefully in her leather covering.

Katrin supposed she too should stir, climb to her feet, and

return to her father. She wanted, with all her being, to stay where she was. To drink in the company of this man, soak up his presence. Comfort beyond comfort.

When he looked at her, his gaze seeming to caress her face, it was almost—almost as good as a touch.

"Ye ken," she told him softly so as not to disturb those around them, "there is still time for ye to turn back."

"And ye," he said implacably.

"I do no' feel I can."

"Nor I."

"Finlay—ye be no' a warrior. Nor sworn to my father. Ye might go on your way off north out o' all this to some other chief's hall. There might ye ride out the storm that besets us, play yer music. And after"—she drew a breath, long and unsteady—"I will find ye."

"I am no' sworn to your father, nay." Finlay let that implication hang in the air, and Katrin felt the impact as she took his meaning. They had made no promises to one another, not even when they lay in each other's arms, when they were joined into one being.

It came to her now that mayhap they did not need promises.

Tears came to her eyes. "Please. 'Twould do me much good to know ye are safe."

"I would do most anything for ye, Katrin. No' that."

"Why?" she asked, desperate.

"Ye wish me to go into the north—"

"Anywhere, into safety."

"—and await ye. But Katrin, it has taken me all my life to find ye. And for me to tak' mysel' off again not knowing what might befall ye, whether ye will ever be able to come to me—do no' ask it."

She said nothing, just blinked away her tears fiercely.

Swiftly he said, "Lass, ye be a strong woman, and dauntless. But ye ha' no idea of the battles to come."

"I should, having heard your tales." A pit of dread opened in her stomach. "I should ken fine wha' it means to be a warrior." Why else did he think she feared so that he should endanger himself? An old, old fear.

He shook his head.

"Finlay, if ye maun stay, at least say ye will lay aside that sword. Engage our men wi' your music as ye will. Wi' yer bold tales. Wi' your high spirits. But when we reach England and the battles commence, at least say ye will remain at the rear of the company, out o' danger."

He said only, "We ha' a long march ahead o' us, and a hard one. Best go, lass, and tak' your rest."

May I no' stay here wi' ye? But she could not speak those words. Her duty lay beside her father. She had quite boldly chosen that duty, and must stand by it.

But she swayed on her feet when she rose, and moved unsteadily as she left him, feeling every step in her soul.

CHAPTER THIRTY

THE NEXT DAY, just as Reagan had predicted, they moved out in a great swarm of men, one giant, ponderous creature crawling its way across the moor, darkening the yellow autumn bracken. Many days' travel they had yet before rendezvousing with King David and his men, and then turning southward.

Toward England.

For Katrin, looking after her father grew ever more difficult and ever more demanding as they kept up with the now-vast army. She didn't know what Reagan considered a slow pace of travel, but she could tell Da struggled, valiantly though he tried to hide it. With every step away from Murtray, she missed her home more. And each moment, full to the brim with caring for those around her, another longing increased steadily in her heart. She ached for Finlay. Aye, to be sure, she could feel him back there among the men. But that only seemed to emphasize the distance between them. She wanted to be with him so he could gift her with one of his smiles. Caress her with those beautiful hands. Bless her with kisses. How had this happened, that he'd come to mean so much? Was it merely the physical connection forged during those four nights they'd spent together? The stories he'd told? Mayhap she hadn't realized at the time just how deeply those had touched her.

Though she looked for any opportunity at all to pass back through the men, doctoring minor scrapes and injuries taken along the way and making sure everyone was decently fed, she won no more than passing encounters with Finlay, and often not even that. Sometimes at night, she could hear him play and would lie with her ears stretched, staring at the sky, almost— almost remembering something too precious to recall. But as they crossed the back of Scotland and grew wearier and wearier, more worn, those musical sessions all but ceased.

To what did she lead him? She asked herself that again and again. Should she try once more to persuade him to return home? That journey would be as naught to him. But she had no words to say that had not already been spoken, and she feared looking too hard at just why he followed her.

What, oh, what if she led him to his death? An old fear, it seemed, an ancient one.

Sometime in late September, the vast army arrived in Perth, where it became still more vast. Here, near King David's stronghold at Scone Palace, at a place called the Bridge of Earn, the king's forces waited, to be swelled by those from farther west.

The day was a bonny enough one for autumn in Scotland, with a blue sky scudded by clouds of white and gray, the light slanting through to show a scene worthy of stealing Katrin's breath. She and all of Da's men, who had already trodden so far and were so weary, fell silent against the greater undulating rush, as did the MacLeods, MacDonalds, and Campbells around them.

She barely noticed when Reagan O'Hanlon stepped up beside her. From his superior height, he slanted her a knowing look before he said, "What d'ye think o' this, then?"

"I think I am a long way fro' home."

"Aye. Sorry ye came yet?"

In a way, she was. Not sorry to be standing at her da's side, nay. But she regretted leading Finlay here, and that they seemed so very small now among this seething throng of men. So unimportant.

She did not answer him directly. "How can any army, English or otherwise, stand against so many?"

Reagan shrugged. There was no such thing, here, as privacy.

Her da stood only a short distance ahead of her, straining—as did they all—for any sight of the king. She had no opportunity to clutch at Reagan and beg him, *Persuade Finlay to turn back, I pray. 'Tis no' too late.*

She could not. She feared their fates were cast. So many fates…

"Where is the king?" The question was being repeated on every side.

"There," Reagan told her. "Ye see the tents."

Would David summon Da? Da and all the other chiefs who had risen so loyally to his call. It did not happen that way after all. No sooner had Reagan stepped away to his men, and Katrin seen to the distribution of water to all their own, than word passed from lips to ears—the king was on his rounds and would soon be there to welcome them.

In due time, another sort of hush fell, one that seemed to spread out the way a wind does across a barley field. He came with his generals, and on foot.

Katrin supposed she should be impressed at being in the presence of the king of all Scotland, a man whom she had never before so much as dreamed of meeting. And, aye, her first sight of him surprised her. A young man was David, overly large in his regalia with the appearance of a warrior. Not unhandsome, with a brown beard and a decidedly long nose.

She should have been reassured by his manner, by the fact that he showed fully willing to stand at the head of his men and would, in fact, lead them across the marches into England. The king of all Scotland! For aye, he moved confidently among the new arrivals and showed little doubt in their cause.

Katrin watched as her da went forward and was greeted by his liege lord, she as silent as the men around her. She noticed a man taking the place at her side no more than she had noted Reagan's arrival earlier. Not till he spoke in a musical voice did she start, her heart leaping.

"Men who call themselves chiefs and kings make the decisions and send those who harbor true hearts to meet their fates," he mused very softly indeed. "So 'tis. So it has ever been."

Katrin gave him a close look. "Ye can turn back yet. There is still time." She had seen others deserting along the way. No one tried to stop them.

Finlay shook his head, not looking at her now.

"Why not? Finlay, please—"

For answer, he reached out and linked his fingers through hers, where they hung at her side. Fierce, hot tears stung her eyes. They stood so, linked amid the swarm of men.

Da came back to her armed with a modicum of information. They would camp and muster here a few days before the troops would be assigned to various leaders, and they would move off south to England.

Word flowing through the ranks as they set out to make a decidedly poor camp was that England stood near empty of defenders, all King Edward's men sent over the water to France, caught in the continuing conflict there.

This should be easy, whispered men to other men as night fell and those from one contingent mingled and spoke with the others. There would be spoils. The English would learn of what the Scots were made and would not try to subdue them again. A blow for Scottish autonomy.

But even before night fell on that wide, open plain, an air of unreality descended upon Katrin. It felt not as if she was part of a great, undulating sea of men, about to attack England, but as if she moved through one of Finlay's stories. None of this could truly be happening. She must be dreaming back in her own bed at the keep, musing on words the bard had said, not marching toward death and pain and devastation. She would wake and go about her duties, as familiar to her as breathing.

Yet even that next morning, which dawned wet and much cooler, such a waking did not come.

Finlay had once more attained a distance from her, back among the ranks. Though she tried several times to seek him out, she still had many distractions, including both Da and the immediate needs of their men. Da and Reagan, in company with Earl Randolph, went forward to meet with the king in the white tent. When Da returned, he confirmed they would soon move out southward, for England.

Not liking the exhaustion in her father's eyes, or the way he moved, Katrin soon sought out Reagan. His men sat in a rough circle, paying little heed to the pandemonium around them, calmly playing at dice and talking among themselves in low voices. Several of them, including Daffid and a man called Malcolm, gave her friendly nods. Reagan got to his feet and stepped to her side as soon as he noticed her.

"What is it?"

"Da says we will leave here soon. How far is it to England?"

He gave her a look, all hard-eyed and steady. "Far."

"I am no longer certain Da can make it. It has been days since he's had enough to eat." Since any of them had. "Wha' condition will he be in when we arrive?"

"Give the man some credit." The wings of Reagan's mustache twitched. "He is stronger than ye think, and as stubborn as yourself."

"I do no' suppose ye can talk him into going home before we cross the marches."

"I do not suppose I can."

"Then—is there any chance ye can find him a mount? Surely Earl Randolph would stretch to such, for so loyal a vassal."

Reagan examined her with tawny-eyed sympathy. "I ha' already tried. Your father says he will not ride when his men are walking." He hesitated. "Ye have to give him respect for it."

Och, why and why had she ever started on this accursed journey? She should have kept herself, her da and—and Finlay home.

Too late now. She found herself on the wheel of fate.

Reagan laid a hand on her shoulder. "Trust, lass. Perhaps 'tis a lesson, this, ye need to learn."

CHAPTER THIRTY-ONE

T HEY CROSSED THE border into England on a cool, windy day
that promised rain, without Finlay even realizing his feet
met foreign soil. In the past, he had been in England a time or
two, though not to stay. It was not a harper's country, and he'd
always ducked back to Wales or Scotland as soon as he might.

This seemed completely different.

It was the whispers all around him that told him the truth.
Word spread, as it tended to do, from man to man. Even back in
his earliest days as a warrior, in Erin, it had been so. Fighting men
developed a sort of second sense and an ability to dispense
information with very few words.

Now everyone, without exception, was exhausted. They had
tramped a very great distance over rough ground to join the
king's forces near Perth, and that mostly on empty stomachs.
They had been fed well enough at the start of the journey
southward, but since then the rations had been poor and few,
even though for the Murtray clansmen, Katrin did her best to gain
them what food and drink she could.

Finlay longed to be with her, and many times he questioned
the wisdom of this journey. Should he have tried to keep her back
from it by force? Should he have told her the truth before they
left? If the worst happened, he might never have a chance.

Still and all, from the very start of this, when he'd located her
at Murtray, he'd known that truth was not his to share beyond
the telling of his stories. She had to realize it for herself. Else how

could she ever believe?

Ye be the young woman in each of those tales. The lass Liadan, who stood in the sunshine watching the man she loved at his ablutions. Bradana, who tramped across Dalriada for the sake of love. Darlei, the princess with the stubborn heart. Hulda, she who fought so valiantly for her independence and her love.

She would not believe all that just because he told it to her, he who had made it into stories.

So he kept an eye on her when he could. He tramped along at Gregor's side. And he wondered what this turn of the wheel would bring.

FINLAY HAD NOT lied; the distance they had to cover was great and near impossible to fathom. Katrin did not try to fathom it. She had become one small piece of the moving pattern, all of which followed the call issued by those who rode fine horseflesh at their head. Their commanders. Their king.

Time blurred right along with reality. Even though young and strong, she struggled, though not so badly as some others around her, including her da.

Och, he still would not admit it. And their pace, though pressed, was not overly demanding, just inexorable like a boulder rolling downhill. Walking beside him as she was, she knew when he began to flag and did all she could to lighten his load, including carrying his weapons. It was the reason she was here, was it not? It was what Geordie would have done.

She told herself over and over that she *was* Geordie, that she now existed only to fill his place. But Geordie would never have yearned so persistently for the company of a single man, back in their ranks, sought him out at every opportunity, nor stretched his ears as she did for the sound of his harp.

Finlay seemed to be holding up to the march better than

most. He had not lied about being accustomed to tramping great distances. To her knowledge, he had not lied to her about anything. She worried for him, though, since rations—shared among so many—were short. She did her best to assure herself that Finlay had what he needed, along with all the Murtray men.

A drop in an ocean, they were. An ocean seething toward storm.

By the time they crossed into England east of a place called Carlisle—an event that in fact Katrin missed—the great army had grown restless, unhappy, and very, very hungry. Reagan estimated they were some ten thousand men or more, and though they had spread out through the countryside, procuring food where they could, it was never enough. Already, men had deserted, and those around Katrin grumbled for a host of reasons.

She was shocked to find that England looked very like Scotland, so much so that here at least, where they entered that foreign place, it proved impossible to tell one from the other. That made her wonder a little. The ground they trod seemed the same, as was the sky above. Was any of this worth the dying?

She stretched her ears and listened to those around her. This border area, so they said, had been disputed and hard-fought over for a long while. Indeed, a chain of castles stood here in defense, as did a very ancient wall, and feuding was a longstanding pastime. Now, though, they had reason to believe those castles, with their ruthless English knights away to France, should stand mostly empty before them.

The great body of the army turned and headed eastward, and Katrin's sense of unreality deepened.

They paused and wallowed, the great sea of men moving the way a sluggish tide might against a shore. Reagan came back through their ranks to find her, his face near expressionless but with concern in his eyes.

"Wha' is happening?" she asked him.

"There is a castle ahead, a place called the Peel of Liddell. There may be supplies, and word is we will lay siege."

"Oh." It would be her first taste of battle. "And after that, will it be done? Will we go home?"

He shook his head, regret in his eyes.

"How d'ye fare?" he asked her abruptly. His manner did not fool her. He cared, that much she could feel.

"Da is flagging." She glanced to where her father had seated himself among a number of Murtray men. "He will no' admit to it."

"I can try to find him that mount, if ye think he will now accept it."

Slowly and with regret, she shook her head.

"And for ye?" Reagan's tawny gaze touched her face and flickered over her body. He seemed so unfazed by the hard distance they had covered, and the low rations, that she could not help but admire it. Could not help but respond to his strength also. A warrior this man was, to the heart.

"I am well enough," she told him, and the wings of his mustache twitched around a smile.

"Ye be a woman in a thousand, Katrin MacMurtray. Let me see what I can do."

He moved off back through the ranks, and Katrin could not help but wonder if he would encounter Finlay. If Reagan touched with him, it would be—almost—like her touching with him.

Word came down later that day that they would indeed lay siege to the Peel of Liddell, but the various factions of the army were scrambled, and the MacMurtrays, along with some of the MacLeods and other western forces, found themselves passed from the leadership of the Earl of Moray to that of Laird Robert Stewart, and left to the rear of the action. Katrin barely saw the castle that fell under attack, a wooden structure with a motte and bailey. Like so much else of this venture, it did not seem real, and she had difficulty believing that some few miles ahead of her, men were dying.

She felt as if, slowly but surely, she lost track of herself. Was this what she'd come away from home to find? Bewilderment and destruction? Nay, the fight had never truly been part of it. The goal had always been protecting those she loved. Yet here, so far away from the Highlands, she feared only weariness and death might be found.

Bruised and frightened, not wanting to admit to either, she went searching for Finlay and found him deep back among the ranks, most of whom sat or sprawled on the ground. Many of the Murtray men, those who had never trained fairly for war but had spent their days fishing or farming, had a dazed and confounded look in their eyes as they listened to what happened up ahead, for little enough could be seen. Katrin recognized that look all too well, because she harbored the same feelings.

"Mistress, wha' are they doin'?" asked Gregor, the young clansman who seemed to be always at Finlay's side. "Will they burn down yon castle?"

"Will there be more food, fro' inside?" asked another man before Katrin could answer.

"I hope so."

She touched Finlay on the arm. He had fastened his green gaze to her—still bright even though he must be as exhausted as anyone—and not looked away. A rush of emotions swept her. She wanted to be with him, anywhere but here—back in her chamber, where she'd experienced ecstasy in his arms. Away in the forest. Out in a wee boat. Alive in one of the tales he had told.

"Can I speak wi' ye?" she asked, and he nodded.

There was, nay, no privacy, nor hope of it. They stepped away, watched by many eyes, and she moved close to him, so that when she spoke, it might be for his ears alone.

"It seems the fight is at hand. If we are no' part o' this battle, 'tis certain we will be part o' the next. I wanted to say—"

What *did* she want to say? Standing there looking up into his face, into those eyes that studied her back so patiently, so undemandingly, she did not know that there were words for what was in her heart.

"Ye need no' follow me," she said. They were not the right

words. She needed to tell him what he meant to her, how being in his company, how lying in his arms had changed her very existence. "If it means yer life—ye need no'." *Please. Please save yourself.*

He leaned close. For one glorious moment she thought he meant to kiss her, and she closed her eyes because she longed so for the sensation. Kisses to her palms. The corners of her mouth. Her cheeks and her brow.

But he only spoke in a whisper that touched her face. "I need no'. Yet, alanna, I will."

CHAPTER THIRTY-TWO

THE CASTLE AT Liddell took three days to fall to siege, and afterward was burned to the ground. Finlay, who watched it all from a distance—for not all their vast forces were required to accomplish the deed—felt sick over it, yet also hopeful. It did not seem that the English could stand against so mighty a force as theirs, even if near half the Scottish army had spread out wide to steal and pillage, mostly food. Surely they would be able to go home soon.

The Murtray army had so far not wetted their swords—or spears or hoes—but they suffered from hunger and a great deal of homesickness. Chief MacMurtray passed through their ranks often, and Finlay grew steadily more concerned about the old man's appearance—for that was what he now appeared to be, a man aged. Like sons suddenly witnessing their father come to old age, the men around them whispered of it. Anders MacMurtray was much loved. If for no other cause, these men would fight to defend him.

Chief MacMurtray shed warmth and concern upon all of them equally. Tired as he might be, he never failed to listen to his men's fears and concerns, or to confirm or refute the rumors that came to them with honesty. Aye, he told them, the English governor, Lord Shelby, had been executed by the Scots. And aye, much of the Scots army had spread out through the countryside in marauding waves, an action he denied to his men, hungry as they might be.

"Ha' we nay more honor than that?" he asked.

And aye, the people of the nearby town of Carlisle had offered King David a ransom that they might be spared the perils of the savage Scots army. So terrified were they of the Scots, the men congratulated one another when they heard it. They supposed wreaking havoc on the English countryside would indeed be an easy task. Finlay, who had fought hard battles long, long ago, did not feel so certain.

They turned eastward toward a town called Durham, said to be a wealthy plum just sitting there for the plucking. Would further ransom be paid? This looked to be more of a venture in pillage than any series of battles.

As soon as he was able, Finlay sought out Reagan, hoping to learn his opinion of things.

"Wha' d'ye think will happen?" he asked the Gallowglass, having found him amidst his own band of men. "Will it be all theft, pillage, and burning before we go home?"

Reagan shrugged. "If the bulk o' the English army is indeed away in France, 'twill be a short and profitable venture, this. But"—the big Irishman hesitated and gave an odd shake of his shoulders—"I have a feeling..."

"Aye." Finlay had it too, and put it down to warrior's instinct, even though he had not been that for some time. "I do no' like the feel o' it."

"Nor I." Reagan looked at him. "If it does indeed grow ugly, I will do my best to protect her, harper."

"As will I."

Reagan raised his eyebrows. "Are ye as proficient with that sword, then, as with the *cláirseach?*"

"Nay." Not any longer. "But old training does tend to return when a man needs it."

"Let us hope. I would hate to have your music stilled—for so poor a cause as this."

If Finlay laid down his life, it would be on Katrin's behalf.

Reagan said, "I am planning to send my men to forage. If they come up with anything, I will make sure ye get some."

"Give my share to Katrin and her father."

"Come now, Finlay—even a legendary harper cannot live on air."

THE NEXT DAY, the army moved on to the city of Hexham, where King David ordered his forces to spread out and find what sustenance they could. Hunger among the ranks had grown dire. More and more men—sometimes even whole clan sects—had deserted for the long walk home. Need overtook morals on every side.

Which was about to be proven in the most grievous way. For no English forces appeared to repel the Scots. They took what they wanted and set their sights on the wealthy priory that lay just ahead. Like the savages the English thought them to be, they plundered it without mercy.

Anders MacMurtray, when he heard of it, was outraged. He gathered his men and spoke to them. "We will no' participate in this. D'ye hear me? Murdering holy men, even be they English, well, there is nay honor in it. We shall no' stoop to such a thing."

"But chief," said one of the men standing not far from Finlay, "those who sacked the priory collected stores and riches. They ha' food. We be hungry."

"I know it. I am hungry also. But 'tis far more important to ha' yer honor than a full belly."

The Murtray men said nothing, did not emit so much as a mutter, such was their respect for this man. Finlay wondered how long Anders's edict could hold. If the men around Finlay were as empty as he, with their stomachs stuck to their backbones, and seeing the forces around them acting to serve their needs with the apparent approval of their commanders, would they not also run amok?

The next day they continued east toward the city of Durham. The Scots were now growing confident in their belief that nothing could stop them, and the lust for plunder was upon them. Finlay sought out Katrin, who stood for once away from her father, gazing ahead with troubled eyes.

She was holding up well. Like the rest of them, she looked weary, and her honey-colored hair hung in a tangle that she no longer even attempted to tuck under her helm. But she stood poised on the balls of her feet, undefeated. At the sight of her, Finlay's heart rose impossibly. The woman he loved, had loved, would always love.

"Mistress."

Her gaze flew to him and kindled. In that instant it felt as if they were alone, despite the seething mass of humanity around them.

"Harper." She edged closer to him. "Ye ha' no need to call me that—mistress. Given wha' we ha' been to one another."

If she only knew…

"Another town lies ahead. Reagan says there is a monastery between us, and it. D'ye think this horde will again attack and slaughter more holy men?"

"Perhaps, if the town does no' pay to spare them."

She made a face. "All this happens wi' the king's approval. I begin to think he is on a campaign to collect ransom, more than aught else."

"Do no' let anyone hear ye say so." Finlay lowered his voice. "Ye maun tak' comfort in knowing yer father will no' let the Murtray men participate in such."

"Nay"—she glanced at him—"he is a stubborn old man and will let them starve instead. D'ye wish to know just how stubborn he is? Reagan has managed to find a horse for Da to ride, and he has refused it—refused it wi' great indignation. 'The Chief o' Murtray to ride when all his men are afoot? How might that be a thing I could countenance? Am I to appear weak before our men?' That is wha' he says.

"I did point out to him that King David and, indeed, Earl Stewart both travel ahorse at the head o' their men while displaying no apparent shame. Will Da survive whatever battles may come? I will be there at his side to defend him. But if I fail…"

Aye, an old fear of hers, and one that had haunted her long. "Mayhap," Finlay said softly, "there will be nay battles. When the king has collected wha' he feels owed to him, perhaps we will turn around and go back home wi'out a fight."

"I hope so, Finlay. 'Tis my dearest hope. But I begin to think in life there are things ye maun face, and fears ye maun conquer. I am no' certain we will get out o' this yet."

He thought she would turn away from him then. Instead, she reached out and touched his hand, just a fleeting brush of her fingers on his. But it brought back to him all they had shared in their four wondrous nights together.

Did she remember?

If only she would—*remember*.

CHAPTER THIRTY-THREE

THE NIGHT BEFORE Katrin's world came apart, she had a dream.

She had not been sleeping well, an empty stomach and an overly full mind not being conducive to it. The army seethed, with men continually coming and going from it, restless and plundering. King David continued to send his men raiding while he awaited a ransom from the monastery and the city beyond.

Before attempting sleep, Katrin had moved back through the ranks—not wanting to admit she searched for Finlay—and had found him in company with a piper and drummers from the neighboring MacDonald clan. Musicians trading stories, it seemed. He had given her a smile that warmed her to her toes, and she'd sat alongside them a while before taking herself off again to make sure Da had all she could provide for the night.

But being in Finlay's company even for so brief a time must have sparked something. For when she did fall asleep after, she dreamed of him. That was, she dreamed she was in one of the stories he had told in her father's hall, with a man who felt very much like him.

She was back home at the settlement perched above the sea, the stretch of shore she knew so well. Only—the keep in which she'd grown was not there. Instead, above the stretch of coast that looked so much the same stood a roundhouse, the sight of which sounded depths in Katrin's soul.

She knew this place. Yet she did not.

In the dream, she walked up from the shore, feeling the stones beneath her feet, to the timber-enforced doorway. Slipped like a wraith inside. The interior opened out in front of her, smoke-filled, with soaring pillars that held up the wheel of the roof. The scent, warmth, and familiarity of the place assailed her.

A man stood there, beside the fire, in the act of donning armor. Not armor such as that with which she was familiar, but rough leather— again, known to her even as it was not so.

At the sight of him, her heart leaped so painfully it shook her whole body, her whole being. Tall he was, with fair hair turned mostly to gray. A face lined by the years yet still handsome, and eyes that, when they turned to her, contained her entire world.

She knew that body of his, as she should well do. A warrior's body now aged. It had collected many a scar over the years in defense of this place, though he tended to disregard the injuries he acquired.

She'd been so sure her fears might at last settle. He was past the age of going out to fight. Yet here he stood donning his leather armor. His sword.

She hurried to him. "Wha' are ye doing?"

He turned his eyes on her, gray eyes speckled with green. All at once they were young again, fleeing together across the face of Alba. Her Irish lad, her exile, her love.

But nay, they were both aged. And he should go to fight no more.

"We are under attack," he said, continuing to fasten the lacing of his heavy vest.

"We are." She had herself, while down upon the shore, sighted the raiders on their way in, a howling, raving crowd of them. Men they'd believed defeated long since.

"Well, then."

She laid hold of his forearms. How long had she loved this man? "Adair," she said. "Adair, ye need no' go. Ha' we no' two braw sons?" She had labored giving them to him, as well as a bonny daughter. Her beloved children, birthed half of Alba and half of Erin, and wholly of their love. "Do our sons nay stand ready to protect us?"

"'Tis my place, Bradana. I did no' take the name of chief lightly from your grandsire. I am sworn—"

"Ye be a warrior nay more."

He gave her a hard look. "If ye believe that, ye do no' know me as well as I thought."

"I know ye. Well. Well! But time does pass, my love. Stay back. For me."

"Alanna." For an instant he closed his eyes as if calling up an inner strength. Not the kind of strength needed to go and fight one more—one last?—battle but that needed to deny her. "I must go. Should I no' be there and should we fall—"

"Stay back and defend the roundhouse. For me. With me. I will stand beside ye."

"Bradana, I would do near anything for ye. All I can. I do no' think I can be other than who I am."

She leaned into him. "Try. Try."

He thrust his sword into the loop at his belt and took both her hands in his. Raised them one after the other to drop kisses into the palms. Planted the tenderest of kisses at each corner of her mouth, upon each cheek, upon her brow.

"Know I do love ye. Always."

Could a woman ask the man she loved to be what he was not? Tears filled her eyes, blurring his form into that of a young man as he stepped away from her on his way out.

Her sons brought him back to her following the battle that proved hard-fought but victorious. They bore him on his shield with tears running down their faces.

KATRIN WAKENED BEFORE dawn with the remnants of that terrible dream in her head, a sense of loss so deep it felt like a mortal wound. A daunting harbinger that, for this day, would prove true.

The weather had turned cool, with lashes of rain moving through one after the other, adding to the general misery. Da rose groaning and cursing under his breath, though he tried as best he might to hide his discomfort from Katrin.

She eyed him with a new understanding in her heart. Was he so different from his ancestor, Adair, whom she'd just seen in her dream? Finlay, so she reflected, had not told them that part of the tale, how the valiant Adair had died and the devastation he had left for his wife. Nay, why should he so spoil a beautiful tale?

Mayhap he did not know that part of it.

She made sure Da ate some breakfast, though she could take nothing for herself. Soon after, King David—likely reading the mood of his troops correctly—unleashed them once more to pillage. He awaited payment on the morrow from the good people of Durham. Meanwhile, he released his restless Scots, some of them under the direction of his man, William Douglas, to continue raiding.

In truth, Katrin could find no other word for it, save *unleashing*. Well into the English countryside and as yet unopposed, they had done little more than raid, pillage, and burn.

When Da heard of it, his face went white. Not the man to disobey his king, he nevertheless called his captains to him, Reagan and Robran.

"Tell our men no' to stir a foot nor a muscle. We will no' take part in this shameful thing. The people o' this land—they are folk just like us."

"They are English," ventured Robran.

"And they ha' no' yet raised a blade against us."

"They will," said one of the clansmen standing by. "Best mayhap to kill all we can beforehand."

"Nay." Da drew himself up like a chief of old. "I do forbid it."

Despite her sympathy for her restless and hungry clansmen, Katrin could only agree. Defending one's own seemed just and right to her, as did standing strong for one's country. Dealing death for the sake of it was something else again.

But she was a woman—soft, many would say—and men were men. They muttered over the decision, being after all this time not loath to exercise their weapons. But they continued to obey their chief and, when others of the vast army moved out, merely watched with envious eyes.

Reagan rejoined his men, none of whom moved out. Katrin turned to find Finlay at her side.

Their eyes met and she saw he wore a guarded expression. He touched her arm and she felt it throughout her body.

"Mistress, wha' is it?"

She shook her head. "This is no' just, is it?" she asked him. "Sacking towns and killing everyone found. Stealing and ruining and burning. Is this wha' we are?"

His gaze, grave and level, met hers. "The king has come wi' the intention o' doing damage. If there is no English army to fight, he will do it otherwise."

"It is cowardly. No' worthy o' us."

"Yer father agrees. 'Tis why he held his men back."

"Yet we are part o' this force, and thus part of all they do." Even now she could hear others in the vast field of men laughing and boasting as if drunk with the deeds they had done. "Finlay, will ye make a tale o' this?"

He shook his head. "If I do, 'twill be o' the valiant Highland chief who held his men back from dishonor."

In the end, it did not matter. Only a short time later, Laird Douglas's party came back with great haste, bloodied and shedding alarm. They went immediately to the vanguard where King David had camped, awaiting his ransom, and consulted with him.

From the right flank where the Murtray party was situated, Katrin could just barely see the king's tent. Some confusion reigned when the party encountered him. The monster that was the army stirred like a great spider.

She took advantage by going to join her da, who had risen from his seat on the ground. Many among the ranks had done the same, all looking in one direction. Katrin had noticed this before—fighting men had a kind of instinct for events that would prove dangerous.

Like this one. A cold trickle crept up her spine, perhaps an instinct of her own. Were they come to a fight after all?

If it did come to battle now, would this Scots army be too exhausted to fight? They had, aye, the sheer weight of numbers. But would that be enough?

They fought for Scotland, and to many of those here, that was sacred. But they were a long way from home.

She had no doubt that for the majority of those around her, home was where they wanted to be.

She glanced aside as Finlay took up a place beside her. He looked grim, less the harper now but steely-eyed like another of the warriors. He had no home, in truth, to which he might return. The world was his home, or mayhap the world he wove with his stories.

He was here only because of her. Because of the choices she had made. If the ill feeling clawing its way through her proved true and the worst happened, if ill befell him, it would be her fault.

Could she live with that?

Nay, and nay.

"Wha' is it, Da? Can ye tell?"

It was Finlay who answered her. "Someone heard the men comin' in shouting about an army. An army ahead."

"An English army? But—" She said no more.

Reagan moved forward with his two commanders and joined the party that surrounded King David, listening to what had occurred. It took some time, and when he did return he came directly to Da, as grave a look on his face as Katrin had ever seen there.

"Chief MacMurtray," Reagan began, and then paused. Katrin knew him for aught but a hesitant man. Sure of his ground and of his stance upon it, he tended to stride straight ahead. But now he clearly groped for words and, indeed, before he spoke, he sought Katrin's face.

His tawny eyes had gone cold and grim.

"Wha' is it?" Da asked.

"There is an army ahead."

"Eh?"

"The raiding party King David sent out has returned wi' the news. An English army. They were engaged—with heavy losses."

All around them, similar words were being repeated. The huge animal that was the Scots army responded, but in that moment Katrin could not quite tell how. Dread? Gladness? Anticipation? Dismay?

Perhaps all of those.

"Oh, God," she whispered. An army. An enemy force. Just when she'd begun hoping the king might grow weary of all this and turn for home.

"How large?" Da sked.

Reagan shook his head. "Not half our number, if the scouting party can be believed. Mayhap not a third as great."

Da straightened a bit. "Tha' is good, then. We can defeat them." *And go home.*

"Aye, the balance is favorable," Reagan agreed. "The king confers now wi' his earls and captains and prepares to move forward into position."

"When?" Da asked. "When will this battle take place?"

Reagan shrugged. "'Twill come when it comes. When it does, Chief MacMurtray"—again he flicked a glance at Katrin before focusing on her father—"I ask ye to stay well back. I will assign two o' my men to protect ye, and your daughter."

Da stiffened with indignation. "I am chief o' this clan, and as such, I will fight."

"Forgive me, Chief MacMurtray"—Reagan's voice was steel—"but ye hired me to fight this battle for ye. And stand in as your son."

"My daughter," Da said, "has taken the place at my side."

It was an incredible statement and one that rocked Katrin back on her heels. After all his protesting of her presence and all the persuading she'd had to do in order to accompany him, did he accept her at last?

He told Reagan, "I pay ye nay to protect me but to lend strength and skill to my company."

"Aye, and that I will do. Yet there are considerations, chief, which surpass that o' the silver in my pocket."

Another incredible statement, in its way, just like the one that had come before it. The Gallowglass was saying Da now commanded his loyalty as well as his sword.

"I will hang back," Da granted with dignity, "that ye may lay all yer might into the enemy when we encounter them."

Word soon came down that would occur almost immediately. The news crept its way through the ranks of men. Now that they knew what awaited them, they were to separate into their divisions and march forth across the wet, broken moorland.

It might be as well, Katrin decided, that after all she would have little chance to dread the coming battle or contemplate what their fate would be. Indeed, she had become separated from Finlay in the ensuing confusion—had he slipped away from her?—and had not even time to seek him out once more, gaze into his eyes or touch his hand. If either of them were to perish in what must come, and she had no chance to say goodbye…

The scene from her recent dream flashed into her head. The woman, Bradana, parting from the aged man she adored. Had they spoken a proper farewell?

Taken up completely with her father, with the rapid movement up front, and the sheer force of the impetus when the Scots army began marching in earnest, she had time for nothing more than to feel the wheel of fate jerk into motion beneath her feet.

⚬⚬⚬

CHAPTER THIRTY-FOUR

WORRIED AND DESPERATE, Finlay searched for Katrin as the army started moving. They had become separated when the body of Murtray's men pressed forward to their chief, seeking answers. Now he could not see her anywhere. After all their waiting, on this cool and rainy morning with fog lying like a blanket over the rough moorland, things moved all too swiftly. He could feel the rush of it, a vibration running through the men, a kind of buzz of conversation, questions, muttering, like the heave of the sea beneath a tiny boat.

He felt edgy, his stomach queasy. He could have eaten no breakfast even had any been on offer, which it was not.

The persistent mist clouded the world. The land here was a broad, rough, and ragged plain that undulated up and down, now torn by the hooves and boots that trod across it. No one could see much of his surroundings, which only added to the dread. Did their commanders know where, exactly, this English army lurked? They might be anywhere.

And whence had these forces come? They'd been told England lay empty before them, and so far they'd glimpsed naught of significant opposing forces. Could the information coming back to them be wrong?

Uncertainty bred fear, and fear ran through Murtray's men, who were now so very far from home. Finlay could feel that too. No doubt everybody there could, and it united even as it shook them.

"Come, march wi' me and my da." Of a sudden, Katrin was there beside Finlay as if she'd materialized from the very mist, her hand on his arm and desperation in her eyes. No more than he did she know what this day would bring. But she wanted them to face it together. And was he not here for the express purpose of fighting at her side?

"Come along," he bade Gregor, and they moved up through the ranks.

The Gallowglass band was, as ever, just in front of Chief MacMurtray's position. Reagan had donned his helmet, and the fog swirled around him like the remnants of a dream, adding to Finlay's sense of unreality. Mayhap he did dream all this, no more or less than one of the tales he told. Like the memories that came to him in his dreams.

Suddenly Laird Robert Stewart appeared at their head with one of his captains, on horseback. He shouted at them, "This division—ye are under my command! Forward, but let the rest o' the army move ahead o' ye!"

Why? In the long-ago battles Finlay had fought, he'd always been in the vanguard, or close to it. Did Stewart wish to keep them in reserve, should the fight go badly for the rest of the forces?

A humble harper, not even a proper warrior, had no chance to ask. Over the strange and foreign land they moved, unable now to see even their own flanks that spread out ahead and to either side. Orders from the other commanders came back to them muffled.

If their scouts could be trusted, an army awaited them, one of unknown size. How far ahead? It must be some distance yet, for the commanders made no effort at silence. But it could all end here. For him. For Katrin, for both of them. One final turn of fate's wheel. Had he found her only to lose her before she knew him?

All too possible. In battle, men died. He knew that to the root of his soul, knew it better than he knew his own name. For, aye, he had been here before, though not in this life. In this life he had eschewed the path of the warrior. This he had done for the sake of the lass who walked at his side.

Yet he found himself here anyway. An irony the likes of which life seemed so fond.

Katrin must have felt his gaze upon her, for she turned her head and their eyes met. An exchange took place, one as intimate as when he'd been with her in her chamber. When they'd lain together, two bodies—and two souls—became one.

He might never have that again, but by God, he would stand strong beside her, whatever that required.

The mist stirred and floated around her. It had wetted and darkened her hair. Her face looked pale, but as she gazed at him, light took hold in her eyes.

His world lay in those eyes.

The commanders were not being quiet. They shouted to their men and to one another. Far away to the front, Finlay could hear the king's voice raised. No silent approach, this. To one side of them, a drummer started up a beat. A piper far on the other side took it up in a tune. To his astonishment, Finlay realized he knew it—the march tune he had made for the Gallowglass.

With a breathless laugh and a look for Finlay, Katrin also took it up. Her voice rose bold but muffled by the mist, disembodied like a murmur from the past. His own tune, aye, and the words they had made together.

> *Come all ye who would valiant be*
> *Who would follow the train o' bright glory.*
> *Where battle brings us gory fates*
> *We follow them both soon and late.*
> *The Gallowglass gang to die!*

After a moment's hesitation, Finlay raised his own voice, a fitting complement to hers. His heart bounded and rose. The men around them stared before beginning to step in time with the rhythm. One by one, beginning with Gregor, they joined in, a score of voices deep and strong. Courage rose among them with the tune.

> *For fight they will wi' sword or spear,*
> *With blade and axe, their numbers dear.*
> *The heart o' courage lingers here.*
> *We will follow wi' strength o' eye.*
> *They lead us on to victory,*
> *May the Gallowglass never die!*

Anders slanted them a look and grinned. Reagan, still at their head, glanced back with a grin also. In a neighboring company, other voices took it up.

A kind of battle cry, the song was. A defiance of fear, and fate. How many of those who sang would survive? In what future might their ancient song be sung?

Katrin reached out and snagged Finlay's fingers. Clutched tight. Would anyone notice? Did it matter if they did?

The sun rose, and the mist brightened strangely all around them before beginning to lift and giving way to a cold rain. Men continued to mutter as they tramped. Back so far in the ranks as they were, surely the fight—if ever they did sight the English troops—would be long over before they reached it?

They stopped moving. Waited, and waited some more. Many of the men sat down even though the ground was rough and sodden. Just ahead of them, Chief MacMurtray lowered himself to the ground with the help of one of the Gallowglass soldiers. They waited some more.

Eventually, Sir Robert Stewart rode back, shouting orders.

"The English army lies just ahead. We will take position and hold. Our division is to keep back—the king and Earl Moray will take the lead for the time being. Understand? Hold and wait!"

The tension, which had backed down a few steps during their singing, cranked up impossibly high.

Finlay sensed raw fear and uncertainty in the men around him, many of whom—just like Katrin—had never experienced such a conflict. Waiting before a battle was hard, but that was not the worst of it. The worst came when the world broke apart and a man committed himself to the killing, and death sprang up from the very ground.

He did not want that for Katrin. He did not want it for himself. He must heed O'Hanlon's advice and get Katrin and her father to the rear when the battle began.

If he could.

The clouds moved across the moor as the rain came and went. Bit by bit, Finlay saw the vast army around him, shifting, shifting with their commanders directing them. The breath caught in his throat. No matter what forces the English possessed, surely they could not overcome so vast an army as this?

As the mist crawled away behind them, he saw where they were. Sprawled across a rise, all uneven and grizzled green, with a steep slope in front of them. To be sure, most the Scots army was in front of them now, two units having moved ahead. Across from them he saw another rise, this one topped by a stone monument. And there—there…

The English army looked vast, but nay, it could not number much better than half their own. Their position, though—did they stand the easier ground? Hard to tell with the masses of knights and horsemen and footmen obscuring the way. Finlay thought he glimpsed a wall, and much broken ground on the Scots' side, which would complicate any kind of concerted charge. But his place was not to give the orders. He must try to protect those around him, even if it cost his life.

He turned to Gregor, still at his side. "Stay near to me when it begins."

Gregor's brown eyes had widened with fright. "When will it begin?"

"God knows."

It once more started to rain, as if to add to their woe. A cold autumn rain it was, and heavy. It further obscured the limited view they had.

One of Robert Stewart's captains came through on horseback, reinforcing his order. "Hang back. Hang back till ye're needed!"

The army—their army—had split into three distinct detachments, the two that had moved forward poised to descend the slope. Earl Moray commanded the foremost, and the king—no one could call him a coward—led the other, visible on his mount even through the rain.

Across from them on the opposite side of the gully, the smaller English army had also broken into three. Finlay's keen eyes saw they had many more mounted knights, men no doubt highly trained in warfare, who even at this distance looked lethal. And there was something about the disposition of their warriors...

The entire Scots army shifted like some great beast taking a breath, and moved forward.

Katrin, who still clutched Finlay's fingers, turned to him.

"I love ye. I want ye to know that full well, before—" And she kissed him right there amongst her father's men.

The years blurred and convulsed around him. He was an Irish warrior standing outside in the sun, gazing into eyes of blue. He was an exile, learning the price demanded and paid for such a love. A second son, fighting against all odds to keep hold of the heart with which a wild Caledonian princess had gifted him. He was a Scotsman willing to risk all he was to say to the Norsewoman who should be his enemy but could never, never be—

"And I love ye."

Did the wheel of life jerk and turn? Or was that but the ground Finlay felt shifting beneath his feet? For here he was, as ever, risking—risking it all again.

He wished with sudden, sharp desperation that he could tell all of it to her, who they were and who they had been. But there was no time, and if things went badly, that time might never, never come.

Her father's men, standing so close around them, did not seem to notice the exchange, their very beings focused on what happened up ahead. But everything within Finlay narrowed to awareness of the woman whose mouth hovered just below his. His life, she was. His heart. His very being.

How strange and terrible, the ways in which a man's life unfolded. He had spent most this lifetime aware of her, though not knowing who or where she was. He'd spent years searching for her and had found her at last.

Only to quite possibly see it all end here in the pouring rain, on this forsaken patch of foreign ground.

"List to me," he told her. "When the battle begins ye must heed all I tell to ye, aye?"

She did not say what she might, that he was a harper, not a warrior, and she had better training than him. Her gaze clung to his and she nodded.

Then she turned to her father, on her other side, and spoke to him.

"Stay near to me, Da, when it begins."

And Anders MacMurtray replied, "Daughter, it already has. May God protect us."

CHAPTER THIRTY-FIVE

K ATRIN'S HEART POUNDED so hard she could feel it in her ears and in her fingertips. Her eyes stretched wide in an effort to see everything at once as a warrior should, each flicker of movement, great or small. The surge of a flank, the charge of a horse, the flash of a blade.

She needed to survive this. For her da's sake, she did. Was it not why she was here?

If only Finlay were not. If only he were safe back at Murtray or on the road far, far to the north of here with Brada on his back.

She feared having him here. *She feared.*

She did—for Reagan, up ahead of her, who, once their division began to move, would take the brunt of the fight. For her da and all their clansmen whom she'd known from birth. For the man who stood so quiet beside her.

She felt connected to all of them. As if their group were one great being.

Ahead of them, a loud cry arose. The forward division went charging down the rough slope and the battle—the terrible battle—began.

Men twitched all around her. They shifted on their feet and cursed. For all they could do at the moment was stand as ordered, and watch.

Watch as Katrin did, with growing horror.

The English army was, nay, not so vast as their own. But as the Scots charged them, their mounted forces parted along with their footmen. A forest of bowmen appeared. Shifted positions.

Began to fire.

The breath caught in Katrin's throat as she saw what the forward ranks of the English had been concealing. The bowmen.

The bowmen.

A hail of arrows crashed into the advancing Scots forces, far more lethal than the rain. Men went down so quickly and so thickly, it did not look real. Despite their shields they folded, row upon row, and the whole of the Scots army rippled with the effect, even though their commanders continued to urge them on.

Katrin could see it then, how the lay of the land favored the English rather than the Scots. The charging Scots were held up by the rough ground and a stone wall near the bottom of the gully that separated the two forces, and were slain by the sleeting arrows. They stumbled on the broken ground as many more fell. With screams tearing from their throats, others ran on.

Katrin had never experienced a battle and was ill prepared for the sheer noise of it, a crashing blast that washed back over their waiting division like a wave upon a shore. Howling, screaming, bellowing, a racket of fighting and dying. She wanted to run. She could not, for those she loved stood here, and so also would she stand.

"The archers!" she cried to no one. "The archers!"

So many of them. They stood in ranks behind the screen of their footmen and knights, and fired. Fired again and again. Was there no limit to the numbers of their arrows?

And whence had they come by their thousand when the Scots had been told England lay open before them, all the English soldiers in France?

A lie. A deadly one.

The Scots army shifted down the slope, closer and then closer to death. They possessed archers also, but not so many. Most of their vast forces consisted of footmen armed with spears, far less effective on this broken ground. For a spearman had to get within reach of his opponent before he could take him down. An archer could slay him from afar.

Their own archers fired to good effect. Yet even some of them fell to the enemy fire.

Beside Katrin, Da began to swear. A warrior, if an aged one, he could see what was happening and how the battle went. All of them could see.

Laird Stewart's commanders came through again. Katrin saw Reagan, still at the head of their company, speaking to one of them. Gesturing wildly. He wanted in on the fight.

Despite her dismay and horror, Katrin's heart bounded, unable to do anything but respond to such courage.

A warrior, was Reagan O'Hanlon, to the bone.

A warrior headed out to die?

Soon after Laird Stewart's commander rode on, Reagan came back to speak with Da.

"They are holding us in reserve. We will go in soon." His gaze slipped over Katrin and latched on to Finlay. "Ye will be ready?"

"It does no' go well," Da rumbled.

"Nay," Reagan agreed. "Not yet. But a battle can change swiftly. Be ready."

The rain slackened, and then came down so heavy that Katrin could no longer see the stone monument on the opposite rise. Time slowed and, like a trickster, sped up all at once, and the sickness inside her grew.

The one thing that did not change was the sound of it—the groaning and cursing and screaming and pleading and exhorting that made one great, ululating cry. It filled Katrin's ears, and her mind.

She could not have said how much time passed before they were given leave to move. When the order came, they swung around the flank of their own army and charged down the slope through the rain. Into the flying death of the arrows, which did not cease.

Da drew his sword, a hard look in his eyes. Unlike many of the Scots forces, he had a shield. Katrin could only hope it might protect him.

They pushed forward and steeply downward. A cry went up. "The king! The king—he is struck!"

Katrin turned her eyes to the place where King David had been holding a front position since the battle began. His knights had gathered around him in a clutch. She could not see—

"Keep moving!"

Reagan glanced back at them. Finlay touched Katrin on the arm and began to speak. She could see agony in his eyes—he wanted her to fall back, her and Da. But it was too late, too late. They could not hold back for the press of men behind them and around them moving in a great wave. For the sake of courage, she would have to fight.

They charged. Into the hail of arrows. Into the deafening sound of it and the death all around.

The broken ground underfoot made it almost impossible to go at a steady pace. Ahead, Katrin saw the Gallowglass engage the enemy, and her heart reached for Reagan.

Let him survive.

Then the battle was upon them and it did not seem anyone would survive.

The arrows took out fully a third of their company before they engaged the enemy, either maiming or killing them outright. Snarling faces were everywhere—with some part of her mind Katrin imagined they were ugly English faces, but she did not truly focus on that then. The deadly barrage of arrows came from behind those faces, piercing into flesh, felling men she knew. Horses thundered past them in an effort to cut off their charge.

She could see the wall now, the one that intersected the broken ground, with dead heaped around it like sea wrack on the shore after a storm. Men were climbing over the dead and dying.

Beside her, Da was hollering, "Murtray, Murtray!"

The Gallowglass were now in the thick of the fighting. She

had one glimpse of Reagan swinging his great claymore with both hands. He wore armor but had no shield. Her heart leaped to her mouth in a sudden conviction that he would die.

They would all die.

But for a moment—one suspended in time—the enemy began to waver and fall back. Men died by the scores, the hundreds. Yet the Scots had so many more men.

Did the king yet survive? And her Da...

In the noise of the conflict, she could barely think. The Gallowglass at the head of their company kept the knights and some of the ugly faces at bay for the moment, but could do naught about the arrows.

Da was screaming, trying to push forward, the warrior in him coming to the fore. Then he was not. Though he'd been running but an arm's reach from Katrin, he disappeared as if winked magically out of sight.

She gasped, "Da!" and attempted to turn. But his men followed him, their motion like a boulder rolling downhill. She saw faces of men she knew, twisted in fear and agony. She saw the fallen. Others of the fallen, for if Da were not still beside her, there was but one place he could be.

She went back, facing now a forest of spears held by their own men. Scanning the ground, searching, searching. She found him not far back with two of his clansmen hunkered down supporting him, his grizzled head between their younger ones. For an instant, her heart stood still.

Dead?

But nay, for one of the young spearmen, named Rabbie, gestured to her. "Mistress."

She threw herself at them, down onto the ground. Feet continued to pound past and sometimes over them.

"The chief is struck!" cried Rabbie unnecessarily.

Aye, so he was. She met her father's eyes and beheld the agony there.

The second young man, Davey, possessed a shield, which he

held not to protect himself but his chief where he lay. For the arrows still rained down.

One had gone through Da's thigh.

It looked monstrous there, obscene. Yet she knew in her heart it was not a mortal wound—at least, it need not be, if she could get him away out of this.

She looked at the sweat-and-rain-streaked faces of his men. "Ye maun help me. Let us get him fro' the field. Finlay—"

She looked around for the man who had been so attached to her in both body and spirit that she assumed he'd moved with her now. He was not there.

He was not there.

Desperate now, she tried to look around. But they were at ground level with feet thudding by, over and around them, and she could not see him.

Oh God, oh God, she could not see him!

"Help me. Carry yer chief."

Her first duty must be to her father. Get Da away, even if she felt like her heart had been torn out by the roots, and her very spirit flayed.

They rose to their feet, Katrin doing her best now to cover them with Davey's shield, which he had handed to her. Still, looking around, she could not glimpse a red head—one particular red head—through the rain.

Had he fallen? Did he lie somewhere beneath all these feet? Bleeding his life away.

Bleeding *her* life away. Because at that moment, she knew, if he lost his life, hers was lost also. She might, aye, live on. But to what purpose?

They moved against the tide of that mighty horde, fighting their way, Da groaning and protesting all the while. Saying he wanted to go back and fight. That his men should not be allowed to go on through battle without their chief.

A fine sentiment, but Da's face was the color of bleached stone and all the courage in the world would not help him stand.

"Hush, Da!" she shouted. "Ye canna. Trust in Reagan. Reagan is there."

Was he, though? Or had he too fallen? *Like Finlay.*

Not like Finlay. She would not permit that thought; she would *not*. She shot another desperate look behind. No one there. Not following.

Gasping and cursing—for Da was not a small man—they carried their chief back up the slope. Out from the range of the arrows, Katrin aching all the while to turn and look behind her. To see Finlay loping after them. Aching, aching to go back.

She could not. She had her da, and the army still surged down the hill toward what now seemed like certain defeat.

"There," she told the two bearers, gesturing to a clump of bracken turned yellow with the autumn. They were not the only ones to make their way back out of the battle. Others were wounded. Some walking, some crawling, some collapsed and more than likely dead.

The two young clansmen laid their burden down gratefully and looked at her.

"Mistress Katrin, should we go back?"

Back into that hell of pain and terror.

She looked at Da, now barely conscious. Would he order them back? Should she?

She could not.

"Nay," she said. "I need ye to help him. Sta wi' me."

CHAPTER THIRTY-SIX

FINLAY COULD NOT say when Katrin disappeared from his side. He'd been determined that above all else he would keep hold of her, stick to her the way a thistle sticks to a man's plaid. That he would get her and her da out of the battle. But they now thundered downhill in a huge, screaming, caterwauling, unstoppable mass. One moment she was there, the next not.

Horror washed over him in a drench colder than the rain. This battle had drawn upon the roots of his soul. He'd been a warrior once, more than once, and being here in the midst of it all did not seem so very strange. Even though his harp banged upon his back in its wrappings, his sword did not feel unfamiliar in his hand.

But Katrin! He'd spent his whole life searching for her. How could she be gone from him?

An arrow skimmed past his cheek, so close the point laid open the flesh. Had he not been turning his head to look for Katrin, it would have taken him in the eye. Around him, other men fell.

The Gallowglass company, just ahead, were fully engaged. Another few steps and so would he be, and those around him. Gregor. Where was Gregor? He too had gone.

Ahead and to the left lay the broken stone wall, a portion of it fallen or never completed. Who could tell, obscured as it was by the dead and dying? Indeed, a great groan seemed to arise from the very ground, a terrible susurration of sound.

The Scots' charge was further hampered by a depression in the ground, a kind of pit filled with yellowing bracken around which they had to divert. A number of the attacking Scots had fallen into this hollow, where the English archers, pressing forward now from the other side, fired upon them. Volley after volley after volley—

They would lose this fight. The ancient warrior within Finlay knew it.

He and those of Murtray blood had caught up with the band of Gallowglass who stood strong. They faced off against the English knights who charged at them, their steeds terribly wounded yet coming on. Reagan O'Hanlon fought with a snarl on his face that made him near unrecognizable.

The rain had slackened and Finlay caught a flash of steel—a pike coming at him—and turned. His sword came up instinctively and then he was engaged. Fighting to stay alive.

The seething mass of the Scots army pushed. Pushed and gained a few paces of ground. A moment or two of respite.

O'Hanlon looked around and saw Finlay. His eyes registered astonishment.

"Where is the chief, Harper?"

"I do no' ken."

"And Katrin?"

Pain stabbed Finlay to the heart. He shook his head.

"Go. Find them."

Find her.

Finlay heard those words thunder in his mind. Then the battle surged back at them. Howling faces and steel on every side. He had a last glimpse of O'Hanlon's face, streaming sweat and blood, as the man turned. The great claymore with which Reagan fought flashed and intercepted a blade that most surely would have taken Finlay's head. A great nudge from the Gallowglass sent Finlay sprawling into the soaking turf.

He landed on his back and felt Brada break beneath his weight. Sword still in his hand, he saw rather than heard Reagan shout at him, "Go."

Saw an enemy blade take the Gallowglass in the shoulder so he fell.

Fell.

A mortal wound? Who could tell? It had looked so.

Finlay wanted to get up and fight on. Every fiber in him longed to avenge the man who had just saved his life, quite possibly at the cost of his own.

But O'Hanlon's men had gathered around him, and anyway Reagan's concern was all for the chief he served. For Katrin.

Did Reagan love her? He worried for her, that was certain.

Finlay struggled to his feet, the gouge to his left cheek streaming blood, and looked around. Tried to look around, for it proved impossible. The last of Murtray's men plodded past and he laid hold of them, one after another.

"The chief? The chief's daughter?"

At last one answered, "I saw our men carrying him fro' the field."

"His daughter?" Finlay repeated on the ragged edge of desperation.

"She were wi' them."

It felt cowardly to leave. The warrior, that ancient warrior deep inside him, insisted it was. To move off and hie away while still others thundered into that morass of death.

Yet if Murtray's men carried him from the field, he must be injured, perhaps mortally so. And Finlay possessed one last bit of the story that Anders MacMurtray needed to know before he left this world.

That knowledge, as much as his longing for Katrin, spurred Finlay from the field. Others moved in the same direction as he, not many. The turf lay littered with dead and dying. A vast massacre, the arrows had wrought.

Others made their way on foot, limping and creeping, some helping their fellows.

He could not see Katrin or the chief anywhere.

The battle moved away from him. Up here on the moor, he could still hear it, the bellowing, the terrible screams of horses and of men. But it echoed like a memory down through time.

For a blessed moment he closed his eyes. Pictured a young woman with yellow hair standing in the sun outside a round-house. A graceful lass with a gray deerhound at her side. The woman he loved, gazing into his eyes.

Here.

He turned and made off toward a kind of ridge covered in dying bracken. Men took refuge here, a few lying, their fellows trying to stanch the flow of blood from hideous wounds.

He found them behind a screen of bracken, the old man lying stretched on the ground and the three others gathered around him. His relief at finding them, at seeing Katrin, went beyond expression. The chief looked dead. He had an arrow through his thigh, and his face had gone the color of daubed wattle.

By all that was holy, had he reached them too late?

He stumbled forward. Katrin looked up and their eyes met. She shot to her feet.

He wanted little more than to embrace her. For she was here, alive and whole, from what he could see. But the two clansmen looked up also, watching with what appeared to be astonishment.

Somehow, he kept from clasping her tight. The emotions flashing between them and what he saw blazing in her eyes would have to be enough.

"Ye be hurt." She lifted a hand to his cheek.

"'Tis naught." *Reagan saved my life.* He could not tell her that now. Mayhap later. "The chief—"

"He's alive. The arrow head passed through, but I think it nicked bone." She blinked at him. "'Tis bad, a grave wound. We canna find a physician."

"Are there any to be had?" They had not thought of that, had they, while rushing headlong into battle.

"If there are, they will be busy elsewhere. The king was struck. Did ye see?"

Finlay nodded.

"I do no' ken if he lives."

"He leads yet the center company," Finlay told her. He had seen that much during their own charge. "But I think we will lose this battle."

"Och, aye. Curse all that sent us to it. Come, we maun do what we can for Da. Do ye ha' any skill in those hands besides for harping?"

"Nay." But she did. He remembered her treating his wounds when he returned from battle long, long ago. In the small roundhouse this was, the place where they dwelt. Her touch gentle and comforting. Healing in its love.

He did not say that either. He did not know if she was ready to hear all they had been to one another.

"Let us see wha' may be done."

Anders was not unconscious after all. He opened his eyes when Finlay hunkered down next to him and said weakly, "Harper."

"Chief."

"I am that glad to see ye alive."

"And I, ye."

After some discussion, they decided the best course was to break the shaft off the arrow, a process that proved painful to Anders in the extreme.

What followed proved even less pleasant, so much so that, at length, the chief did pass out, a relief to all involved.

Katrin scavenged from her clothing to bandage him. Not until that task was accomplished did she turn to Finlay.

"Your face—"

"Skinned by an arrow."

"Let me see what I can do for it."

They had discovered a muddy rivulet of water, one no doubt formed by the rain. She wetted a scrap of clothing and washed the blood from his face and beard, and aye, it was so like those days long past that he had to close his eyes again, absorbing the feel of it. Of her. If he opened his eyes, whom would he see? His Irish lass bent over him with her golden hair all hanging down or Katrin in her filthy armor, love and concern brimming in her eyes?

It scarce mattered. The love was the same.

Just the same.

"I canna bandage that," she said. "I canna do much at all for ye, but 'tis clean as I can make it."

He opened his eyes and found himself back on the muddy, broken plain. He took her hands in his.

She leaned forward and lightly dropped a kiss upon the wound. "Ye will ha' a scar there."

"Alas."

"Nay matter, I do no' mind. Ye may be ugly as a boar's backside and I would no' mind. No' that ye are." The smile in her eyes failed. "How do we get my da away out o' this?"

Finlay did not know.

"Wha' frightens me, Finlay, is that I ha' already had my miracle. When I saw ye walking out o' that battle to me—"

"Aye." It must have been akin to what he felt seeing her there kneeling on the ground.

"I do no' ken if I will get another miracle. If I deserve one."

Finlay hesitated to tell her. "I saw O'Hanlon go down. Before he did, he saved my life."

Her eyes filled with a rush of tears. "Dead?"

"I could no' tell." Finlay glanced over his shoulder toward the great, seething battle. How could it be otherwise?

"Och, God, och, God," she wept. "A great man. I cared much for him."

Finlay could not find it in him to mind. If she loved the Gallowglass, well, O'Hanlon was a man worthy of her admiration. Of her respect. And his own heart hurt with seeing him fall.

For an instant, there on the edge of the soaking battleground, the world wavered around him, life and life and life overlapping in loss and pain.

In love.

Softly he touched Katrin's hand. "Let us see to your da." All that they could do, for the time being.

CHAPTER THIRTY-SEVEN

PANIC CLAWED AT Katrin's belly and up through her throat, threatening to choke her. She needed to keep calm, to think clearly, but she had never been so frightened or so sick to the heart.

She gazed around from the place where she knelt on the broken moorland. Behind her, the battle still raged like a seething, flailing creature somehow intent on destroying itself. The ground between lay strewn with dead and injured in every unspeakable condition.

The things she had seen.

She gulped down her sickness and blinked her eyes. Men were streaming away from the battle, leaving it just as they had, in twos or threes. Some helping or carrying others of the wounded away. Some clearly in flight.

Despair most terrible touched her heart. She did not know how they were to get her da safe away.

What of the rest of their men? Men she had known all her life and liked full well. Many no doubt dead. Some still back in the horror that was the battle. Was she to desert them?

She represented her brother, here. With Da down, she supposed she now represented her chief. Should she return to the battle?

How strong was she?

All her life she had rebelled at not being given leave to train as a warrior, that she might stand and defend herself and those she loved. Now she had that chance, and duty rose before her—her duty to get Da away—while men continued to die for her. For them.

Reagan.

Her heart bled for him. With his great strength and his quiet amusement, his calm patience and forbearing. The consummate warrior he was, and she grieved, grieved for him.

If such a man had fallen, they were lost.

That realization got her to her feet. She looked around again.

Their little band of five made a pitiful sight, wet to the skin and bloodied. The two young clansmen who had carried Da out from the thick of battle looked exhausted and white with fear. Finlay…

It would live in her mind forever, that moment when she'd seen him emerge from the fighting like a dream come from the past. Aye, she'd had her miracle and could not expect another. All she could do was reach for one.

She turned to the two young men hunkered beside their chief.

"I am sorry to waylay ye, but ye will no' be able to return to the battle. I need ye to carry him awa' out o' here. I believe that is our duty now." Da had no heir. He must, so, return to Murtray.

Rabbie climbed to his feet. "Mistress"—his blue eyes, wide with shock, looked earnest—"I do no' doubt that pullin' us fro' yon battle has spared our lives. Any service I may perform for the chief or ye—I stand ready."

"Aye, so. Davey, your shield"—for that young man had it yet upon his shoulder—"can we use it as a litter for him?"

That had been done in the old days, as she knew. Had not Finlay told of it in his stories? But that had been in the days when shields were larger. This one bore a crack right across, and they had to yank several arrows out of it.

And the chief was not a small man. As they tried to load him onto the makeshift litter, the shield came apart.

"Here, use Brada's wrappings. Fro' my pack."

Finlay's cheek had resumed bleeding. Trails of blood trickled down as he shrugged off his pack and swung it to the ground. Something within gave off a mournful sound, and when he unwrapped the harp, they all stared.

The beautiful instrument's back had broken in two, now held to the bow only by the strings.

"Och, Finlay!" Katrin cried.

"Nay matter," Finlay said, placing the shattered instrument into the pack once more. "The wrappings are strong."

Katrin wept as they spread the leather on the ground and lifted Da onto it. Carrying him so would not be easy. And they were so very far from home.

Two men came slogging through just as they prepared to lift their burden. One of them was the drummer who had walked beside them for a time. He still had his drum, not burst, and his face was gray with strain.

"The battle is lost. Lost!" he called to them. "The English knights are coming after us, killing all they can find. Best flee!"

Katrin's panic threatened to choke her again. She dared not take the time to look back down the hill, but aye, she fancied she heard hoofbeats and screaming.

"Come, hurry," she told her group.

Finlay shrugged his pack onto his back. With one of them at each corner, they lifted Da and started off following the drummer and the others who fled.

A hard and arduous process. Da's weight was such that he dragged the sling to the ground.

At last, Davey said, "Let us fold the cloth and try again. Rabbie and I will hold the chief higher. Mistress, ye lead the way. Harper, keep watch fro' the rear."

They shifted Da and tried again, the two strong young men hefting him to shoulder height. Better yet, how long could they continue?

Others fleeing the battle now streamed past them. When Katrin heard hoofbeats pounding, she paused and turned in terror, expecting to see a line of English knights bearing down on them.

What she saw instead gave her a sudden rush of hope. Their own men. Not only that—a face among them she recognized for that of Laird Robert Stewart.

One of their own commanders.

Abandoning her group, she ran toward him.

"Laird Stewart, Laird Stewart!"

For one terrible instant she thought he and the horsemen with him would not stop. Perhaps it was her voice—a woman's voice—that made him draw his mount to a halt in the soaking turf.

He streamed with wet, a combination of sweat and rain, but he appeared untouched. He gazed down at her with incredulous amazement.

"The battle is lost!" he bellowed.

"Aye, but my father—" Wildly she gestured behind her. Rabbie and Davey had laid their burden down. They made a piteous sight. "He is the chief of Murtray and sworn to John Randolph, Earl Moray—he answered Laird Randolph's call and now is sore injured."

"The Earl of Moray is dead."

"Oh! But my laird, surely ye—If ye can only help us get him awa'—"

Sir Robert shot a withering look at their group and a second at Katrin. "Nay time. Ye must make yer own way."

And he spurred his mount, which bore a grievous wound across the chest, away. The other riders followed, throwing up sodden clods of turf and muddy water as they went.

Anger arose in Katrin's heart. Anger and a sense of betrayal so terrible it felt bottomless. Their own commander had abandoned them—abandoned her father in all his loyalty—to the aftermath of this terrible battle.

"Come." Someone touched her arm. Finlay. "We canna tarry here."

The screams behind them grew louder. Nay, they could not tarry.

After that, they walked. The rain had mostly stopped, but the world was a sodden place without refuge. Night came on, which, as Finlay said, speaking softly and steadily into her ear, was a good thing. It would lend them cover.

They needed it indeed, for the English army, the knights for the main part, were in hard pursuit. Katrin had heard—and seen—them riding down any number of her countrymen. So far, her little group had escaped notice, but she knew it could only be a matter of chance, and not a good chance. They walked a narrow blade of danger.

Please, she beseeched every power she knew, in her mind. Though she did not know precisely what she requested. Just *please.*

Her two stout bearers tired and often had to lower Da to the ground. Whenever they heard the sound of horses coming behind they all dropped and cowered flat in the bronze heather, Katrin throwing herself over Da's body.

He did not regain consciousness, not once, and blood soaked her makeshift bandage. They dared not stop to care for him.

She did not know what she would have done without Finlay's voice in her ear, soft and steady, lending reassurance. Without his hand at her elbow when she faltered. Without the sheer strength of his presence as they moved off into the unknown darkness of the night.

And then—

And then.

She should have known they could not escape notice forever. They moved so slowly with their burden that many had outstripped them. Most of the English knights had fallen away, but now, just at nightfall, squads of soldiers came hunting, their orders no doubt to find and kill any Scots stragglers. Screams behind them increased in number. Always distant enough.

Then not distant.

A hoot, a cry like a hound sighting its prey.

They had been seen.

The English soldiers howled after them, and somehow Katrin's stunned mind managed to count them. Five. Aye, so, they themselves were four strong if Rabbie and Davey laid their burden on the ground. All exhausted. Spent.

They would not leave this patch of ground, this piece of English moor, alive.

She drew her sword and turned with the litter and its two bearers at her back. Instinct made her do so, and determination. She would die here, aye. Far, far from her home. Perhaps that had always been meant—she, the warrior.

With a hard shove, Finlay bumped her aside. He too drew his sword, moving not at all like a harper but like a man who set himself to fight.

For her.

"Nay!" she cried.

It came from the heart, that cry. From the soul. From a place so ancient she could no longer remember it.

"I will hold them," Finlay told her. "Go. *Go*."

"Nay." She could not. She would not.

"Yer da needs ye. Yer clan needs ye. Go."

"I need *ye*!" she wailed. The soldiers already bore down on them, rushing in. She swiped at one, and he leaped back. Finlay engaged another, a man with an already-bloodied head and a terrible smile on his face. Finlay, not like a harper at all but a—

"Katrin!"

Her da's voice calling to her. He'd come awake and reached for her through the falling gloom, reached with one hand and with his eyes.

"Go!" Finlay shouted at her again, and threw himself into the fray.

Threw himself to the wolves.

Weeping, she went.

CHAPTER THIRTY-EIGHT

Katrin never remembered much of what followed, at least not in any detail. They ran. Somehow, over that broken ground and in the dark, they did, her two bearers giving valiant service. After a time, they reached a stand of trees, one alive with others who also fled. The hunted.

Katrin hunkered down beside her father and said, "I maun go back."

"Nay," Da said. He'd remained awake, distressed and cursing, insisting he did not need to be carried even though he did.

"Finlay," she said.

That moment, that one terrible moment, now superseded all the others in her mind. Whenever she closed her eyes, she saw it again. Finlay, throwing himself forward.

So she and hers could get away.

He must have succeeded in delaying their pursuers, for the English soldiers did not come after them. Even though, aye, the wood rustled with life, they were left alone.

He could not possibly have survived. He was a harper, not a warrior, and even the best of warriors—Reagan—had gone down. Exhausted and with no shield, Finlay fought armed only with love.

His love for her.

Nay, he could not possibly have survived. But he must have hung on long enough to allow for their escape.

The pain of it stunned her, made it hard to breathe and harder to think. She realized but one thing: she could not waste what had been given at such a price. At all cost, she must get her da away to safety.

How, she could not imagine. They were stranded in hostile country miles and miles from home with nothing. No food. No supplies. No clothing.

Would others of their clan come behind them? Had any survived?

It grew cold that night, and they had no shelter. Wet to the skin, the four of them huddled together for warmth and Katrin slept not at all. By morning, when dawn bled in from the east, she felt sick to the very death.

She once again robbed from her own clothing to rebandage Da's leg. When they moved off, he insisted on walking, supported between his two young clansmen. Katrin did not think he would get far.

They needed food and warmth. Da needed a proper physician. Katrin could still hardly think on these things. She saw only Finlay.

Finlay.

They filled their bellies with water from a stream and hid when they could. Katrin had no doubt the English still hunted them, and after the atrocities at the ransacked priory, any landsman they met would be sure to point them out. Nowhere to ask for help. Da grew steadily weaker, but refused to let his men carry him.

Again and again that day, she peered over her shoulder. Searching, aye, for pursuers. But also hoping, *hoping*. Hearing words echo in her mind.

I will find ye. Always.

Like a tribe of wounded rabbits, they moved on through that day, keeping to the gorse and heather, finding their direction by the sun that broke through from time to time. It shifted far to the south at this time of year, and Katrin—now leading the way— kept it behind her right shoulder.

Many other rabbits traversed the country around them. She could hear as well as sometimes glimpse them, and sometimes mounted knights still moved through. Not their own.

By hiding in the wet gorse, they escaped notice.

That miracle may have been due to prayer. She heard Rabbie praying often. She prayed also, in a blind sort of way, desperate prayers that went out to who knew where, especially when the riders moved past. *Do no' let them see us. Please, please.*

She once heard Davey mutter, "I want my ma," and it wrung her heart because she did not think he would see his ma, or his home, again.

Da was in too much pain for prayer. He sweated and tried not to groan, but he kept moving. For another night they crouched in the heather, freezing. Starving. Davey wept, and the rest of them pretended they could not hear him.

A deep and terrible sort of despair took up residence in Katrin's heart.

Not long into the next morning, they came to a ruined structure. Those fleeing the battle had by now spread out and the pursuers came less frequently, yet Katrin felt anything but safe.

Though the place stood tumbled stone from stone and overgrown with bracken, Katrin thought there might be some remnants of food there—a foolish thought, as it proved, since something else entirely awaited inside.

"Ye wait here," she told Da and his two young helpers, one supporting him on either side. They had become, so, like one being.

"Nay—" Da began. She ignored him.

As she stepped to the door of the dwelling she drew her sword. And was met, when she stepped in, by what was very nearly her own reflection—a man, as dirty and tattered as she, standing in a like attitude with a sword in his hand. Five other men sat in dirty straw behind him. Eating.

Her heart leaped sickeningly. She stared into the man's dark eyes and he into hers. After a startled moment, he lowered his sword and she did the same.

"Curse me," he told his fellows, "'tis a woman."

Who were they? Dressed in Highland garb, they were so smeared with mud and wet she could scarce recognize the tartan. Not English, that was the important thing.

"Fleeing the battle, are ye?" the man asked. He was perhaps thirty and had a gap in his front teeth. A foolish question, but then, he no doubt needed to establish she was not English either.

"Aye. I ha' my father, sore wounded, and two o' our clansmen." She jerked her head. "He is Chief MacMurtray."

"Is he, then?"

She directed her gaze at the other four men, only one of whom had got to his feet and at the food they shared. By God, she was hungry.

"Did ye find that food here?"

"Nay, this place is long empty. We stole that, we did. Fro' a house. Wee Jacky stole it." He indicated the man on his feet who, indeed, was very small.

The man to whom she'd been speaking thrust out his hand. "Ranald MacLeod," he introduced himself.

"Katrin MacMurtray."

"Bring yer men awa' in. We will share wha' we have."

It turned out that Ranald, Jack, and their companions had also been recruited under Earl John Randolph's banner, and had become separated from the rest of their clan during the battle.

"A rout, that," as Ranald put it. "How so many could be brought low by so few is beyond me."

"'Twas the archers," Katrin answered, "so I am certain."

The other three MacLeods were Jamie, Gus, and Tam. Jamie was wounded but not badly. They were making for home.

"Ye can travel along wi' us if ye've a mind," Ranald offered. "We can help ye wi' yer chief, then."

To say that Katrin felt grateful would fall far short. These were not their own men, nay—God alone knew what had happened to their own men—but they were fellow Highlanders banding together.

They shared their food, which was not much, a fact that made the gesture mean even more. Katrin wanted to wolf down what she was offered. Instead she consumed it slowly and made sure Da ate all his.

They sat in a circle on the rough stone floor and spoke of the battle, or spoke around it, for there were things none of them wanted to mention. The hideous sights seen. The savagery on both sides.

As said Tam MacLeod with a shake of his head, "'Twas cruel to put they horses through that. I saw a gey many go down." He was a young man with a slash to one arm and horror in his eyes.

So had Katrin, and it had bothered her also.

"Aye, so we will travel together," said Ranald, and Katrin felt touched by the fact that even if Robert Stewart had forsaken them, they'd found hearts far more loyal.

She and Ranald spoke of it as they moved out, leaving the ruined hut.

"We saw Laird Stewart come through after the battle," she told him. "I asked for help for my da. Da was sworn to Earl Randolph, ye ken, who was in turn sworn to him, and answered when he called us up."

"And what did the fine Laird Stewart do?" Ranald asked, not without a touch of irony.

"He rode off." The words felt sour in Katrin's mouth. "Abandoned us. Saved himself." She had a flash of Finlay throwing himself to the wolves, in sharp contrast.

Nay, do not think of that.

"I am no' surprised," replied Ranald. "He is an important man, aye? Wi' an important skin to cherish."

Katrin trusted Ranald MacLeod instinctively—or Rannie, as his fellows called him. He led his poor little band as she led hers, and in the days that followed, they often walked together. She found him easy to talk to.

When Da grew worse and could no longer walk even with

his clansmen's help, Rannie offered his own men to spell them. He did so with a grave courtesy that would put to shame the highest in the land.

They spoke less and less frequently of the battle. *Did ye see that the king got struck wi' an arrow? In the face, nay less—*

Did he live?

For a wee while, at least. Now, who knows?

Rannie was obviously curious about Katrin. *How did a lass like yoursel' end up in battle?*

I took my brother's place at Da's side wi' my brother perished.

They spoke more of home. Rannie headed for the Isle of Skye and wanted nothing more than to reach there.

Katrin wanted one thing more. As the days crawled by and the distance grew, she became more and more certain she would not have it.

Getting Da home—alive—would have to be enough, if she could manage a deed so impossible. Only then would she be able to try to imagine how to live without the man she loved.

⊰ ❖ ⊱

CHAPTER THIRTY-NINE

RANNIE AND HIS men provided them with what food they could. They proved dab hands at theft, and young Gus set snares whenever and wherever they stopped for the night.

All too soon, Katrin lost any hope of guessing where they were. Rannie had chosen a route that differed from what the army had followed on the way down—no doubt many of those in flight did so. He moved due north, pressing the pace when possible, and announced it gladly when he estimated they'd crossed the border and were back in Scotland.

She breathed a little easier then, but not a lot. These marches, disputed territory for centuries, were prime for English invasion, which meant they remained far from safe.

She knew one thing for certain—they would not have made it back to Scotland at all but for Ranald and his band of MacLeods. Da soon took a fever, and the wound in his thigh, far from clean, caused constant pain.

None of them had hope of getting clean. Katrin had never been so filthy, but at least back on Scottish soil she began to sleep better. And to dream.

Most of the dreams were brief, terrible things, memories from the battle. She awoke sweating, screams caught in her throat. Once or twice she awoke weeping, and she not the only one of their group to do so.

She dreamed over and over again of Finlay throwing himself to the English so she could get away. The look in his eyes just before he'd leaped forward. So terrible—and so brave and bright—was that memory, she had to build a wall around it lest the pain strike her down.

And then there was another dream, deep and wonderful and terrible all at the same time.

A quiet chamber where she lay dying. How she knew she was dying, she could not say, but aye, this she knew. She lay upon a bed covered in furs, with a bolster beneath her head, and she could see her own hands lying upon the covers. Aged hands they were, thin and frail, skin over bone. Yet hers all the same.

A woman bent over her, and the odd thing was that Katrin both did and did not know her. She had a thick braid of brown hair that fell over one shoulder as she leaned down, and eyes the color of the sea on a windy day. Not precisely young either, this woman, but of middle years.

"Mam," she said, "ye maun try to drink something."

A cup was tilted to Katrin's lips. The smell of the contents turned her stomach.

Was the woman—this woman—her daughter? To be sure, she must be. Katrin's mind groped for a name but could not find one.

She croaked painfully, "Where is your father?"

"He is here." The woman glanced over her shoulder. "I bade him tak' some rest, but he would no' leave ye."

Katrin nodded. She should let her beloved husband go find some rest. But she wanted him. Needed him. "Have I been selfish?" she asked her daughter. "Have I asked too much of him?"

"Nay, mam. The two o' ye tak' as ye must fro' each other. Now drink. The healer says ye must. For Da, if no' for the rest o' us."

The rest. She frowned with the difficulties of thinking. How many children did she have? How many grandchildren? Already it faded away, and her not yet gone. How would she remember later, when she needed to? How would she remember him?

In sudden panic she demanded, "I want your da. I want him now."

The woman—her daughter—gave a sad smile. "Now, there is the Caledonian princess."

She rose and moved away. A man took her place.

He too was aged, with a mane of white hair that flowed over his shoulders and blue-green eyes like the sea on a windy day. A strong face, broad in the forehead, lined from the years. All the years.

"Deathan," she said, and reached out to grip his hands. "Deathan, I must go ahead. I fear I must go ahead without you. I did so try to stay. Stay here with you."

Tears flooded his eyes. Strong he was, and so seldom had she seen him weep. When they'd lost their wee babe that time so long ago. When his brother, the chief, had died, leaving the place open for him. when her deerhound had perished—

Many things he might say to her now. He could beg her to fight against the weakness that beset her, to try harder. To stay with him.

For he could no more live without her than she could without him.

Instead he told her, his voice a fog of grief and pain, "I understand."

She reached for his face, stroked the grizzled beard that grew upon his cheek. "I am sorry."

He bent his head over her hands and whispered, "I will follow ye, Darlei. As always, I will find ye."

His tears fell upon her fingers, the last thing she felt in that world.

Katrin awoke in the heather, her heart hammering. For an instant part of her was still there in that dim room, part of her still with him. As always she would be.

She had no doubt of what she had seen. A past time, a past existence, it had been. Part of the third story Finlay had told, of Darlei and Deathan, yet beyond what he had shared. Was it merely a story? Or something more? *A life the two of them had in truth shared.*

If so, a terrible parting. Yet he said he would follow her. An aged man, had he died soon after? Or did he mean he would follow her from life to life? Would thus find her.

As, perhaps, he had.

Katrin lay there staring up at the sky while the wonder, the possibilities, and the belief washed over her. What if the stories Finlay had told were not just stories? What if the scenes she beheld in her dreams were real memories? She, Liadan, who had stood in the sun, she, Bradana, who had played on the harp, she, Darlei, who had learned to defend herself, and she, Hulda, who had fought her way back to him?

Had Finlay come to Murtray for a purpose far more vital than entertainment? Had he told her those beautiful tales for a reason—so she would remember him? Recall all they had been to one another…

No stories, no dreams. Memories.

And if she had remembered? If she now recalled and founded a belief in life after life after life after life…the memories, the love? Only too late.

For he was lost to her now, was he not? Dead somewhere back on the broken ground of a foreign land.

Life gave no assurances. Neither did love—none other than the repeated promise from the man she loved that he would find her—as Finlay had. They were not promised a life together. But och, how would she live on, having glimpsed and heard all of what they'd shared?

She rose feeling much like that old woman, in the chilly dawn. Her party made their way steadily, if slowly, north and westward, the country becoming more hospitable as they went. Here, householders sometimes gave them food and often a roof for the night, wanting in return only to hear news of the great battle fought in the south.

From one such householder who had heard from other soldiers passing through, they learned that King David had been taken prisoner, and it pierced all of them to the heart. Caught hiding beneath a bridge, it was said, his reflection in the water betraying him to the English knights. He had taken not one arrow to his face, but two. Despite that, he had fought his captors most valiantly before being taken.

He had been hauled away south to London.

A blow for Scotland, that. One from which Katrin did not know they might recover.

So many lost. So many—

But nay, she could not let herself think of that yet.

Her main worry remained her da, whose condition deteriorated steadily. At a place called Lanark, they found a physician who treated Da out of pity, since they had no silver to pay.

After, he took Katrin aside. An older man, the physician had kind gray eyes. He did not give her false hope.

"Mistress, I take it ye still ha' far to travel?"

"Aye. Far."

"If ye were not on a journey, I would recommend removal of that leg. But he would not withstand travel, after."

"I maun get him home." It had become her one goal, if a half-crazed one.

The physician shook his head. "I will tell you truly, I doubt he will make it."

"But—" Katrin gulped back her panic. "He is strong."

"Aye, so he may have been. Once."

Katrin took that like a blow to the gut. They were all debilitated. Beyond spent.

"I will give ye some medicines to take with ye. For the fever."

"I ha' nay money to pay."

"No matter."

Aye, he'd been kind. But he'd been terribly certain.

If Da did not make it home, what was she to do? What would become of the clan? Their chief gone and no heir. Many of their men who'd gone away to fight would not come home. They would be left destitute.

She would have to step up and lead, if she was the only one remaining. Marry one day and provide—

Nay, she could not think of that either. Not yet. Possibly not ever.

She decided on that day, standing outside the physician's home in the autumn sunlight, that she would do best not to think at all. Just get Da home, if she could.

She gestured to Rannie, who stepped up to her.

"Katrin?" They were long on a first-name basis.

"Rannie," she said for his ears alone, "the physician does no' think my da will make it back to Murtray. 'Tis a long way yet. If ye and yer fellows wish to go on wi'out us, wi'out the burden we have been—"

He studied her with his gentle, dark eyes. "Well, now—'tis hard news to bear, that."

"Aye." She did her best not to cry but she was tired. *Tired.*

"Wha' ha' ye there?" he asked.

"Some powders the physician gave me."

"Those just might do him some good. So we will carry on helping ye for the now, as we ha' been, aye?"

"Ye be a good man, Rannie MacLeod."

"I would no' be too certain about that." He gave a weary grin. "But I do my best."

"Ye shall ha' yer reward in paradise."

"Aye, just so long as that does no' come too soon."

CHAPTER FORTY

WHEN FINLAY WOKE in the soaking grass, he did not know where he was. Indeed, at first he did not know *who* he was. He lay blinking at the lowering gray sky and tried to determine it.

His brain refused to work properly. Filled with a swirl of dirty gray mist, it failed to fasten upon any of the familiar touchstones that usually came to a man at waking. A room, a bed, a day of the week, or the tasks of that day. He merely *was*, without *who* or *when*.

Some facts did filter through to him. It was raining, big drops that spat down from the sky. He felt cold, and he hurt all over. The left side of his face stung badly. And some great weight pressed him to the turf, pinning him from the knees down.

In the distance—or mayhap not so distant—was a great roar of sound. It seemed to come at him in waves like a heartbeat, louder and softer. Some ancient knowledge within him stirred and told him that was the sound of a battle.

One in which he had fought? Aye, that made sense.

Whom had he been battling? Dacha's men? But nay, surely they had defeated Dacha long ago. Mican's crew, then. Aye, they had been defeated also, but the young bucks of that clan had risen up much later, when he was aged, and came to attack…

He had gone out to fight them despite his age. It was what a chief did. He had not returned home from that fight, home to the woman he loved.

He blinked at the sky again, doubtful it was that battle either. Despite the pain throughout his body, he did not feel aged. He did not—

With a great effort of will, he sat up. It was not easy, and he had to battle for it because once in a sitting position he could see he was surrounded by dead men.

One lay across his legs, but others—five in all, for his mind succeeded in counting them—lay heaped around him, one or two staring with sightless eyes at that same sky.

By God. *By God.*

He drew great, gulping breaths of air, staring around himself. Away back the way he was facing, the ground sloped downward, littered with other dead men. At least, he assumed they were dead, or if not, they should be on the move. For aye, that was fighting he could hear away in the distance. And at a length, he could just glimpse a stone monument that seemed to float above the ground.

Other men ran past him, all going away from the conflict, none of them so much as glancing at him.

A thought came to him, clear and bright. He must get home. Home to Liadan. She would be worried for him.

That knowledge, above any other, got him to his feet, an act that took all his strength. Once there he surveyed the dead men who surrounded him.

Not dressed as he was, in a kilt and leggings, but in leather and metal armor, and rough tunics. A word filtered into his mind. *English.*

He had a sword in his hand, the hilt clutched so tight he had not released it even when he fell, knocked flat, no doubt, by the man who'd landed across his legs.

Despite the rain the blade bore flecks of blood, and the men around him bore terrible wounds.

Had he been the one to slay them?

He staggered a bit and raised a hand to the side of his face, which felt flayed. Upon inspection, he found he bore other wounds also. A slash to the chest, not too deep. A narrow cut to one arm. His knuckles, bashed and laid open.

By God, he hurt.

But it seemed he was alive in this place where so many others were not. And he had a purpose, a guiding purpose that at the moment he could not quite recall.

A man ran past him up the slope. Near enough that Finlay might almost have reached out and snagged his arm. He wore a kilt liberally splashed with blood, and his breath labored so hard in his lungs, the sound of it preceded him.

Finlay called out, "Where are we, man? Wha' is this place?"

The man's feet faltered and he stared. A trail of blood ran into his eye and he blinked it away. "Eh?"

"Where are we?" Finlay repeated.

"England! The battle is lost, man, and the king taken!"

The king. The Ard Ri? A great shame that they had not been able to defend him.

"Get yoursel' awa' out o' here," the man advised, "if ye want to live." And he pelted off.

Finlay wanted to live, aye, for he must get home. To Liadan. She would be waiting. Standing outside in the sunlight.

Again he assessed his situation. He wore a pack, though its contents rattled every time he moved, a fact that caused him a measure of grief he did not comprehend. The dead men surrounding him all bore weapons. He put his sword into its scabbard and without real intention searched the dead men. One had a pack with a few coins, which he took. Another a small store of food, which he also took, along with a good knife. Two knives—one for his belt and one for his boot.

Not very honorable, stealing from dead men, but he needed the means to get home. Had he not promised to return to her? In the confusion of his mind, only that promise remained.

When he bent to search the dead men, he grew so dizzy he thought he'd fall. His searching fingers found a great, bloody lump at the back of his head—surely he'd struck it on a rock when the big brute knocked him down.

That was why he could not remember. It would come back to him.

He had to take great gulps of air in order to stay on his feet. Men still streamed past him. He supposed he should take the same route, since it was away.

He set out for home, though he did not at once know where that lay.

HE SLEPT BENEATH a tangle of gorse that night, if sleeping it could be called. He seemed rather to slip in and out of consciousness, shivering in the cold, for he was soaking wet. When morning came, he ate some of the slain man's food—not a lot, for his stomach rebelled over it—and drank from a stream. Moved off with the rising sun at his back.

Why west? He did not know and merely followed instinct.

When he heard hoofbeats coming from behind, he ducked into the dying heather and lay flat like a hare before the hawk, though he did not know quite why he did that either. Knights came pounding through, cutting men down. He saw two fall at some distance from him. Three. Four.

He lay in the turf until the earth stopped shaking, and wondered how he was ever going to get home.

After that, he walked. And walked. *He walked.*

He hid when the pursuers thundered by, but that became less and less necessary as he gained some distance from the battle. He rested when he had to and consumed the dead Englishman's food. He slept. He dreamed.

The dreams, deep and sometimes wonderful, sometimes terrible, added to his confusion when he woke from them. He dreamed of his wife, Liadan—aye, he knew it was she—but most distressingly, she wore a number of differing faces. That of a lass standing beside him in the sunshine, a proud woman with a deerhound at her side. A princess with silver eyes. A Norse warrior sailing out in a boat with a prow like a dragon, determined to battle for his sake.

For his sake.

He woke shaking, not always with cold but with a welter of emotions. Fear on her behalf. Longing. Love.

How could she be all those women, and yet one? How was he to return to her if he did not know where she was?

He discovered that the pack on his back held the pieces of a harp, now shattered, its spine snapped in two. For a long time he held those pieces in his hands and pondered as to why he possessed such a thing, and why, if it was ruined, he had not discarded it. Why he did not discard it now.

For he wore a sword also, and he was a warrior. Was he not? He had slain five men back there at the place where he'd awakened.

How could he be a harper as well?

❖

CHAPTER FORTY-ONE

THE SEASON WORE on as Katrin and her band traveled, each day blending into the next, borne on the necessity of continuing to put one foot in front of the other. The farther they moved from the borders, the more they relied on the generosity of their countrymen and women. Householders continued to gladly lend them a roof for the night in exchange for no more than an account of the distant-to-them battle, and provided what food they could.

Once, at the cottage of a widow, they stayed three days while helping the woman prepare for winter, but Katrin dared not linger longer. Da yet clung to life, but no more than that. His fever raged, and sometimes he was out of his head.

Twice, he asked for Geordie. "My son—I want to see my son before I die. I maun leave Murtray in good hands."

"Da, ye are no' dyin'." But Katrin knew she lied to him, as did everyone in their stalwart little group.

He had no hands in which to leave the clan, but hers. Which at the moment were battered, and burdened, and filthy. She need only get him home.

Offsetting the hospitality they received, the way grew more difficult. They covered less ground per day, and on a few mornings, while sleeping out, snow fell. Katrin slept curled around her da in an effort to keep him warm, the clansmen on either side of them. Sometimes she dreamed of Finlay standing before her in his fine green cloak, his gaze compelling on hers.

Sometimes she did not dream at all, her heart too weary.

At Oban, they met the sea. Da was seen by another physician there, it being a sizeable town, and the man bent to charity.

He merely shook his head over Da's condition.

"The wound is filthy."

"I ha' kept it as clean as I could."

"Ye will lose yer father to the fever, I do no' doubt."

"Can I get him home first?" It had become her one goal, with Finlay gone.

Do not think of that.

The physician, a Master Roderick Campbell, gazed at her long. She thought he would answer harshly, for he seemed that sort of man. But to her surprise, he softened.

"Ye travel farther north?"

"Aye, to Murtray."

"I ha' a client wi' a horse and cart who might take ye part o' the way. He is himsel' going home fro' a consultation wi' me."

"I ha' a party—"

"At least your father may ride."

When she went out from the physician's house, though, she discovered she would soon not have a party. Rannie and his mates very apologetically told her they had found a ship they might take over the water to Skye.

"We ha' just arranged for it," he confessed with regret in his eyes. "I hate to abandon ye here—"

He held out his hand, but she went into his arms instead, giving him a fierce hug. "We would no' have got this far wi'out ye. I will be forever grateful. Ye maun do as ye must."

"Aye, but how will ye get home?"

She told him about the physician's offer.

"Ye be a courageous lass," he declared in parting, "and I am that glad I met ye."

"And ye, all o' ye"—she included the others in her glance—"are men o' honor."

She shed tears at that parting and blessed those who went

from her. Then she, Rabbie, Davey, and Da awaited the physician's client, hoping against desperate hope he would appear.

He did. It was snowing when they set out north and homeward. Truly homeward now, for was not the sea there beside them just the same as at Murtray? Snow covered the ground before they'd traveled half a day, and when their benefactor, called Andrews, reached his own home, he offered them a roof for the night. They accepted and slept warm by the fire.

Once again, Katrin dreamed.

A strange and terrible dream was this one, and no mistake. For she dreamed she awakened affrighted in a dim and dark place, one she did not immediately recognize. She rose from a bed as at some signal given, with haste. Trouble. There was trouble at hand.

Not alone. A man arose also from the bed beside her. She turned to look at him, and it was as if she saw him twice—once with the discerning gaze acquired over the course of a long life, and again with the eyes of love.

He had aged, this man, this husband she adored. Ach, when had that happened? While they tumbled through the years living and loving together, so comfortable that she had not heeded the passage of time? But ja, many the years had been. His mane of auburn hair had turned silver. His beard also, and the hair upon his chest with which she was so familiar.

The feel of him—the feeling remained the same.

From beyond this chamber they shared, she could hear voices calling, footsteps pounding past. Men crying the alarm. Hurrying for weapons.

Attack. Their holding here on the edge of the sea fell under attack. They would go forward to fight and possibly to die.

Standing there beside the bed they had shared so many years, she drew a breath.

"Norse," she said. "Again." It had been a number of seasons since they had fallen beneath the eye of the wolves from the sea. She was Norse, ja, but so long had she lived in this Scottish stronghold with him, she very nearly failed to remember it.

Ignoring her need to dress, clad only in her sleeping gown, she walked around the bed to him. Her hair hung over her shoulder in a braid, the fair strands now liberally mixed with white.

"Quarrie, husband, do not go out to battle." Surely she had said these words before, in another time? "Let Airlee"—their son, their firstborn—"lead the fight."

Her husband's lips twisted in a wry smile. "I will be more than glad, Hulda, to let Airlee lead the fight. But"—his eyes hardened to granite— "I will be there. I will stand for this place I love."

Her stomach tightened into a knot of pure pain. Not this. Please, by any god who listens. Not this again. *She could not bear it.*

"Husband"—she reached for him, put her hands to either side of his face—"I have a bad feeling for this. What if I asked you keep from going out?"

"Wha' if I asked ye the same?"

"Then I would hold back."

"Would ye?" Clearly he did not believe her, thought she would lie to him if she must.

She pressed her body up against his. "I fear—"

"Stop wi' fearing, wife. Ha' ye learned naught? We always return to one another, aye? No matter wha' comes between."

"Ja, but the between *hurts. It hurts so."*

"Hulda, ye ken I would do anything for ye. Aught but lay aside my sword."

"Quarrie, if we are to be parted now, if we do manage against the tide of time and fate to meet together in another life—will you promise me one thing?"

"What more to promise than that I will return to ye? I will find ye, Hulda. Always."

"And when you do, in the next life, let it not be as a warrior. Because I cannot endure this fear upon fear of losing you in battle. Even after all this time, I cannot."

"And wha' else should I be, than wha' I ha' been?"

"I do not care. A smith, a trainer of horses, a builder of boats, a carver of stone—any man who does not march out to die."

"A harper?" He said it lightly, as if in jest, but his eyes were serious, holding her gaze, holding her soul.

"Aye, that. A harper to play sweet songs for me and tell all the old tales. Give me those ancient songs and I promise to fall right back into your arms."

"Ah, Hulda." A glimmer of a smile touched his face. "Ye would fall into my arms anyway."

She would. But she said, "It is a promise, then. You will return to me as nay warrior but a bonny harper instead."

And she kissed him, kissed him to seal the pledge, and so he could not say what she suspected he must—that a man was who he was, whatever time and fate made of him.

When the searing kiss ended, she whispered against his lips, "For love of me, husband. Keep this vow for love of me."

Katrin woke from that dream shuddering with cold and shivering in the dawn, a hollow place opened up inside her. She—she had been Hulda, aye. Finlay had also been an habitant of the tale, one Quarrie MacMurtray. And—

He had done as she had asked.

He had done as she had asked.

And it had not mattered, for she'd lost him anyway.

CHAPTER FORTY-TWO

KATRIN AND HER party reached home on a cold, clear day with snow in the wind and the ground iron-hard beneath their feet. She brought her da back alive, but so weak she feared every breath might be his last. Those breaths came with a hard rasp. She was no longer sure what kept him clinging to his life. Stubbornness, perhaps, for he had run out of any other strength.

As, in truth, had Katrin and her companions, Rabbie and Davey. They were so tired and spent, so starved and chilled, they moved by rote more than by will. Their makeshift litter fashioned from Brada's wrappings had long since fallen to pieces and been replaced by one they fashioned from spruce boughs. The three of them rotated toting their chief, to provide some respite. Da was not as heavy as he had been, for the weight just melted from him.

Since parting with the physician's client with the cart some distance north of Oban, they had covered most the rest of the distance on foot. Katrin's hands were a mess, the palms blistered over other blisters, those of her companions in like condition. None of them spoke to one another, being too weary for words.

A stop at the fortress of a friendly neighbor to the south broke the journey, and when the chief could not persuade Katrin to leave her father for the time in his care and travel on without him, he provided a pony and litter for the rest of the distance.

Da needed to die at home in his own bed, and that could only occur soon.

When they breasted the rise that led from the headland and

on down to their own holding, now accompanied by some of the neighboring MacEwan men, she could have wept. Davey did weep, the tears trickling unchecked down his face, and Rabbie turned to Katrin.

"Mistress, I did no' think we would mak' it. I did no' believe."

"'Twas your valiance, yours and Davey's, that got us home."

They received a fierce welcome and homecoming. Others of their men—not many—had filtered home ahead of them, and they had brought word of their chief being lost, Katrin and many others with him.

Katrin saw her father into the hands of their own physician, who looked very grave indeed at the sight of him, and went to her chamber to wash and don clean clothing, a luxury for which she had not dared let her mind reach.

But once there, she merely stood in the center of the chamber and stared. *This place.* This was where she'd been with Finlay. A glorious joining it had been, of body and spirit, which now seemed no more real than Finlay's stories. The dreams she'd had on the trail. Both of which had seemed as real as life.

She crumpled to the floor, where she huddled like someone broken, and sobbed. One of the maids, Janet, found her there and tried to help her up. Called for a bath and stripped her of her clothing, all the things she wore going straight into the fire. Fit for naught but burning, so the kindly Janet declared.

After that, she was fed and put her to bed. There were things Katrin knew she needed to do. See to her da, be with him if— well, *if.* Make sure Rabbie and Davey had the reward they deserved.

But all that slipped away from her once she was laid between the clean blankets, and after the briefest of battles, she let it go.

How long she slept, she did not know. She slept without dreaming now, feeling safe for the first time in days without number. Not until Janet gently shook her awake did she remember where she was.

Home.

"Mistress, I am that sorry. 'Tis the chief. He calls for ye."

If ever there was a sentence to draw her from her rest, it was that one. Katrin rose with her heart thumping and, pausing only to wind a shawl over her sleeping gown, went out with her hair hanging loose down her back.

Da's chamber lay mere steps away. When she reached it, Katrin found Janet's words had not been quite accurate. Da had not called for her; the physician had.

There were others in the room ahead of her, the place in shadow with only dim light coming through the windows. Disoriented, Katrin struggled to grasp the time of day before deciding it did not matter.

Da's advisors were there, as was the physician, who turned to her with a look of deep regret.

"Mistress, I think his time has come. He will no' hold on much longer."

Already had he held on so long. All those terrible, hard, and dangerous miles from England, him wanting only to be at home.

She started forward. The physician stopped her with a hand to her arm. "'Tis no' the wound taking him after all, nor even the fever, but an inflammation o' the lungs. Ye can hear wi' what difficulty he breathes."

She could hear that, aye. All that way home, and she unable to keep him warm or dry.

She nodded and went to the side of the bed. Knelt down and took Da's hands in hers.

He was awake, aware. His eyes met hers and clung, even as he fought for breath.

"Lass."

"Da. Och, Da. Nay, do no' try to speak."

"There are things—maun be said."

Were there? Katrin supposed so. She wanted desperately to reassure him, this man who had guided his clan so well for so long. Seeing him as he was, she wanted even more than that, for him to find relief.

"Ye ha' a valiant heart," he told her. "As brave as ever I ha' seen. Thank ye for gettin' me home." Those words did not come easily or quickly. He fought for them.

Tears flooded Katrin's eyes. She squeezed his fingers hard.

"I place the clan's welfare in your hands, Katrin. There is no one I consider worthier. Promise me—"

The wheezing in his chest rose to a terrible storm and she had to wait with him through it, till he found breath to speak again.

"Anything, Da—"

"Promise me ye will marry. A good man. Someone who will stand beside ye and help ye lead."

Och, but she did not want to give that promise. Anything *but* that. She did not want to wed where there could not be love, and for her, all love had fled the world.

But—

There was love, and there was duty.

Even though she knew that very well, she did not speak.

"Katrin, lass?"

"I will do my very best to defend this clan in any way I can."

His fingers, still gripping hers, tightened spasmodically. "Lass, ye canna stand alone. Other chiefs will see it as—weakness."

He was slipping from her, sliding through her hands. She saw the mist come to his eyes.

She gave him what promise she could. "I will wed, aye Da, if I can find the man worthy o' the place."

"Wise lass." He closed his eyes before he whispered, "Och, yer ma is here, come for me. And Geordie!"

As simply as that, the breaths for which he'd been battling ceased. The chamber became horrifyingly quiet until Katrin, her head lowered to her father's shoulder, whispered.

"Go to them, Da. Go on!"

The wheel of life turned. Of all the things she had learned, both joyful and terrible, she knew that. Finlay had told her they traveled on its torturous turning from life to life, meeting and parting, and meeting again.

Let Da meet those he loved. Let him find joy in it. But for her—

By God, she felt so alone.

She knelt there beside her father's bed a long while until she found the strength to rise, shake off the paralyzing grief, and assume the mantle that had fallen upon her. She now led the clan, and for her da's sake, if not for that of all the folk who relied upon her, she must do well by them.

Keep her promise? Och, well, that was another matter. For with Finlay gone, where was the man worthy of the place in her heart?

CHAPTER FORTY-THREE

For Finlay, the dead Englishman's food did not last nearly long enough, and the weather deteriorated around him. He knew not where he was, and he avoided cottages with instinctive wariness just as he avoided towns. His condition grew steadily worse as he moved north and westward, putting one foot in front of the other as he had for so many years on the road.

He chose his direction by the same instinct that impelled his feet, that kept him battling. As if there was something inside him that knew where he should be bound, even if he could not name that place.

Often, upon waking under some hedge or beside a wall, he had no idea who or where he was. When he was walking though, pieces of memories tended to come floating in.

They were akin, these memories, to the things he saw in his dreams, so much so he wondered if it was merely those dreams he recalled, and not actual memories at all. He saw most often the bonny, golden-haired girl standing outside the roundhouse in the sun, smiling. Smiling at him.

But there was, too, the tall girl with the deerhound at her side. And the wild-eyed lass riding a brown pony, laughing and looking back over her shoulder at him. And an older woman, aged, standing in the firelight, who stared into his eyes and said, "When you return to me, in the next life, let it not be as a warrior. Because I cannot endure this fear upon fear of losing you in battle. Even after all this time, I cannot."

All these memories—if so they were—warmed even as they baffled him, brought a measure of comfort upon his dogged and terrible journey. When they faded, he was lost again, left with a single conviction: *Four women. All the same woman.*

His wounds healed, the cuts on his hands first, even though he had to use them most. The lump to the back of his head. The slash to his cheek healed badly, but covered by beard, it did not seem to matter.

From time to time, he glimpsed others who might be refugees from the battle, fleeing like himself. A few called to him but he did could not be sure of them, friend from foe. Was he still in England? The place of that terrible conflict. He had no way to tell. He grew steadily weaker, the great vitality housed within beginning to flicker and wane.

A cold day it was when he followed a mere track of a road, barely a rut between the dying heather, through an area mostly empty of habitation. To his right, a stream flowed. To his left were the heights of five mountains, those of which it seemed he should know the names.

Ahead, a rare sight—a small hovel of a cottage, huddled stone on stone beside the track. He knew very well he should make his way up and around the brae to avoid it, but he lacked the strength.

He meant to trudge on by as swiftly as he could. But in quickening his pace he stumbled and went down beside the drystone wall that fronted the track, his fingers grasping for it. They missed, and he went down.

He felt the hard, cold ground coming up to meet him, and then no more until a voice sounded in his ear and a pair of determined arms urged him up again.

"Here, now. Here, now."

He came to himself, at least bits of himself, and obeyed that strong urging. Someone helped him to his feet. Supported him as he struggled.

"Awa' in wi' ye now. A few steps more, only."

The next he knew, he awoke in a dim room. A fire burned nearby, but it did little to lift the gloom cast by a low roof and no windows he could see. He felt warm but curiously wooden-headed, and so weak he had no words for it.

"So ye've come awake, ha' ye?" A voice, the same surely that he had heard outside, along the track. A woman's voice.

She appeared beside him and eased herself down with a small groan of discomfort. She was aged, with a crown of silver-white hair and a face full of weathering, her voice cracked by time.

"I was beginning to wonder if ye would wake at all, and me wi' ye stretched out here beside my hearth. Wha' to do wi' ye?"

Finlay said nothing in reply, did nothing save stare at her.

"Fleeing yon battle, are ye?" she asked kindly. "The one awa' in the south?"

"Aye." His voice did not sound like his own.

"Aye, so I have had others moving through here, a few, and some hurt sore bad. I ha' helped them as I may, being the loyal Scotswoman tha' I am. But I am a widow on my own, ye ken, and ha' no' much to spare."

"Wha' is this place?"

"Kintail. Laird Campbell's land. Where are ye bound, laddie?"

"Home."

"And where might that be?"

"Cursed if I can recall."

She pursed her lips and tutted at him. "Och, ye ha' a great, terrible lump to the back o' yer head. I reckon that's knocked the sense out o' ye, but I do no' doubt all will come back in time."

Finlay doubted it.

"Wha' is yer name?"

"Ardahl. Ardahl MacCormac." It came from nowhere.

"Aye, and does that no' sound like a name fro' Ireland? What ye be doing here, then?"

"I am no' sure."

"Well, ye sound like a Scotsman true, and no' Irishman I ever met. When my husband, Ernie, was still alive we sometimes hired Irish lads for the harvest, ye understand. They did no' sound like ye. But ye no' be wearing a tartan. Just that gray kilt and nay plaidie at all."

"The only name I recall is Ardahl."

"Well, I canna help that, but mayhap ye'll remember more as yer head heals. Wha' I can help is the state o' ye. Ye need feedin'. Ye are naught but bones, and I am no' surprised ye went down outside my door."

She was kind. "Ye be kind."

"Tush, tush, ye let me do as I will. One thing for certain, ye canna be out in the cold or ye will lie down beneath a gorse bush and die. 'Tis snowing out there, ye ken."

"Is it?"

"Aye, so, but ye be safe and warm here. My name be Molly, but ye can call me Mol, as everyone does."

She bustled off and returned carrying a wooden bowl. With one arm, remarkably strong for an aged woman, she urged him up. "Drink o' this. Broth, it is."

He drank obediently. The broth was thin but warm and went down easy.

"There now. Ye rest and sleep as ye need, for 'tis the best healer, and we ha' nay other to hand."

And as she moved around the tiny place, leaving him to that rest, she began to sing in her ancient, cracked voice. An old song that surely he knew.

He slept and woke and slept again. Molly cared for him as if he were her own son, and a wonder that was, for it had been long and long since he'd known a mother's care.

Sometimes when she knew he was awake, she chattered to him with soft Highland words. Mayhap she did that when he slept also; he could not say. He dreamed, but not anything he remembered upon waking.

She had little to give him beyond broth and care. For all he knew, she beggared herself to feed him. No one came to the door, and it made him think it must be a lonely life she lived most the time.

She had a few animals, a cow at the other end of the bothy and some hens outside, for once he grew stronger she fed him eggs. The cow, so she said, was nearly dry, she having sold the last calf earlier on.

"No' but that her milk would be good for heartening ye."

His strength returned, under her care. Frighteningly, his memory did not, save in those elusive pieces.

Thoughts of a woman who loved him. Of long journeys upon the land. Most of all, though, memory lay in the music, in the songs Molly sang. Those stirred something in his heart and in his mind.

"I ken that song," he said one day as he sat combing fleeces for her. "I just canna remember the name o' it."

"'The Lover Lost,'" she told him, and just like that the whole of it came flooding upon him, words and all.

"Aye, so." Arrested, he stared at nothing, his fingers poised.

Molly came and sat beside him. "D'ye still no' remember yer place or trade, Ardahl?"

"Nay."

"For here's a curious thing. Ye carry a sword like any warrior or clansman returning from yon battle. All right and proper. Yet—I had a wee peek in yer pack. I hope ye do no' mind."

"I do no'." God knew, what was hers had been his, and what was his must be hers.

"Let me show ye wha' I found."

She went and fetched his pack from beside the wall. Tattered and filthy it was, but she opened it carefully and extracted—

Aye. A harp. The one he carried. The pieces of it.

For an instant, his senses swam. He went so dizzy he had to clutch the old woman's arm.

"Wha' is it, lad?"

He took the broken back of the instrument into his hands. It had not fractured cleanly. The pieces had come apart jagged.

Like his heart.

A name appeared in his mind. *Bradana.* But nay, that was not it. *Brada.*

"My harp. This is mine."

Her face brightened. "But the sword?"

"Mine also."

"A curious thing, that! Is there nay a song about it?"

"The minstrel boy to war is gone, in the ranks o' death ye will find him."

"Aye, that is it. What a lovely voice ye do ha'."

He hadn't realized that he'd sung the words. He felt odd. Unsteady. His fingers caressed the shattered wood in his hands.

Molly said, "Here is the rest o' it here in yer pack. I do no' think it can be repaired."

"Nay. Och, nay."

But the songs were still there. The songs remained with him.

CHAPTER FORTY-FOUR

Finlay remained with Molly and worked her croft as the winter came on, even though his heart longed with a deep and persistent ache to reach home. Since he could not remember where home might be, it seemed best not to stir even after his strength began to return.

He felt he owed her, this old woman who had doubtless saved his life. Strong as she was, she struggled visibly with the chores she faced, doubly difficult in the cold, and those tasks grew easier and easier for him.

She called him Ardahl, or lad, or more frequently laddie. As the days passed, a rare and true affection grew between them.

She sang the old songs for him, all that she could recall. And like a dam breaking, those songs brought others to him, words and tunes and all, his fingers twitching for want of the strings. With the songs came pieces of memory. Places he had sung and played. Grand halls and humble cottages not unlike this one.

The pieces of himself, coming back to him, and with them an increase in his longing.

For the girl with the golden hair who stood in the sunshine.

Sometimes her name whispered in his mind so fleeting he could only just catch it. *Liadan.* But the love, oh, the love found him in full.

He and Molly sometimes sang together at their work, and then in the evenings to pass the time, his smooth voice blending wondrously with her sweet, fragile one. She clapped her hands like a young girl in delight over their singing.

"So many songs ye do know," she said one evening after he'd begun recalling more tunes than she knew. "D'ye think ye were a shanachie?"

"Aye, I do think so."

"Then why the sword? And why awa' in the battle?"

That refused to come to him. Indeed, he scarce recalled the battle, though he knew full well he had come from there.

One market day when the weather was not too harsh and Molly had some eggs to sell, she persuaded Finlay to accompany her. She gave him her husband's kilt and plaid to wear, and even his boots, as Finlay's own were too worn.

"How braw ye look," she said, smiling. "Everyone will think ye my long-lost son."

Finlay wondered then if in her heart Molly wanted him to stay. Part of him would not mind. Yet the wheel of his life turned with him upon it, toward what he needed quite desperately but could not quite see.

Folk in the market town of Kintail were curious about him. Molly was forced to pause and explain his presence again and again. He gleaned news of the battle, which was being called the Battle of Neville's Cross, and what a disaster it had been for the Scots. The king captured and held in chains in far-off London. Scotsmen killed in their hundreds. Scots lords taken for ransom, or slain.

"It has broken our back, it has," one old man declared, and Finlay thought of his harp, no doubt shattered against a stone.

When folk in the town asked where he was from, he answered only, "North and west o' here," quite certain of that much, though not sure how he knew.

When a woman eyed him up and down and asked Molly outright, "Will he be stayin' wi' ye, then?" He and Molly exchanged a look but gave her no answer.

They were quieter on the way home, both with thoughts crowding their minds. Would Molly ask him to stay? To become in truth the son she likely thought him?

The last thing he wanted to do was hurt her feelings. But he felt as if a great wind lay at his back, pushing him toward what he could not see.

They had nearly reached the croft when Molly began to sing softly in time with her footsteps, as one did to make the way shorter.

An instant memory flooded Finlay's mind. Walking—nay, marching—with a great body of men. Someone walked beside him. A lass, a woman she was, though dressed like any warrior and wearing a sword at her side. Much as Molly had just done, she raised her voice, soft yet clear, in song.

Come all ye who would valiant be
Who would follow the train o' bright glory.
Where battle brings us gory fates
We follow them both soon and late.
The Gallowglass gang to die!

It hit him like a boulder rushing downhill, did that memory. Fair shattered him. All at once he was there inside the memory with all the attendant emotions. Fear and dread for the battle to come, for aye, it was into battle they were bound. A deep sense of connection with the woman beside him and love, *love*—

"Ardahl? Ardahl, lad, wha' is it?"

He had stopped walking. Molly stood on the track in front of him, gazing up into his face with worried eyes.

"Be ye ill? Is it yer head?"

"Nay." He reached out for something—anything—and clasped her hands. "There is someone. I remember—"

What had happened to her? The woman who had walked beside him so bravely and sung to raise the hearts of those around her? Had she died in the battle?

That thought delivered him a second tremendous blow, one that nearly took him to his knees. So many were said to have died in that fight. A rout, by all accounts.

"Ardahl?" Molly began to look frightened. "Wha' is it, lad?"

"Memories. Coming back to me."

"Aye, well, 'twas bound to happen." But the old woman continued to look concerned. "Let us get ye home."

Inside, she sat him down and raked up the fire before fetching him a warm drink. Days had now grown short, and a wind rose to play around the stones of the tiny place with a wail like a woman grieving.

"D'ye want to talk about it?" Molly asked, sitting down beside him.

Did he?

"Sometimes it does help. When my man died—surely the worst memory I hold, for he died right out there upon that hillside, working the land. Just dropped down as if stricken by the hand o' God—I did no' think I wanted to go on. And I could no' speak o' it, no' at all. My neighbor, Esmie, a wise woman who's since died also, forced me to. She sat me down right where ye be and told me to let it all out." Molly's faded eyes were kind. "It did help."

"There was a woman. Marching beside me on the way into the battle."

"A woman!"

"Och, so, how could that be? Indeed, she dressed hersel' like a man and carried—carried a sword. She raised her voice as we went, just the way ye did outside, to sing."

"Ah, then. Is that a memory or fancy?"

"A memory, I think." A memory. "I loved her. So very much. I love her still."

"Her name?"

"I canna recall. Her face—'tis a strong face and a beautiful one. Fair hair, ashen brown. And the smile in her eyes—" Longing struck him, so powerful it near doubled him over where he sat.

"Och, lad." Molly's eyes grew round. "And ye do no' ken

wha' happened to her?"

"Nay. *Nay.* When I came to mysel' after the battle, I was alone." Save for the dead men. "She never would ha' left me, nor I her, unless—"

Sympathy flooded Molly's eyes. "'Tis a terrible torment, no' knowing. If she did survive—where would she be?"

"I know not. But how could she survive so terrible a battle, and she a woman?"

"Did ye no' survive? And ye a harper!" Molly gave him a wobbly smile. "Ye never know."

That was the trouble, was it not? Among all the other questions that beset him, Finlay might never know what had become of the woman who'd walked beside him.

The one who held his heart.

THE WINTER CAME down swift and hard, and Finlay stayed in the little stone cottage with Molly. At first he told himself he would linger only till the weather eased and he might be away. Then he reckoned he stayed to help the old woman with all the difficult chores she performed so arduously. Hauling water up the snowy slope from the burn. Tending the beasts and guarding the roof against the wind.

His body mended and his strength came back. The gouge to his cheek was an ugly thing, but his wild red beard covered most of it. He worked hard through the days and slept well at night, though when the dreams came, they consumed him.

A bright confusion of scenes they were, all jumbled and twisted so he could scarce make sense of them. If they were meant to make sense. And no ordinary dreams, for he inhabited them, walked, breathed, and sang in them. It was as if the wheel of his life spun, giving him random glimpses, and him not knowing where the pieces fit into place.

It came to him slowly over the long months of that winter, came with an otherworldly kind of knowing—that the women he was seeing were all aspects of one. The woman that he loved.

She who stood in the bright sunlight outside the roundhouse. She with the great deerhound at her side and she with the defiant, silver eyes. She who sailed a dragon boat, and she who had walked, bravely, into battle at his side, singing.

The one thing he did not doubt was that he loved her, with a deep and unwavering devotion as fundamental to him as his breath. Where she was, he could not say. Nor did he know if he would ever be with her again in this life. Whether she be alive or dead.

But och, each time he woke from a dream or even when he recalled one—cherishing the thought of her—his heart ached to be at home. At home in her.

Old Mol watched him throughout that winter, glad that he stayed and at the same time worried for him. She proved patient with his silences and willing when he sought to talk the pieces through, weaving the threads of them into something resembling a pattern. She sang with him and laughed with him, and he knew it would be hard to leave her, just as he knew that time would come.

So it must.

It came on a day late in winter when a watery sunshine bloomed, arguing that against all odds spring would arrive. They sat by the fire together, sharing a scant breakfast of oatcakes and weak herb tea, and he recounting a dream he'd had wherein he sailed in a tiny boat far out on the ocean in company with the woman he loved, and a great gray deerhound.

"D'ye think she was yer wife then?" Molly asked.

"Aye, so she must ha' been."

"And she is the same woman, ye say, as strode into yon English battle at yer side?"

He smiled at Molly. "I ken it makes nay sense, but aye, 'tis so."

Molly hesitated. "Ye ken, lad, ye are welcome to stay wi' me. For good if ye choose."

"Aye, I do ken that, Mol." When her name came from his lips, it near sounded like *Ma*.

"But I ha' watched ye all this while and I feel there is a place ye need to be. This dream ye keep having"—for he'd had it more than once—"o' yer lass marching to battle at yer side."

"Aye?"

"Wha' is she wearing? Besides the sword, I mean."

"Why, as I ha' told, she is dressed like a man entirely. Leggings and a leather jerkin for armor and a cloak over all—"

"A kilt?"

"Aye, so."

"All the troops among whom ye be walking in this dream— they are kilted also?"

Finlay narrowed his eyes.

"Wha' color the plaid? Wha' pattern, lad?"

He gazed at her, arrested.

Molly leaned forward and laid her hand on his arm. "Find the plaid, and ye may find her."

So he would. If yet she survived.

CHAPTER FORTY-FIVE

K ATRIN LEANED FAR out over the ramparts so she could see what was happening in the bailey below. Winter had nearly gone, and the land lay raked by the storms they had endured. Near-endless storms there had been, as if they had not enough to bear without.

The ground below was a sea of muck, that being one of the woes that beset them. Another was a winter ague that had spread through the guards and many of their families. Katrin had fought it off early, surprised she had the strength. These days she seemed to have strength for naught more than facing one day after the other, doggedly.

The ancient songs had fled her life, and with them all joy. All meaning.

Aye, well, that was not strictly true. There was meaning still in shepherding her clan, in leading them through the hard winter and keeping their heads up in what seemed to be the new Scotland. News had filtered to them only rarely during the cold, dark months. None of it had been good. The king remained in English hands, and the barons had been knocked back on their heels.

God alone knew what would become of Scotland.

But that did not concern her now. The welfare of her own people and protecting her holding did. Da would want her to stand tall, to lead their folk, and so she would.

A curious thing, though—for most her life she'd half envied

Geordie, wondering why she had not been born male so she might follow Da and better serve the clan, march to war, and defend. And now she was doing just that. Fate had presented her with her heart's desire, and the pity was—

The pity was, her heart was dead within her.

Everyone around her knew it, or at least suspected. When first she'd come back from England, they had tiptoed around her, giving her time to heal. The weight of the battle—for Rabbie and Davey had spoken of it, as had the others who succeeded in making their way home—added to Da's passing made it understandable that she should be changed.

But as time passed, they grew disappointed and perhaps a little impatient with her continued malaise. Da's advisors, who so tangibly longed to help her, lost their enthusiasm, if not their kindness. Rabbie and Davey, with whom she remained close. Even her maid.

None could help her, though. Her heart had become a barren place. A desert.

"D'ye want to fall to yer death?" a voice beside her demanded, and a strong hand caught the back of her cloak. Davey. A lad no longer, he had grown into a man during their tortuous journey home and now regarded her with level blue eyes. "Lean out any farther, mistress, and ye will land on yer head below."

"Aye, so." She could not but agree. Mayhap a part of her would not mind falling to her death, if it would halt the pain. The longing. But nay, for Finlay had paid too high a price to buy her life, had he not? "I would no' die, Davey, cushioned by all that mud."

"Aye, so. What are ye thinkin'?"

"That 'twill be a hard year ahead."

"Could scarce be worse than the winter." Davey himself had been down with the ague for a fortnight. She'd thought she might lose him.

Sometimes it seemed there was naught but loss. First Ma. Then Geordie. Reagan. Finlay. Da.

"We will get through somehow." Davey tried to sound braw. "Though we are gey short-handed."

They had lost so many in the south, only a portion of those that had gone off managing to make their way home again, and some of them maimed.

"'Twill get easier," he went on, clearly searching for something that could lift her spirits, "as the weather improves."

Would it?

"So many widows," she mused, "and bairns wi'out fathers. I canna forsake them. We maun provide."

"Aye," he said softly. "They do trust ye, mistress, to mak' the best decisions for them."

"Do they? I am no' so sure about my father's advisors." Aye, they had left her alone for a time after she'd arrived home. Let her grieve. But then they'd begun to badger her, if as gently and persistently as possible.

To Davey, with her eyes on the sea that crashed against the shore below, she said, "They want for me to marry. Someone suitable."

He gave a hard laugh. "Aye, well, that will be a fine trick, wi' so many perished."

There was that. A definite dearth of men beset them.

"They say 'twill strengthen the clan to ha' a man at the helm."

"I canna imagine a stronger leader than yoursel', Katrin. 'Twas ye got yer father home."

"'Twas all o' us. But Davey"—it was a cry from the heart—"wha' good did it do in the end?"

"It allowed the chief to die at home where he wanted to be, and be buried here as well."

"Aye, ye are right. Ye're right. 'Twas important." Far be it from her to take anything from the valiant effort he and Rabbie had put into that cause.

"'Twill get better," he repeated kindly. "So I promise."

She reached for his hand—deeply scarred in the palms—that

lay beside hers on the parapet, and clasped it. With false lightness, she asked, "Will *ye* marry me, Davey?"

"Me? Nay, I am no' man enough for that!" Besides"—he hesitated—"I ha' been speaking wi' Red Alice. Her Neil did no' come home, and she wi' the two wee bairns to look after." His voice had turned serious. "She needs someone, and I care for her, for them. But I donna ken—"

"What?"

"Whether she will ever be able to care for me, after losing Neil."

Aye, there was the crux of it. So many hearts broken, so many lives shattered.

"She will be that fortunate to ha' ye, Davey."

"Ye think so?"

"I know it."

"'Tis a funny thing. We were so sure we did the right thing when we marched off and awa' to that battle. Obeying our chief, who answered to his own laird. But it has all gone wrong and our very lives are changed."

"Scotland hersel' is changed," Katrin agreed softly. Hanging in the wind and twisting slowly. Who knew what would become of them?

"Still and all," said Davey, who despite all the hardships seemed determined to search out the hopeful, "we ha' survived and ha' a chance to mak' somewhat of our lives."

"Aye." They had survived, as so many had not. How could she complain then? Even if, for her, all the songs had faded into silence.

"Mistress," said old Dougal, who had once been Da's closest advisor, "a letter has come. Brought by a messenger just this morning."

The aged man gave Katrin a close look with careful eyes. He likely did not want to upset her and found that these days much did upset her. Try as she would to receive him, others of the council, and the clan's folk who came to her with patience and kindness, she felt brittle enough at any point to break.

She had watched Da's advisors whispering about her after they tried to reason out the steps they thought she must take, to lead their clan. Did they think she could not see?

"Wha' letter?" she asked him. "From whom?"

"It comes fro' Oran MacGill, our neighbor, ye ken, to the south."

"I ken fine who he is." Katrin's skin crawled. She did not like MacGill, had never quite trusted him, even though he and Da had dealt fairly together.

Dougal drew a breath. Katrin could almost feel him bidding himself to remain patient.

"He sent a runner, a young man who has fair winded himself. He came all the way in due haste."

Katrin turned and looked at the old man, dismay stirring in her heart. "Is there trouble? Did the young man say?" By God, what else might befall them? What fresh and terrible horror?

They were in the small chamber behind the hall, where her da had always conducted his business. She turned to Dougal and held out her hand.

"Is that the letter ye ha' there? Gi' it to me. I ha' best read it."

Dougal swallowed. "Mistress, I ha' read it."

"Eh?" She narrowed her eyes at him. "Was it addressed to ye, then?"

"Nay, mistress."

A rare anger stirred in Katrin's heart, mingling sickeningly with the dread in her stomach. She felt so little these days, was careful to let herself feel little. But like a vixen besieged by hounds, she experienced the desire to turn and fight.

"Then why ha' ye read it?"

"Mistress Katrin, ye maun understand. I, and your father's

other advisors, are doing our best to deal wi' the situation. To protect both yer welfare and that o' the clan."

"Am I no' the chief?"

"Nay, mistress."

What had he said? Katrin blinked at him, trying to make sense of it. When she did, the rage flared and clawed its way up her throat. Following all the hollow emptiness, it almost felt good.

"Am I no' my father's heir?"

"Well..." Dougal struggled visibly with the answer to that question. "Since there is nay male heir, aye and nay. If ye wed—"

The hand Katrin still held out in demand of the letter began to tremble. "Gi' that to me."

He did, extending it silently. Since the room was dim, she took it to the low-burning fire and unfolded it there.

She could read, if not particularly well. The script upon the page was ornate and difficult to decipher, but it was, aye, addressed to her.

How dare her father's advisors, however well trusted, withhold it from her? Keep from bringing it to her until they'd had a chance to discuss its contents, no doubt. She wondered—without much sympathy—how Dougal had drawn the dubious duty of facing her.

Slowly she puzzled the letter out. Heat rose to her head, making it feel like it would explode.

Her neighbor but one—for MacEwan held the stretch of coast between them—was Oran MacGill. They'd long had what might best be called cordial relations with him.

Now he wrote offering to solve Katrin's current dilemma by doing her the great honor of making her his wife.

I apprehend, mistress, that as a woman standing alone at the head of a great yet much-damaged clan, ye find yourself in a perilous position. Prey to any unscrupulous lord or baron who might happen along. Since your father has left nay heir, I am prepared to offer ye my protection in the form of marriage to be performed as soon as can be arranged. I am sure that ye will see the wisdom of this and I accept your gratitude in advance.

Katrin read it once. Twice. The parchment trembled in her hands. She raised a stricken face to her father's advisor.

"He offers, here, to marry me." Of course, Dougal already knew that.

"Aye."

"He does me the great favor of offering."

"He does, mistress—"

"He is twice my age."

"That scarcely matters."

It might not to Dougal. Nor might it to Katrin's shattered heart.

"It is, mistress, a solution to the predicament in which we find ourselves."

"Predicament?"

"There is currently nay heir to Murtray—"

If he said so one more time, she would beat his head in.

She thought furiously. "Oran MacGill is already married, is he no'?"

"He states in the letter, if ye read on, that his wife has most fortuitously died—"

"*Fortuitously?*"

"That is the word he used. He is thus a widower."

"He wants the lands. Naught but the lands."

"He will be able to defend them."

Slowly, in defiance of her rage, Katrin turned to face Dougal more fully. "Ye are never telling me to accept this—this vile offer?"

"We ha' discussed it and—"

"Ye ha'?"

"I and your father's other advisors."

"Get out o' my sight."

"Mistress!"

"Get out before I say or do somewhat I will regret."

The old man moved stiffly toward the door, turning back at

the last moment. "I hope ye will consider, mistress, wha' yer father knew full well. Ye maun exist, now, solely for the benefit o' this clan."

"Do no' tell me my duties. I understand them."

He went out. With fastidious haste, Katrin fed the parchment to the flames of the sleepy fire.

⬥

CHAPTER FORTY-SIX

BURNING THE LETTER from Oran MacGill did little good. It had already been read and debated by Katrin's advisors. MacGill's messenger still lingered, awaiting a reply. The damned matter would not go away.

If Katrin had felt besieged before, she now felt ravaged to pieces. She awoke with a knot of dread in the pit of her stomach and thought of little but her predicament all day long.

Had she not earned the place of chief in her own right? Had she not marched to war at her da's side? Got him home again against terrible odds? Could she not be trusted to lead the people with whose welfare she had been entrusted?

If she wed Oran MacGill, Murtray would cease to exist in its own name. Aye—she might bear sons, though the very prospect of them being Oran's sons made her skin crawl. But they would live beneath MacGill's banner evermore.

Her father's advisors might argue that MacGill offered them protection, for that they continued to do in the days that followed. She viewed it as a great loss of independence.

She remembered Oran MacGill. Aye, indeed, she did. And as she pondered his unwelcome offer, other pieces of memory began falling into place within her mind.

The stories Finlay had told there in her father's hall before all this began. Had he told them by chance, or by intention?

It seemed now she recalled Finlay's every word, burned into her mind as he was burned into her heart.

She took to walking great distances out from the settlement to escape her advisors as much as the eyes of her clan's folk. She walked northward up the coast to the place where Adair and his Bradana had come ashore so long ago, that he might fight the battle that won this very holding for him. She walked south, where Deathan and his Caledonian princess, Darlei, had once met together. She even walked up into the forest to the place she imagined a half-ruined cottage had once stood—the place where a Scotsman and a Norsewoman had taken refuge together in an effort to ease their all-consuming need for each other.

And the truth, in all its surety, took hold inside her, deeply rooted, unshakable. Whether Finlay had intended to tell her so or nay…

She was the young woman back in Ireland who had stood in the sun with him. She the denizen of old Dalriada, who walked with a deerhound at her side. She the Caledonian princess, unwilling to surrender control over her life, and she the Norse maiden who had battled for that self-rule.

Again and again, life after life, the two of them had met and loved, reclaiming one another in a deep devotion that refused to perish. She was her own ancestresses reborn, who had loved— and lost—him, only to find him over again.

He had tried to tell her, Finlay, who must have known the truth and needed to make her see it. He had told it to her in beautiful words. Sung it to her.

Now that she had found that truth, he was gone from her again.

And it was her fault.

She came to that last conclusion while tramping her lands to the point of exhaustion. Reliving the ancient tales Finlay had told, word for word. And reliving the dreams that had since beset her.

Twice had she forbidden him, her love, from returning to her as a warrior. Once—as he'd told—when she'd returned as Hulda from the Norse lands to stay here with him. And again when they were both aged and he went forth to defend this place they both loved. What was it she had said then?

"*Quarrie, if we are to be parted now, if we do manage against the tide of time and fate to meet together in another life—will you promise me one thing?*"

"*What more to promise than that I will return to ye? I will find ye, Hulda.*"

"*And when you do, in the next life, let it not be as a warrior. Because I cannot endure this fear upon fear of losing you in battle. Even after all this time, I cannot.*"

"*And wha' else should I be, than wha' I ha' been?*"

"*I do not care. A smith, a trainer of horses, a builder of boats, a carver of stone—any man who does not march out to die.*"

"*A harper?*" He said it lightly as if in jest, but his eyes were serious, holding her gaze, holding her soul.

"*Aye, that. A harper to play sweet songs for me and tell all the old tales. Give me those ancient songs and I promise to fall right back into your arms.*"

When Katrin put those pieces of memory fast together in her mind, it nearly took her to her knees.

For he was a warrior, this man she loved. As Ardahl back in old Erin, he had been. And that—like his love for her—had traveled with him from life to life.

Until she had forbidden it to him. And for love of her—for love of her he had taken up the harp instead of the sword.

That had not kept him from following her into battle. It could not keep him, because the man was who he was.

The man she loved was who he was. And had he not vowed to follow her?

The thing was—the thing was, he'd abandoned his training as a warrior early on, in this life. Had he not—had she not forbidden it to him—might he have possessed the skills necessary to survive that terrible battle in the south? To fight his way free. To follow her yet again.

So deep did that question cut, Katrin could scarce endure the wound. So fierce the pain, she could only flagellate herself and flay her soul raw, until she could scarce feel at all.

Aye, for feeling nothing was better than knowing she had

caused the loss of what she best loved.

It did no good to apply reason, to remind herself that Reagan—a warrior without equal—had not survived that devastating battle either, nor her da, ultimately, nor countless others. Grief and self-blame did not answer to reason.

"Mistress Katrin, I implore ye. Ye maun send a reply to Chief MacGill's letter. His messenger has been kicking his heels here for days, and I cannot imagine what Chief MacGill will be thinking. 'Tis the height o' discourtesy—"

It was old Duncan who beleaguered Katrin this time, but her father's other advisors stood in a ring around her, having caught her as she came home wet and exhausted from yet another tramp. They abandoned their disapproval and now appeared desperate.

Desperate and concerned. Aye, everyone showed concern for her. "MacGill will think I am considering his offer, making up my mind, no doubt. Do women no' tak' an unconscionable amount of time making up their minds?"

They exchanged looks. They no longer knew how to handle her.

"Mistress, he holds a certain amount o' power here along this coast. 'Twould no' be wise to antagonize him."

Katrin turned to look Duncan in the eye. "He holds a certain amount o' power? As his ancestor did?"

"His ancestor, mistress?"

"Aye, Duncan. Surely ye ken that he is descended from Mican MacGillean."

"Who?"

"Did ye no' listen to the bard Finlay's stories when he was here to tell them? He told o' Mican MacGillean and his treachery."

They exchanged yet another glance as if they thought she had indeed lost her senses.

"Aye, mistress, everyone listened to Finlay's wonderful stories. But those were just that—stories. Tales meant to entertain."

"Were they?" Or had they been direct appeals to her, to remember?

"Even if the bard's tales were true," Dougal objected, "the quarrels o' which he told were ancient ones, almost fro' the beginning o' time, and have nay bearing on the present day."

"So ye would ha' me wed wi' a man whose forebears had nay honor, would ye? Who might well ha' treachery at his heart?"

"Mistress," Dougal said, "I would at least ha' ye answer his missive that we might ha' nay quarrel wi' him now."

"Fine." Katrin tossed her head. "I will answer him. Send his messenger back saying my answer is nay."

Her advisors shifted around her uneasily. "Ye canna do that," ventured one. "Ye maun send a letter right and proper—polite—in reply. Ye may no' realize it, mistress, but wi' the country in the present perilous state—"

"I understand precisely what state the country is in." Near broken. Even its leaders, such as Robert Stewart, held in ignominy.

"Then ye will comprehend 'tis wise and politic to keep a neighbor like MacGill sweet, since we may one day ha' need o' him."

Katrin lifted her chin and looked the old man in the eye. "Would ye ha' me lie to him then? I will no' wed wi' him. Best to be honest about it."

"But then—wha' will become o' us? Wi'out an heir—"

"I canna think on that now. Gi' me some room to breathe, for heaven's sake."

She fair shouted it at them, and they backed off, Dougal lifting a hand to warn his fellows.

"To be sure, Mistress Katrin, ye be still grieving yer father and all the others lost in the south."

Aye, she still grieved. No end to her grief.

"Shall I write to Chief MacGill," Dougal suggested, "and advise ye require more time to consider his offer?"

"Nay. Ha' I no' said I refuse to lie to the man?" Katrin thought of MacGill, whom she well remembered. At least twice her age, aye. He was loud and bluff and opinionated, and as far the opposite of Finlay as a man could be. Och, after so many generations, he might well have little in common with his treacherous ancestor.

Katrin was in no frame of mind to take the chance.

"I will write to him," she decided. "And I will be courteous."

She sweated over that letter. She did not read or write easily, and in the end kept her reply as simple as she could, thanking Oran MacGill for being a strong ally to her father in the past, saying that she hoped he would be the same to her in the future if the need arose, but stating with certainty she could not accept his offer of a marriage alliance—for she had no illusions it was anything else.

She gave no reason.

Then she walked up to her da's grave, there, where so many of her blood lay sleeping, and told him what she had done. Asked his forgiveness. For in the welter of doubt and confusion that was her mind, she very much feared making another mistake.

Trust, he seemed to tell her in return. *Trust in the turning of the wheel. In the ancient promise.*

Or maybe what she heard was only her own heart.

❖

CHAPTER FORTY-SEVEN

MOLLY KNEW OF an old man two villages away who, she said, had a head full of knowledge. A scholar he had been in his youth, and kept the history of Western Scotland. He might well be able to identify the plaid Finlay's companions had been wearing on their way into battle, if Finlay could describe it to him.

It being too far for Molly to walk, Finlay went alone, choosing a day that at the outset looked to be fine, but which deteriorated into biting wind and snow before he reached his destination.

The old man lived beside a tiny stone church, and sometimes, so Molly had said, served as its caretaker. His daughter admitted Finlay to the cottage, telling him that aye, her father was to home.

"Are ye looking for lodging?" she asked, eyeing Finlay up and down.

"Nay. I am but seeking some knowledge."

That won a smile. "There is naught Da likes better than sharing out knowledge."

Finlay found Pádraig MacKay sitting beside his fire, puffing on a pipe near as long as his forearm. A number of leather-bound books occupied a shelf behind him, but as Finlay was to learn, he did indeed keep most his knowledge stuffed inside his head.

He had quick, dark eyes and an equally quick mind. He listened to Finlay's accounting as if rapt, puffing increasingly denser plumes of smoke from his pipe.

"Ye ha' the manner o' a storyteller," he remarked when Finlay finished. "A fine voice for it. Ye might be a bard."

"I think I was one," Finlay admitted. "I canna remember all of it—yet."

"A bard who went to war."

Finlay hesitated. "A bard in this life—mayhap a warrior in previous ones."

"Aye, so." Pádraig did not look surprised. "And yer blood?"

"Eh?"

"Yer background, man."

Finlay related the bits he could remember of his youth, living in the south, for that much of memory had returned to him.

Pádraig smiled. "This plaid ye would chase down—"

"'Tis the woman I would find."

"Aye, so. One plaid sounds much like others, in the describing. Green, ye say. Wi' red and white? It might be almost anyone's."

Finlay's heart sank.

"Do no' look so downhearted, man. Since yon battle in the south, the accounts ha' been flying. Many are the men who passed through this way, bound north and homeward. Since I collect the lore and the wisdom, all o' it comes to me.

"There is only one chief who wore a tartan woven wi' green and white, who marched wi' his daughter into battle, and that was Anders MacMurtray."

MacMurtray. The name seemed to chime and twine through Finlay's mind. As if a door opened within him, he remembered.

He saw a hall, a fine structure filled with rapt listeners, their eyes fixed upon him as he wove and spun his tales. His own gaze drawn to but one among his listeners. A woman. Tall she was, with honey-colored hair and pale blue-gray eyes. In those eyes lay his entire world.

I will find ye. Always.

"Where is this place?" he asked old Pádraig. "Murtray."

"North o' here, a good distance north up on the coast. Ye will ha' a long trudge ahead o' ye, if ye go."

He would go.

"If ye mak' yer way to the sea and can find the means to sail, 'twill be quicker. So long as the weather allows."

A small, light boat clad in oiled skin, bobbing on the breast of the ocean. A woman with wide blue eyes leaning toward him.

"Adair." She spoke his name.

Adair. He was Adair MacMurtray, come from Erin.

Even as Pádraig's daughter slid a mug of warmed ale beside his elbow, he told the old man sitting opposite him, "I begin to remember. All the things that have been scattered since the battle. They come in pieces and I maun fit them together."

Pádraig leaned toward him, his dark eyes bright. "Then remember this."

FINLAY SPENT THE night with Pádraig and his daughter, tucked into the corner beside the fire with a borrowed blanket. For aye, he knew now that *Finlay* was his name. *Ardahl?* Well, Ardahl had been his name also, once upon a time. As had Adair, Deathan, and Quarrie, each in its turn. Did it matter, a man's name, so long as a single flame burned in his heart?

Pádraig, with a world of knowledge in his head, knew many things. The history of all the western clans and much about their lineage. He told it simply even as Finlay might relate a tale, and helped to slot many of the pieces into place in Finlay's mind.

"The current Chief of Murtray—or he who was Chief of Murtray, for I hear that man has since died—had a great-grandfather, and that man had twa sons. They quarreled, so 'tis told, which is an old habit among members o' that line."

"So it is," said Finlay, remembering.

"The quarrel was a fierce one, and the younger son took

himsel' away to forge his own path in the world. They say"—Pádraig's lively gaze met Finlay's—"he traveled south even into Wales, where he married and had a son of his own. He then returned north, for no Scot can keep awa' fro' Scotland for long."

"Nay." *Alba, land of magic that had taken him to its heart.*

"And his son, they say, won a place as master o' arms for a chief out in the islands. For the blood of warriors was still strong in his veins. But he died in a battle and his good wife from an illness not long after, and his son was passed to others to raise. And that son might have been a warrior also, like so many of his ancestors, and indeed, 'tis said he did start training early, but he abandoned the pursuit. For the harp." Pádraig's dark gaze met Finlay's.

"Me. Ye be speaking o' me." Finlay went breathless, as if struck a blow to the heart. "How d'ye know these things? How, when I do not?"

"Am I no' a scholar? And ha' I no' been collecting such knowledge all my life?" Pádraig leaned toward Finlay. "'Twas fate that sent ye here, lad, to me."

'Twas the turning of the wheel that created his life—life after life.

He struggled to draw breath. "Ye are saying I am a descendant of Murtray?"

"Aye, how else could it be?"

How else, indeed? For he remembered being Ardahl the warrior, and Adair the exile, Deathan the second son who loved a princess, and Quarrie who wed a Norsewoman. The pieces of the past shattered by the violence of the battle fitted together so he remembered not only the pieces, but how—and most of all—why they fit.

Ah, did not memory travel via the blood?

"By God," he whispered.

"Murtray lacks a chief, having left none but his daughter, Katrin," Pádraig told him.

Katrin. The name whispered like music in Finlay's mind.

"And ye be that man they are wanting. I suggest ye get there promptly and claim yer place."

Finlay, as chief? Ah, he cared not for the place of chief, though he would fill it if he must. Had he not always been good at fulfilling his duties?

What he wanted was the place at Katrin's side.

He rose the morning after Pádraig told him all this and, with many thanks and expressions of gratitude, took his leave. Outside, beside the tiny stone church in the cold air, he gazed upon a world reborn. High above the hills the skies cleared, yesterday's snow showers flown. Sunlight shone through in racked beams, ladders of light reaching northwestward. Leading him where he needed to be.

CHAPTER FORTY-EIGHT

"I MUST LEAVE ye," Finlay told Molly with real regret, as he stood outside her door in the sunshine. He wore his pack already on his back, and though he owned little besides the shattered harp, she had tucked some goods inside for his journey. Foodstuffs she could ill afford, and her husband's plaid.

She stood looking up at him, for she was a small woman for all her strength, and tears glittered in her eyes.

"Come wi' me," he said impulsively. "If I mak' a place for mysel' at this holding to which I journey, there will be one for ye also." She had been like a mother to him, more of one than he had ever known.

"Dear lad. Bless ye for asking, but I would delay ye on yer journey, for I could only go slowly."

"Then," he said, despite the all-consuming urge that possessed him, "I will go slowly also."

"Nay, and nay. For ye go to begin a new life, all the dreams now flown back into yer head. And am I no' near the end o' mine? I belong here where my man does rest."

Finlay understood that, but sorrow touched him as he bent and embraced her. "Ye saved me," he whispered. "I swear, ye did."

"Go wi' God," she bade him.

They both wept when he started off up the track, away from her tiny bothy. Away from the comfort she offered when only confusion had beset him. On into the light.

As he went, he relived the old stories in his head, all he had told of them in Murtray's hall, stories he had cherished the way he did his acquired tunes, gathered in his time tramping the roads and byways of his world. For did a harper, a bard, not harbor tales to please and delight those who offered him hospitality?

He'd felt a great pull for what he'd learned of Murtray's history and had attributed the meaning of that pull to *her*. The woman who seemed to have somehow been with him from birth, who had belonged to him again and again, life after life.

He could not say why, during this life, he remembered all they had been to each other, though she did not remember also. He knew only that it had become more important than aught else for him to reach her and, if she did not remember who he was, to remind her. To convince her she was his alone. That in the wide world, as promised, he had found her.

He'd never had a way to know then that Murtray was his own place of blood, of belonging. That he was a lost son of that tribe who had wandered and wandered, and now journeyed home.

The wonder of it inspired and uplifted him. He told himself he should have known. For did not memory travel in the blood? Even the things folk forgot they knew.

But doubt beset him also. Aye, old Pádraig—with his vast knowledge—had heard of Anders MacMurtray's death and that his daughter had reached home. That they were a clan without any leader other than she.

To his mind, they needed no other. A woman of strength was Katrin, and devoted to her clan. But what if she still did not realize who he was and what they had in the past been to one another? What if her advisors refused to accept him when he turned up at their door, naught but a wandering harper? He had no real proof of his lineage, only a tale told by an old man.

Somewhere around day five of his journey, he decided there was naught he could do to convince others. He could only cast himself onto the breast of fate, keep the ancient promise he had made to the woman he loved. She would accept him as she might. They would battle together as they must.

Step by step, he journeyed home.

KATRIN HAD TAKEN to walking up the rise to the place where her da was buried, each and every day. Usually she went in the afternoon, when pressure from all that beleaguered her made the need for escape irresistible. The patch of ground was quiet, with a magnificent view of the sea. No one ever bothered her there.

She fell into the habit of speaking to her da, only a few words at first, as one would murmur a prayer, and then floods of them. Words she could say to no one else.

"I do no' want to wed wi' Oran MacGill. Or wi' anyone, to be honest. I will love only one man until I die." And he lay cold already, somewhere. All the beauty of him, all the magical warmth and music, lost with him.

Where had Finlay been buried? It bothered her that she did not know, and bothered her even more that his body, the same she had cherished, might have lain uncared for in the open, naught more than food for carrion.

"Da, it is my fault he was lost." That confession brought hard and painful tears. She crouched beside her father's stone-covered grave and wept like a soul forsaken. For if Finlay was lost, she was also, and the only hope she had was for a life beyond this one, whenever the fates might be kind enough to bring them together again.

In that she had to believe that they would—och, please by all the powers—meet again in some future existence.

"How will I ever forgive mysel'?"

Ye will do yer duty, daughter, she seemed to hear her da say.

Aye, she would do her duty even if that meant living out her life alone. She would do aught she could to lead this clan with strength and mercy, anything save wedding another, lying with another—even if that meant Murtray would have no heir. Aught else, she would do for this place she loved.

Not that.

Forgive me, Da. I ha' a duty, aye, to Murtray. And a far older one to my own heart.

She was not a woman who countenanced despair, and she fought it now on a daily basis, finding her best comfort there among the graves. For her da's was not the only one. Geordie lay here too, and her ma, her grandparents, and everyone else from lost bairns to her most distant ancestors.

Her ancestors.

Were they buried here beneath the plain stone markers, those whom she knew so well? Those she knew because she had walked through their days, lived their lives. Bradana, who would surely be laid beside the grave of her gray deerhound. The Caledonian princess, and the Norse warrior maiden. Did they all lie beside the men they had loved?

That thought near took her to her knees. She did not know which piles of stones were which. Some had been battered and broken down by weather over the centuries. But she wandered among them, and she felt, in the pieces of the past—in their inevitability—a far deeper comfort.

As if, out of the past, her own self whispered to her.

Ye ha' been with him, this man ye adore. Ye will be again.

On this one afternoon, an afternoon hinting at the first breath of spring, she lingered long, feeling the strength of the past like a wave buoying her up. She stood gazing out to sea, past the waves that boldly kissed the shingle, past the islands lying like sleeping dragons.

From here she could almost see Ireland. The place where it had all begun, where lay the very roots of her love.

Have faith. Believe.

She waited till the light began to fade before she went down to take up her duties. Just above the keep she paused and gazed southward along the sea trail. And saw a flicker of movement.

Nay, but surely her eyes played tricks on her. No one was there, lest it was a member of the guard. And this traveler—he did not move like a member of the guard.

Her heart began to pound, high and hard beneath her breast—as if had not beat since she'd watched Finlay throw himself to the wolves for her sake, back in England. Nay, and nay, it could not be…

Yet conviction seized her, claimed her, a kind of knowing that came from far beyond herself. From long ago and far, far away, bringing its own certainty.

The thrill of it stole her breath. Lifted her spirit on a cresting wave that knew nothing of possible or impossible. Her eyes might wonder—but not her heart.

Faith it was that made her catch her breath and run.

She nearly stumbled over her own feet half a score times. The folk she passed stared at her. One or two called out.

"Mistress!"

"Mistress Katrin?"

Aye, she was Katrin. She was Liadan, and Bradana, and Dar-lei, and Hulda, all flying through time, flying toward the man she loved.

How he could be here, she did not know. How he could be alive, when she had left him standing poised to face death itself, a harper with a sword.

I will find ye, always.

FINLAY'S FEET KNEW the stones of the trail, for he had walked it more times than he could count. His eyes knew the set of the land, the rise to his right, the broad sweep of the sea on his left.

Home. He was nearly home.

Here the rough trail turned to a path in earnest as it left the headland and sloped downward. He paused an instant, for from here he could see the keep. Murtray.

There, once, had stood a roundhouse. Over the centuries it had become a fortified house and then a keep, expanded to the proud fortress it was now. Generations of people had put their hearts and souls into it. Their love.

Emotions rose up and nearly choked him. A long while, it felt he had roamed. But had the ending ever been in doubt?

His feet marked the paces as he walked on. Here had he and Darlei strolled together. He and Hulda, so many, many years later.

The light began to fade, the kindling-spring day winding down. Here, where sea met land, where past met present, the light gathered on the breast of the water, just enough to show him the figure of a woman, running—running to him.

She flew to meet him, his love, his alanna, his dearest wife. In whatever guise, it no longer mattered.

For she brought all that was love to him.

<hr />

CHAPTER FORTY-NINE

FINLAY'S STEPS QUICKENED to a run, all the weariness gathered during the long miles and the long years streaming away from him. He could no longer feel the stones of the shingle under his feet. No longer feel his connection to the world. But the wheel of destiny—och, aye, that he could feel, turning, turning beneath him, as inevitable as life and death and love.

Katrin stretched out her arms as she came. And it seemed in the wind that streamed past Finlay's ears he heard laughter and weeping and music, an ancient song. But nay, it was only her voice he heard, for she called his name as she ran to him. "Finlay! *Fin-lay!*"

They met just above the waves, where she crashed into his arms, a sea finding a shore, a longboat finding its harbor, two pebbles beaching high above any marauding tide.

"Finlay."

"Alanna."

Blindly they held to one another, heart to a heart, soul to a soul. Finlay did not know that she wept until their mouths, desperate, met and he tasted her tears. A sweet, salted remembrance of hurts past. Now all lifted away.

How long that kiss lasted, he could never tell. Forever and not long enough.

It would never be long enough, with this woman.

At length she drew from him, not far. In the last light of the day she examined his face, touched his cheek, searched his eyes.

He hid nothing from her, not the gladness, the aching, or the love.

"Finlay, och, Finlay!" She still wept, the tears flowing down her face unheeded. "I remember. I remember it all. Your stories were no' just stories—they were tales o' us together, the two o' us, life after life, through time."

He nodded, his relief such that he had no words for it.

"But I thought ye were dead. Back there in the battle when ye threw yoursel' to those Englishers to get us awa'. Ye sacrificed yoursel'—"

"No' dead, alanna." With one reverent hand, he brushed her hair, pushing it from her face. Here, she was. With him. "How could I possibly die, before I returned to ye?"

"I thought—I thought—we would no' be together in this life." She gulped. "Forgive me."

"For what?" For the life of him, he could not imagine a reason.

"I made ye promise. Did I no'? Do ye no' remember? I made ye gi' me a promise—that if ye returned to me again, it would no' be as a warrior. Aught else, I did say." The tears slid and glittered in her eyes.

"Aught else. Even a bard." He smiled.

"But I never should ha' asked ye to be other than what ye are. It was wrong o' me. And all this while I ha' been thinking— thinking that if ye had the skills o' a warrior, ye might ha' survived."

"As I did."

That made her weep harder, his strong lass who had so seldom wept save for fear of losing him.

"Katrin, all ye ever did was love me. And as ye can see, there must ha' been enough o' the warrior left inside me after all. For here I am to keep the vow I made to ye so very long ago."

They kissed again, this not so much a caress as another vow given anew, and a pledge of faith.

"I remember," she repeated in a whisper. "I remember all o' it now. The beautiful, ancient music ye played. Those were songs of our lives." She gazed into his eyes. "And I believe, Finlay. I believe that love is stronger than time itself. That what has been will be again—forever more."

Finlay closed his eyes in a moment of pure gratitude.

"Come," she told him softly. "Ye are coming awa' home wi' me."

"Home."

"'Tis your home now as well as mine. For I want ye to know ye can play upon yer harp all ye like, but ye will wander nay more." She tugged him by the hand. "Ye are staying here for good, wi' me."

Finlay smiled to himself. He need not tell her now that he was a lost son of Clan Murtray, come home. There would be time for all that later.

They had time. Years and years of it.

"Katrin, wait." He drew her to a halt where she stood facing him, a blaze of love in her eyes. "Before we reach the keep and all the madness that must come o' my return, there is one more thing I owe ye."

"A pledge o' marriage, I hope," she declared.

"That too. But first…"

He clasped her hands, and one by one raised them to his lips. Dropped fervent kisses into the palms. Laid a soft kiss on either corner of her mouth, and both cheeks. The seventh kiss blessed her brow.

"Now," he told her, "now I am come home."

EPILOGUE

NOT UNTIL NEARLY a year later, when Katrin was beginning to show with the child she carried—the lad or lass who would in turn carry their ancestors on into the future—did an unexpected visitor arrive.

Indeed, Katrin and Finlay were far up the shore on one of their rambles, it being a rare chance for them to seize some time alone, and walking hand in hand. A member of the guard, named Archie, came running to find them, a curious look in his eyes.

Trouble? Katrin could almost hear the word spark in Finlay's mind, though he did not speak. His fingers merely tightened on hers.

"Wha' is it?" he asked the man.

"A traveler just come over the hills, asking for Mistress Katrin." Archie drew a breath and announced, "'Tis the Gallowglass!"

"What?" Katrin stared.

"Aye, the one the old chief hired when we went to battle last year."

The old chief. Katrin still experienced a pang when she heard that. Was Finlay the new chief, or was she? He went by that name, aye, but she had an equal part in any decision that was made.

"Reagan? Impossible!" She gazed into Finlay's eyes. "He died at the battle!"

Finlay gave her a rueful smile. "Did he?"

Katrin dropped his fingers and ran, a great gladness tearing up through her. It could not be. *It could not be,* she thought in tune with her footsteps. She'd thought him lost to her.

At the foot of the rise just in front of the gate stood a man. A big man he was, with wide shoulders covered in light chain mail, a sword nearly as tall as he was strapped across his back.

"Reagan!"

He turned from surveying the keep when she called his name, and a big, wide smile broke across his face. Warm and steady, tawny-colored eyes. Flowing mustaches and a countenance grown somehow older. Harder and tightened, but aye, the smile was the same and spread immediately to his eyes.

He swept Katrin with a look up and down before he switched his gaze to Finlay, who came close behind her.

"Harper."

"Master Gallowglass!"

"I thought ye dead." The words burst from Katrin and drew Reagan's eyes back to her. "In that battle—I saw ye fall."

"Aye, I nearly was dead. Lost more than half my men, I did, and still more in the attempt to get what was left o' us awa'. The thing o' it is, I am not so easy to kill."

"Och, by God," Katrin exclaimed. "Och, I am that glad!"

His eyes crinkled. "As I am glad to see the two o' ye here, and together. As should be."

Finlay reached out and clasped arms with the Gallowglass who, tall as Finlay was, topped him by a good bit. The very air seemed to shimmer. This, Katrin knew, would be one of those moments that would live in her mind forever and perhaps one evening be told in song—the day the bold Gallowglass returned.

"I had heard talk that made me hope ye had survived, sayin' Murtray had a new chief married to the old chief's daughter, and that he was a harper. I just had to come and see for myself."

"As ye do." Katrin could not help but beam at him.

His eyes crinkled again, in return. "I do see that ye have been hard at work assuring the future. When is the babe due?"

Katrin laid a hand on her belly in an age-old gesture. "By summer's end. It canna be soon enough."

"I am having trouble," Finlay admitted, "keeping her fro' doing all the things she thinks she can, like training ponies and wielding a sword."

Reagan laughed outright. "I wish ye luck o' that. Will he be a harper as well as a fine warrior, this son o' yours?"

For an instant, Katrin's eyes met Finlay's and softened. "I hope so," they said in unison before Katrin added, "He—or she—will be whatever is born into him, or whatever she wishes. I ha' learned"—she lifted her chin—"to trust in wha' is meant to be, and so leave the fear behind."

Reagan nodded soberly. "A worthwhile lesson for anyone."

"Come inside, man," Finlay invited him. "I hope ye can stay wi' us for a time."

"I cannot." Reagan shook his head. "I am bound back for Ireland, Scotland being no place for me at present. With your king still in chains in England and your fight for liberty bruised and battered—at least for the time being—'tis nay fit place for anyone."

"Aye." Again Katrin glanced at her husband. "We mean to keep close and look after our own. As for Scotland—well, we maun trust that time will tak' care o' her also. She is no' so easily defeated."

Just like our love. She almost thought she heard those words in Finlay's mind.

"Reagan, are ye sure ye canna stay?"

"Nay, I wanted only to make a stop here and see that ye were set right, before I leave Scottish soil. Harper"—he turned again to Finlay—"ye keep singing and telling your stories. They are our past and our path to the future."

"I will."

"And ye, lass." Reagan's gaze softened once more as he reached out to embrace Katrin. "Remain the strong woman ye be," he whispered into her ear.

"Och, aye." Strong enough to love in the face of loss. Strong enough to have faith in a promise given long, long ago.

They stood with their fingers linked, hearts linked, souls linked, and watched their unexpected visitor away. He went as swiftly as he'd come, heading south along the coast road, and once he was out of sight Katrin wondered whether he'd truly been there at all.

Or if, like the dreams that so often flickered through her head, she'd merely glimpsed him on the turning of the great wheel that was her life.

The tiny life within her fluttered and stirred as she moved into her husband's arms, a new song for a future yet untold.

The Song of Finlay the Bard

Do our ancestors journey with us
In the color of our eyes?
In the strength of our limbs,
A fiery mane of hair.
Or does the connection reach far deeper?
Is there a better way for spirit to travel
Than via the blood of family?

Do our ancestors journey with us
In the choices that we make?
The longings of our dreams,
An aching of the heart?
The hint of a tune long remembered.
Is there a surer way for spirit to travel
Than via homesickness for what has been?

Do our ancestors journey with us
In the memories that we hold?
A hint of a tune,
A trill of breathless laughter,

A smile in a pair of eyes.
Sweet sorrow of things lost.
Is there a surer way for spirit to travel
Than via the echoes of what has been?

Do our ancestors travel with us
In the strengths that we possess?
In the lessons learned from past failures
And the longings born of far-off losses.
In the sudden knowing that draws heart to heart
And life to life,
Is there a surer way for spirit to travel
Than in the trading of what is for what has been?

Do our ancestors travel with us
In the binding of our souls?
In trails well-traveled and tales remembered.
In ancient songs that we hear not with our ears
But with our hearts.
Is there a surer way for spirit to travel
Than by the magic of love
That brings us home?

THE END

About the Author

Laura Strickland delights in time traveling to the past and weaving deliciously romantic stories for her readers. Her first love has always been Scottish Historical Romance, and her work has garnered her several awards including a RONE. At home in Western New York, she's been privileged to mother a number of very special rescue dogs. Her lifelong interest in Celtic history, magic, and music, along with her mantra of *Lore, Legend, Love* are all reflected in her writing.

Visit Laura at www.laurastricklandbooks.com